NOTORIOUS D.O.C.

THE SECOND HOPE SZE MEDICAL CRIME NOVEL

MELISSA YI

Windtree
Press

Join Melissa's mailing list at www.melissayuaninnes.com

Published by Olo Books in association with Windtree Press
Cover photograph © 2015 Victor Kuznetsov
Cover design © 2017 by Design for Writers

Yi, Melissa, author   Notorious D.O.C. / Melissa Yi.
(Hope Sze crime novel; 2)
Issued in print and electronic formats.
ISBN 978-1-927341-34-6, (softcover).--ISBN 978-0-9876865-8-9 (eBook)
    I. Title.   C813'.6

To advise of typographical errors, please contact olobooks@gmail.com

For Cara, Mai-Anh, Bernice, and the rest of my posse.
We survived.

With special thanks to Shaun Visser.

1

I'd avoided St. Joseph's emergency room for the past week, but it hadn't changed. Stretcher patients lined the wall and spilled into the hallway. Fluorescent lights turned everyone's skin yellow, even though most of them weren't Asian like me.

I smiled at a nurse who squeezed my arm and said, "Welcome back, Hope!" as a patient's wrinkled mother waved me down.

"Miss. We need a blanket!"

Home, sweet home.

Well, sweet except for the smell of stool drifting from bed 12.

I nodded at a few fellow medical residents. Officially, we're doctors in our first post-graduate training year, formerly known as interns. Unofficially, we're scut monkeys rotating from service to service. I'd debuted in emergency medicine last month and ended up tracking down a murderer who almost killed me.

I had to take a week off, which meant I was late starting my psych rotation. Duty called. I perched on the chair in the psych corner of the nurses' station, near the printer, and grabbed the chart for a Mrs. Regina Lee.

One of my favourite emerg nurses, Roxanne, paused and shoved a pen behind her ear. "Hope! Nice to see you. Are you doing okay?"

I nodded. We hugged. She smelled like Purell, and she was built like me, skinny but strong. Once she told me her Italian grandmothers practically cried when they saw her, they found her so emaciated-looking.

Roxanne glanced at the blue plastic card clipped to my chart. "Oh, no. You got Mrs. Lee. Is it Fall already?"

I frowned. "August eighth?" After sitting in school for twenty-odd years of my life, including most summer vacations, I hate when people call autumn prematurely. As far as I'm concerned, it's still summer until the snow hits the ground. I don't even like to see the leaves change colour. Call it denial if you want. Whoa—I was in psych mode already.

Roxanne shrugged. "Close enough. She always comes here. Especially around now. It's very sad."

"Why?"

"Did you know Laura Lee?"

I hesitated.

She shook her head. "You're too young. Anyway. She was a resident here. Star of her year."

A resident like me. "What does that have to do with Mrs. Lee? Are they related?"

Roxanne pointed to the clipboard. "I'll let Mrs. Lee tell you. It's her favourite story."

Strange.

I glanced at the triage note, even though my mind was on one scut monkey in particular. A blond dude. A guy who appreciated sausages and beer and me, not necessarily in that order. A guy I'd overlooked when I first came to Montreal for my residency, but I wasn't about to make that mistake again.

Sadly, no matter how casually I glanced out of the corners of my eyes, John Tucker did not appear.

I strode through the open door of room 14, the designated psych room. The stretcher and its five-point restraints stood empty, but a woman sat in a chair by one indented white wall. "Mrs. Lee?"

She clutched the clunky leather purse in her lap as she turned to face me. Her permed black hair was streaked with white, but I noticed her strong cheekbones and her skin, still enviably smooth considering her sixty-four years. Although her lips parted, no sound emerged.

"Hi." I held out my hand.

She didn't take it. My hand hovered in the air until I shoved it back in my lab coat pocket. Then I remembered that I was trying to improve my body language and dropped my hand to my side. The smell of bloody stool wafted toward us from room 12, and we both winced before I changed the subject. "My name is Dr. Hope Sze. I'm a resident from psychiatry. Could we—"

She stared at me with such intensity, I faltered.

Her eyes filled with tears.

Oh, dear. She really was depressed. The psychiatric patients who come to the emergency room are usually depressed or psychotic. I set her file down on the desk and scanned the room for tissues. They always kept a box handy on psych.

She said something in Chinese.

"I'm sorry. I don't speak Chinese. But I could get a translator if you like." My parents thought we should be Canadian and always spoke English to us.

She reached a hand toward my face, gazing at me like she was in a dream.

I flinched, not wanting to jerk away, but mildly freaked. Who was this woman?

She checked herself. Her hand dropped to her side and she tried to smile. "Excuse me," she said, in perfectly good English. "It's just that you look so much like my daughter."

I relaxed a little. "Oh. That's nice. Is your daughter, ah, here with you?"

"Not anymore." Her brown eyes met mine. "She's dead. Somebody killed her."

My shoulders tensed. It's an answer you'd never expect. And, even though I tried not to be superstitious, I found it eerie that her dead daughter had been a resident who looked like me.

She blinked. The tears already shining in her eyes dripped on to her cheeks. She ignored them, still staring at me. "I'm sorry," she said. "You must think me very foolish."

"Not at all."

She dabbed her eyes with a tissue she extracted from her purse. "I know you're not Laura. I know she's gone. It's only that I've been without hope for so long."

I twitched. My name, Hope, is a constant sore spot for me. When people mention the concept, I always feel like they're talking about me, although Mrs. Lee was the most poignant example.

She shook her head. "I know what they say about me, that I can't accept my daughter's death. They think it's tragic, but I should move on after eight years."

Although the emerg nurse, Roxanne, hadn't rolled her eyes, I could imagine others would, and Mrs. Lee knew it. To use psych lingo, Mrs. Lee had insight, meaning that she understood her condition. A lot of psych patients don't. They think you're the nutbar who doesn't receive the secret messages from the Cadbury commercial, and they're perfectly sane.

So far, Mrs. Lee didn't seem crazy, just sad.

Somehow that was worse.

Her mouth twisted with what might have been humour under different circumstances. "They even think I should move so I'll 'make new memories' and, not coincidentally, remove myself from their sector."

I nodded. I only knew about sectors because Tucker, who did psych last month, had explained them to me. The Island of Montreal was carved into psychiatry "sectors" according to postal code. If you had mental health issues, you had to go to whatever hospital sector you belonged to. No exceptions, even if it made no sense. We had patients who were literally born at St. Joe's and lived across the street, but they had to get downtown for their psychiatrist.

Mrs. Lee already knew this, which was a little scary. She was clearly an intelligent woman who'd been grieving for eight years. What was I going to do for her? I'd better steer her away from the subject of her daughter's death, even though I really wanted to know how she'd died. Curiosity not only killed the cat, it lured me into medical school—and into fighting crime, although I'd hung up my magnifying glass after my first and only case last month. "I'm very sorry for your loss. Maybe we should start at the beginning. How would you describe your mood, on a scale of one to ten—"

She waved her hand, cutting me off. "I already have a psychiatrist. Dr. Saya is happy to prescribe me medication or let me run off at the mouth, but I don't want to talk about it anymore. I want justice."

Justice. I knew I should get back on track, asking her about depression, but I couldn't resist. "Have you talked to the police?"

She laughed and tossed her tissue in the garbage. Two points. "They know me well. They say I don't have any proof it wasn't an accident. It was a hit and run, you see."

Well. Maybe it really was an accident. I crossed my legs. "Do you have any proof?"

She leaned forward and placed her hands on her knees, eyes suddenly sharp. "You believe me, don't you?"

I hesitated. I yearned to say yes, even though my logic and medical training shied away from her.

She shook herself. "How silly of me. Of course you don't, yet. But I could show you what I have. I have an entire file on Laura."

I had to draw the line at sorting through Laura's gap-toothed elementary school photos and stellar report cards. "I'm sure you do, Mrs. Lee, but—"

"Not that kind of file. Evidence. The police reports. The autopsy." She paused. "I used to carry it with me, but most people here have seen it already and don't take it seriously. I couldn't bear that."

How many mothers could say "autopsy" without breaking down? On the other hand, she'd had eight years to acclimatize to the word. I had to admire her drive, still searching for justice.

But it wasn't my place. The fact that I reminded her of Laura made it even more unprofessional. "I'm sorry, Mrs. Lee. I do know one or two people at the police department. They might be able to help you with...justice." The word tasted foreign in my mouth. I hurried on. "In the emergency room, we deal with medical problems. You seem quite stable. Are you feeling more depressed than usual lately?"

She shook her head. "I feel much better now that I've met you."

I closed my eyes. I couldn't save this woman. I could hardly save myself.

"Please, Dr. Sze. Have a look at her file. That's all I'm asking."

I had to say no. I took a breath.

One of the things I never liked about psych was, when you interview a patient, you're not really an ally. You're mentally critiquing what they say and how they say it while trying to categorize them. It sounds harsh, but a gazillion people came to the ER and said, "I'm depressed." Very few of them were truly suicidal. Some of them were trying to manipulate you. Some of them wanted attention. Of course, this happened in emergency medicine too, which was what I planned to specialize in, but I generally wanted to be on the patient's side instead of inspecting them from behind glass.

This time, though, I needed to keep her behind glass.

I knew what my supervisors would say. I knew what I should say. I forced the sentences into the air, creating a barrier between us. "Mrs. Lee, please, let's concentrate on you. Have you thought about hurting yourself?"

She sighed. "No, I am not suicidal. Naturally, after Laura was killed, I had days of despair, but I never attempted to kill myself. I have never tried to hurt anyone else. I am not hallucinating. I do not have a special relationship with God or Satan. I do not drink or take any drugs except an occasional Ativan to help me sleep, and even then, I only take half a milligram. I know I am at St. Joseph's Hospital in Montreal, Quebec, Canada, and that it is the eighth of August."

I stared at her, wide-eyed. She'd encapsulated a psych interview better than I could have done.

She smiled. "It's practice, Dr. Sze. I've had many, many of these interviews. I could go on if you like. But I am not crazy. I am not going to hurt you or anyone else, including myself. I already have a doctor and I'm not asking for any special treatment. All I am asking is for you to read my file on Laura. You don't even have to meet with me. I could leave a copy in your mailbox."

"Mrs. Lee..."

I should say no. I should concentrate on medicine. Or even on Tucker.

Curiosity killed the cat.

Counteraction brought her back.

I looked into her steady brown eyes and said, "All right."

2

I paged the psychiatrist on call for the emergency room half an hour later, after I'd finished the rest of the interview and written a note.

Dr. Gatien answered. "I'm teaching the medical students. I'll be down in a minute."

"Great. See you then." I wondered why I hadn't gotten called to the teaching too, but I couldn't complain since I was starting the rotation late.

Twenty minutes ticked by. I was still waiting for Dr. Gatien when Nancy, the psych nurse, wandered out of the psychiatry office. She was a freckled blonde woman, the kind that you imagine playing tennis and drinking lemonade instead of hanging around in a windowless emergency room, talking to psychos. Still, the psych office was the only place in the emergency room that looked like an actual office, with an L-shaped desk and a rolling chair, so maybe she felt at home. She closed the door behind her and said, "There's another patient for us to see, a frequent flyer."

"Okay." I checked my watch. "Dr. Gatien said he'd be right down."

She nodded. "He'll be here before lunch."

Nice life. Why did I want to be an emergency doctor again?

The automatic emergency doors flew open, and a medium-built man with a light French accent said, "Hello, Nancy. Dr. Sze, I presume?"

I turned to meet Dr. Gatien. My eyes widened. He looked like Face from the A-team, all tan and white teeth. In other words, younger, more handsome and probably more conceited than I'd expected in a shrink.

I shook his hand and nodded hello at the medical students flanking him. Dr. Gatien introduced the two guys, a plump one named Robert and a medium one named Gary, plus a thin girl, Marcella. Then Dr. Gatien crossed to the nursing station and picked up the chart. "You've met Mrs. Lee. So what's your diagnosis, Dr. Sze?"

Some staff doctors make a point of calling you "doctor" once you graduate from medical school and get your Doctor of Medicine degree. Sometimes it's a sign of respect. Sometimes it's to up your status in front of the patient. And sometimes, like with Dr. Gatien, you get the feeling it's because they're more formal in general.

I cleared my throat. Time to improvise. After all the talk about justice and murder, I didn't really have a diagnosis for Mrs. Lee, but I couldn't let that show. Medicine can be like a circus performance. You have to bark out the right answers and demonstrate the right tricks (intubation, IV insertion), often in front of an audience. You never get applause, only nods of approval, but the criticism never stops. "Ah, some sort of adjustment disorder—"

"After eight years?" He smiled at the medical students. The three shiny, happy white young'uns in white lab coats beamed back at him. I felt a pang. They were only two years behind me in training, but I wished I could be innocent like them again. Even before I solved the murder last month, the patients' suffering, the staff attitude, and the sleep deprivation had sucked the naïveté out of my marrow.

My smile tightened. I didn't do psych well. I wanted to be an emergency doctor, not a Face Man. "I know adjustment disorders are usually due to a short-term stress."

"Within three months, not more than six months, and not representing bereavement, if you read the DSM-IV," Dr. Gatien supplied.

Gary whipped out his notebook and wrote that down.

Dr. Gatien pretended not to preen.

"She's definitely suffering from bereavement," I said, annoyed. "There's no question. Her daughter, a former medical resident, died in a hit-and-run accident eight years ago." I hesitated, then plunged ahead. "Mrs. Lee believes it was deliberate."

"Ah." Dr. Gatien's index finger stabbed the air. "There you have the heart of the matter. She has a delusional disorder."

I shifted from foot to foot and glanced at the medical students. Gary was nodding, fascinated. The other two looked blank. I said, "I thought delusions were based on paranoia or erotomania, that sort of thing." Everyone knows paranoia; erotomania is when you have delusions that your partner is in love with someone else. I know a lot of girls like that.

Dr. Gatien nodded. "Arguably, this is a sort of persecutory delusion. The patient thinks she—or in this case, someone close to her—is or was persecuted. Did you read her chart?"

"Yes, I read what I could. Her older medical records have been archived." I brushed imaginary lint off my white coat while I debated whether to fall into party line or not. I'd started this rotation one week late. I wanted a good evaluation at the end. But Mrs. Lee's tears pricked my conscience. "Are you saying that for sure, the hit-and-run was an accident?"

He sighed. "We all miss Laura Lee. She was an excellent doctor. But as far as we know—which means as far as the police know—it was an accident. Or, at least, there's no proof otherwise." He stopped. His eyes narrowed and he smiled, showing a quick flash of his teeth. "Ah. That's right. You're the 'detective doctor!'"

My cheeks flushed. I was still getting used to my fifteen minutes of fame. In the olden days, after I introduced myself, people stared at me in confusion, as if I'd sneezed instead of saying my name. I had to say, "Dr. Sze. Like the letter C!" But now that I'd gotten some notoriety...

"That's right. I recognize you from the *Gazette*," said the chubby med student, Robert. Both local papers had done an item on me after I solved the murder of Dr. Radshaw, one of St. Joe's favourite doctors.

Dr. Gatien said, "Well, I don't think there's anything wrong with detective work. You need to be a detective in medicine, putting all the clues together. A patient comes in complaining of abdominal pain, you need to check the constellation of symptoms: location, radiation, nausea, vomiting, blood in the stools, as well as reviewing the systems—"

I knew that already. A wave of fatigue sideswiped me. I clenched my teeth, bit my inner lip, and widened my eyes, trying to fight it off.

"—because it could turn out to be something completely unrelated to the abdomen, such as diabetic ketoacidosis." He stopped and winked at me. "I imagine you thought I had forgotten my medicine, being a psychiatrist and all."

Gary chortled on cue.

I forced a smile. "Dr. Gatien, about Mrs. Lee—"

"Yes, of course. What I was going to say is, you should indeed investigate all avenues, as we have done over the past eight years. But be careful. We have a saying. If you have a hammer, everything looks like a nail. If you want to be a detective, everything looks suspicious. Be careful not to fall into any delusions yourself, Dr. Sze." He smiled. "You know what we call that in psychiatry? *Folie à deux*."

Charming. "You two would be cuckoo for Cocoa Puffs" always sounds better in French. After more talk, we ended up discharging Mrs. Lee and retreating to the psych office. I wrote another page in her chart, while Dr. Gatien pontificated to the medical students. Then I felt someone's gaze land and lock on my right cheekbone.

I swivelled in my chair to see who it was. My breath seized up and blood rose in my face.

It was John Tucker, staring right back at me. He was in the nursing station, behind Plexiglas, so he must have been fifteen feet away, but I could still feel his presence.

I forced myself to smile and nod at him like he was merely another resident or friend or comrade. So what if he liked sausages and beer. So what if I'd scanned the emerg a dozen times, checking for his profile. So what if I had to fight the urge to lick my lips and straighten my collar. It don't mean a thing.

But now that he was here, with his intense brown gaze, crooked mouth and eyebrows lifted with a combination of humour and disapproval, I couldn't lie to myself. All day, I'd been waiting to see him.

He shook his head at me from across the room.

I knew why. He thought I'd come back to work too soon.

He shoved his hands in his pockets, but in my mind's eye, I could imagine his strong, capable fingers, his short nails and the slightly tanned skin. Not to mention his lean yet muscled body.

Down, girl.

I forced myself to concentrate on his flaws, like his spiky blond hair. It looked as if he'd been attacked by '80s hair gel this morning. But who was I kidding. Even that was endearing.

"Dr. Sze?" a man drawled.

If guys are too perfect-looking, you have to wonder if they're gay, or at least narcissists. And anyway, I like a hint of non-conformity, that little F-U to the world of fashion police and humourless internists. Bring on the hair gel. Bring on red socks. Bring on the sausages and beer. When you've been in school all your life, even a tiny *soupçon* of revelry is a heady thing.

"Dr. Sze!"

Finally, I snapped my head around to focus on Dr. Gatien and the grinning group of medical students. "I'm sorry." I tried to hold my head up with dignity. No doubt he was about to interrogate me on the symptoms of Rett's syndrome or some other rare disease and make me look even more idiotic.

Instead, Dr. Gatien gave an almost imperceptible smile. "Never mind. I'll send one of the medical students to see the other patient, *detective.*"

The girl, Marcella, giggled. I mentally crossed her off my friend list.

Dr. Gatien waved over the psychiatry nurse, Nancy, to tell us about the next case. By the time we finally emerged from the office, Tucker had disappeared.

And a good thing, too. We were just friends. I was on a strict, man-free diet after a disastrous July encounter with a guy named Alex. The fact that I couldn't stop scanning the emerg like a rabid security guard meant absolutely zip.

Then Marcella pointed to a note affixed to the Plexiglas above the psych counter. "Is that for you?"

I glanced at the note. *DR. HOPE SZE.* I snatched it and unfolded it to read Tucker's spiky handwriting, scrawled with his signature blue fountain pen.

5-7? Page me. T.

3

---

*S*he knows too much. She's dangerous.

So I think, Fine. I'll leave.

But why should I run away again? I like my apartment. I like my girlfriend. I like this corner of Montreal.

Then I think, blackmail. *She knows some shit about me, I'll find out shit about her. If she coughs up some money to keep it quiet, I'll get some cash flow out of it too. Chinese doctors always have money.*

Only problem is, I can't find any good shit about her. Her biggest sin is probably picking her nose on Sundays, and I can't even catch her doing that.

So I go with plan C: kill her.

∽

CINQ À SEPT. Five to seven. Before I came to Montreal, I used to call it Happy Hour.

Actually, I didn't call it anything because I never went out. When I did med school in London, Ontario, we never seemed to take the time. For the first two years, I was in lectures forty hours a week and making love to my books when I wasn't sleeping. The last two years, I rotated through the hospitals as a clinical clerk, doing everything from trauma to mole removal. At the end of the year and each major rotation, everyone partied, but it wasn't the same as taking the time to hang out in a group as a part of life. So this was part of the *joie de vivre* I'd missed before I moved here. If you think about it, isn't it cool that in Montreal, you get happy for two hours instead of one?

So when Tucker's note said "5-7," I knew exactly what he meant. Even though he was probably going to lecture me—again—about coming back to work too soon, I was looking forward to seeing him. And, well, since no one else had mentioned a *cinq à sept,* it could be just the two of us, sipping drinks under a patio umbrella.

Could be, but it wasn't. When I paged him, he told me, "Tori and I are throwing you a welcome back party." Sigh.

Still, after work, he was the only one waiting for me at a picnic table beside St. Joe's main hospital building. He waved as soon as he spotted me. I blushed and tried not to rush over to him. Usually, the smokers commandeer the picnic tables, which offer a fine view of the parking lot and the old brick nurses' residence that houses the Family Medicine Clinic, but at the end of the day, most non-doctors had taken off, and it was me alone with Tucker.

He stretched out his long legs and grinned at me. His blond hair caught the sun like a white halo. I never thought I'd end up with a blond dude. Even if my sig other didn't end up being Chinese, I thought he'd have dark hair.

"How was your first day back?" he asked.

I considered several responses, at least one of them lecherous, but settled on, "I could use a drink."

He laughed. "Thought so." He quirked an eyebrow at me and I knew he wanted to ask about the big P.

In my case, that P stood for the panic attacks I'd been suffering during the past week, since Dr. Radshaw's the murderer had nearly strangled me. I could have ignored his hint, but I felt compelled to say, "Don't worry, I didn't get triaged as a psych patient myself."

"Good. I wouldn't want to have to see you." He meant as a patient. Like I said, Tucker did psych last month. Now he was doing psych combined with family medicine while I rotated on to pure psych. Tucker hesitated and added, "Like that, I mean."

Our eyes met and I looked away first. In July, when he was interested and I wasn't, it was so straightforward. Now, only a month later, we didn't know what to do with each other. He'd visited me lots of times while I was off last week, but usually with another friend, like Tori Yamamoto, in tow. Today, it was just us.

We sat in silence. The sun warmed my face and arms. For once, I hadn't reapplied my sunscreen and I didn't care. I closed my eyes and basked in the warmth. When I opened my eyes again, Tucker was staring at me with a mix of confusion and tenderness before his gaze slid away.

"You want to keep waiting here? We could always go ahead, get a drink by ourselves and tell Tori and Stan to meet us there," I said, trying to sound off-hand.

"Probably not a good idea."

My heart dropped before I caught the look in his eyes and he added, "You, me, alcohol. I'd have you pinned to the floor before you could say 'Uff-da.'"

I let the Norwegian or whatever slide. "Tucker—"

He stood up and shoved his hands in his pockets. "Just friends, remember? It's only been a few weeks since you and Alex."

I stubbed the toe of my shoe in the grass. I'd only been with two guys, in the carnal sense, in my entire life, but right now, I felt like I had a scarlet letter shining on my forehead. How 'bout a great big W, for Whore.

He bent over so he could look me in the eye. "Hope. Whatever you're thinking, forget it. I'd love to have a drink with you. Hell, I'd love to have a drink off you and bend you over this bench—"

My thighs tightened. Oh, he was nasty. In a good way.

"—and God knows, I'm no saint myself. But I'm trying. You're worth waiting for." He stopped short and ran his hand through his hair. Even with the hair gel, the top strands ended up endearingly askew. I reached my hand up to touch them before I caught myself.

He was saying the things I longed to hear. Before Alex, and maybe before my ex-boyfriend, Ryan, I would have jumped him. But now we were both gun shy. Part of me wished we could go back to flirting without consequences or any possibility of a future. I cleared my throat. "Thanks. I'll put that on my c.v."

He leaned close enough to kiss me. I caught my breath. He said, "Hope—"

"*There* you are!" Stan Biedelman hollered from across the parking lot, hands cupped around his mouth. "Did you turn off your pagers or what?"

I checked mine, but it hadn't gone off. Sometimes, the incompetent operators couldn't figure out how to page me. Tucker didn't bother to check his. "Saved by the Stan," he murmured.

I pretended not to hear. I waved at Tori, who popped out from behind Stan and frowned like she knew what I'd been thinking.

Within the hour, the four of us were ordering drinks on a bar-café's *terrasse* under a striped umbrella on St-Denis Street. I marvelled how a café managed to cast a spell negating the exhaust fumes and rumbling car engines.

When Tucker's legs bumped into mine, I edged my chair closer to Tori. He grinned at me like he could read my impure thoughts.

I turned away from him to sip my water and mop up a circle of condensation on the green plastic table. I glanced around to make sure no one else was within earshot before I said, "I can't wait for my drink. I deserve one after Dr. Gatien."

Stan snorted. "What about me? I did ICU today."

"How was that?" asked Tori.

"Same old. Saved some lives," he said.

I refused to be impressed. "Yeah. It must have been so taxing, you were out of there almost before I got out of psych."

He shrugged. "When you're good, you don't have to write five pages of notes."

"You do when you're on psych. At least if you're trying to make up for missing the first quarter of the block. If I miss one more week, I'll have to make up this entire rotation."

Tori made a disapproving noise low in her throat.

I balled up my wet cocktail napkin. "C'mon, Tori, you promised me no more guff when I came back to work. It was my decision."

"Yeah, but we can still make you feel guilty about it," said Tucker.

"No need." I flicked the wet napkin at him with my thumb and index finger. He caught it and slapped it on the table while I said, "I'm already being punished."

"Yeah, you got Mrs. Lee," said Stan. "I saw you guys in emerg. That poor woman."

I straightened in my seat. "You know her?"

He laughed. "Since I was a med student."

Right. Stan was from Montreal, born, bred, and trained, so of course he knew Mrs. Lee after nearly a decade of ER visits. "Did she ever tell you about Laura?"

"Yeah, but I didn't really know her. She was a few years ahead of me."

My jaw practically dropped open. "You knew Laura Lee?"

"Well, she played the piano in an end-of-year play in med school. She was pretty good. Back then, I was doing accounting and thinking about going medical. I didn't actually know her. But after she died, if Mrs. Lee came in when I was doing psych, we talked about Laura playing the piano, and it made her feel a little better."

I don't know why, it hadn't occurred to me until then, that Laura had been a flesh and blood presence at McGill until she died. "How about you, Tori? Did you know Laura too?"

She shook her head. "I'm from Alberta, remember?"

I laughed. Some detective I made. It wasn't that small a world.

Tucker's dark blond eyebrows drew together into a single line before I could ask him. "Oh, no. Don't tell me."

"What?"

He sighed. "I didn't know Laura. But I know Mrs. Lee, and I know you. You believe her, don't you? That someone killed her daughter?"

It sounded so unscientific, like I believed in Ouija boards and spirits rapping the table, once for yes, twice for no. "I don't know. I don't have any evidence to the contrary yet. I'm keeping an open mind."

He narrowed his eyes. "But you're not going to see Mrs. Lee again, unless she comes in—oh, my God. Did you offer to help her find out if Laura was run down on purpose?"

Instead of answering, I turned to Tori. "Have you ever met Mrs. Lee?"

Something about Tori is an oasis of calm and precision. She'd started drawing on her still-dry cocktail napkin with a black, felt tip pen while we spoke. Now we all shut up and watched her. She finished a few strokes before replying. "I know who you're talking about. I saw her in the emergency room because she'd cut her hand."

"And did she talk about her daughter?"

She shook her head and picked up her pen again. "I sutured her up and updated her tetanus shot."

"It didn't look like a suicide attempt, did it?"

She raised her eyebrows. "No. It looked like a cut in the web space between her thumb and index finger. She was washing a glass and it broke." She added a few lines. It looked like a bird's wing.

"So how did you know it was Laura Lee's mother?"

"One of the nurses told me the story."

The emergency room was a cauldron of gossip. Not that our foursome was any different. But she told me what I needed to know. Mrs. Lee was lucid then and now. She did not go around telling all Asian women they looked like her daughter and must read her file.

Tucker threw up his hands. "So you did offer to help her. God, Hope. You want to give yourself an MI before you're thirty?"

I ignored the heart attack crack. "I didn't offer. She asked," I replied with dignity.

"You didn't have to say yes." He stared at me, and I could see his thoughts marching across his face. The same things he'd said when he told me to take a longer stress break: *you almost died. Look after yourself. There's only one you. The patients will take care of themselves.* I found his transparency refreshing, but I didn't need his bossiness.

"I'm not doing anything," I told Tucker. "I'm only reading Mrs. Lee's file. If it doesn't go anywhere, neither do I."

"And if you do find a lead, or think you do?" Sarcasm laced the last part.

I hesitated. He had a point. I hadn't thought it all through. But I knew the right answer. "I'll talk to the police."

"Bullshit," said Tucker.

The waitress arrived with our drinks, so he got to look like a cursing barbarian while I smiled sweetly. Still, he was right in that I might not leave Laura's case in the police's hands.

The waitress set down a martini for me, the first in my life. I took a sip. Yuck. Not sweet at all. Well, at least the olive should be good, and the triangular glass was amusing.

Stan held his beer mug up in a toast. "I guess you're taking that 'detective doctor' thing seriously. Well, *à chacun son goût*." His French was terrible, but at least he wasn't giving me a hard time. I clinked my glass against his and he gulped his Guinness.

Tucker muttered under his breath.

Stan turned to him. "What's it to you, bud? She's a grown-up."

Tori said, "He's worried about her. We both are." She laid down her pen.

I glanced at her drawing. It was a bird in a cage. Was that supposed to be symbolic or something? I suspected as much from the way she refused to meet my eye. I made a face.

Meanwhile, Tucker was so mad, his nostrils flared. "Look. We all go into medicine thinking we're going to save the world, but most of us figure out it's not worth grinding ourselves into powder. Especially if you're already—"

Do not mention the panic attacks. I will kill you.

He caught himself, glanced at Stan and finished, "—in a vulnerable state."

"You're in a vulnerable state?" Stan said. "Let me guess. The Gaza Strip?"

I hardly heard him because I was so busy staring Tucker down. He blinked at the venom in my glare, but he didn't back down.

Neither did I. I'm old-fashioned enough that I like guys looking out for me. But that doesn't mean *patronizing* me. Tori and Tucker were the only people who knew about my panic attacks. Now that Tucker had almost told Stan the Mouth, I could see my secret spewing forth into the halls of St. Joe's.

Forget about the 'detective doctor.' I'd be the *defective* doctor.

Tori put her hand on Tucker's arm, but it was too late.

"I'll put *you* in a vulnerable state," I said to Tucker.

"Hope. Tucker," said Tori. "We've probably all said things we regret. Let's try and enjoy our afternoon."

I fixed my eyes on Tucker and enunciated very clearly. "I haven't even gotten started. For the past week, I've been listening and listening to you guys while I tried to get my head together. Well, I decided to come back to work. You don't have to agree with me, but for Chrissakes, if you're my friends, just support me. Don't tell me I'm wrong, I've screwed up, or I practically belong in a psych ward myself. I'm twenty-six years old, okay? I'm a medical doctor. I survived this long without you mapping out my every move. Lay off."

Tucker opened his mouth. "It's just—"

I stood up so fast, I rocked the patio table. The others grabbed their drinks. My martini stayed standing without me laying a finger on it. "Save your prescriptions for your patients."

Tori reached out as if to lay her hand on my arm, but hesitated and let her fingers flutter back into her lap.

Stan banged his mug on the table. "Hey, I don't have a problem with you investigating Laura Lee. It probably won't do any good, it's been what, almost ten years? But who cares. It's your funeral."

Funeral. Yep. I could have died last month.

I didn't say anything. Neither did Tucker or Tori.

After a frozen minute, even Stan figured out he'd said something inappropriate to a woman who'd had a near-death experience. "Sorry. I'm an ass."

"Me too," said Tucker, mouth twisting.

"Me three." I sat back down. Tucker handed me my glass. I took it, careful to avoid brushing his fingers. I wanted him. I hated him. And I hated him even more for pointing out I was more out of control than I'd thought. In my mind's eye, I saw myself writing a psych note on Dr. Hope Sze. Judgment: impaired. Insight: poor.

"So how about them Expos?" said Stan.

"They don't exist anymore," I said. I'm not a baseball fan, but even I knew that.

"Sucks, huh?" he said brightly. And conversation sort of turned back to normal, but after half an hour, I threw my money on the table. "Thanks. It's been a slice."

Tucker said, "Do you want—"

I cut him off. "I have to grab a few things before I head. Feminine hygiene products."

Oldest trick in the book: invoke menstruation and the men will melt away. It even works on doctors. Tucker sank back into his chair. I marched away to the sound of Stan's laughter.

I had to think. Thinking was easier without Tucker around.

Should I have stayed off longer?

Should I tell Mrs. Lee to forget it?

While these thoughts buzzed through my head, a man walked by with a brown dachshund in a carrier strapped to his chest. It doesn't get more metrosexual than that. I had to laugh.

Montreal was a lot different from London, Ontario. On St-Denis alone, I could hardly count the number and type of restaurants. Vegetarian Thai. Afghan. Vietnamese. A gelato shop. Plus cute clothes and stores selling mainly French CD's and books. If I had money instead of our resident's slave wages, I'd be in heaven.

Maybe literally. A cyclist nearly mowed me down as I crossed the street. He didn't say sorry or even turn around, just kept speeding down the street in his helmet and Spandex. I thought about giving him the finger, but what was the point?

I'd rather window-shop. Tori had mentioned a medieval clothing store. I felt like surrounding myself in brocade and satin and fantasy instead of real life.

"Hope!" called a male voice.

Was that Tucker? I spun around, already gritting my teeth, ready to face him.

But it wasn't Tucker. Or Stan. Or any guy from my residency program.

The guy walking toward me was one I'd know anywhere, any time, even though I hadn't seen him in almost two years. My breath froze in my throat.

His face seemed almost as familiar as my own, maybe more so, since I'd spent hours, days, even years memorizing it, from his gentle eyebrows to his well-shaped lips. I missed his hair, though. It was still crisp and black, but he'd pared it down to a crew cut instead of letting it touch his collar in the back.

Ryan Wu, my first love. My first lover. My only real boyfriend. Live in Montreal.

He was breathing a little faster from chasing after me. That made me think of other, more intimate times I'd seen him breathless.

We stared at each other. I couldn't believe how little he'd changed. I could see the same laughter in his brown eyes. He'd retained his slim build and long runner's legs. A few times I'd wished him fat and bald after we'd broken up, but now I was glad he looked almost exactly the same. I could mentally rewind the clock three, four years, before it all went sour.

I said, stupidly, "You cut your hair."

"So did you."

True. My hair used to spill past my shoulders, but I'd tried a chin-length bob and liked it.

He smiled. I smiled back. Then, suddenly shy. I glanced back at the café. We were a few blocks away, so I could barely make out our table, let alone Tucker.

Ryan nodded at me. "You look good,"

He said it first, thank goodness, which let me admit, "You too."

Ryan sticks to the truth. He was brutally honest, annoyingly Christian sometimes, but not a liar. Such a tonic after Alex, the first Montreal bad boy I got mixed up with.

I wanted to eyeball every detail of Ryan's body. Part of me wanted to make sure he was really here and now, within licking distance. The other part of me wanted to sprint far away from him.

I exhaled. "So what are you doing here? I mean, I didn't know you were in town."

His smile hitched up at the corner and he glanced over his shoulder. A girl in a miniskirt marched toward us on coltish little legs, black hair swinging with every step. She was pretty and she was pissed. I'd never met her, but her expression told me exactly who she was with respect to Ryan.

"Sorry, Lisa," he said. "I didn't want Hope to get away."

"No, we wouldn't want that," she agreed in a high-pitched voice. I looked down at her. She was so short, she was made miniature all over. In other words, the stereotypical Asian doll-like build that made even me feel like a tank, even though I was as Chinese as she was.

"Hi, Lisa, I'm Hope Sze." I tried to smile. I hadn't so much as glimpsed Ryan in over a year and a half, so why did I feel so bereft, meeting his girlfriend?

To my surprise, she held out her hand and pumped mine. She had a good grip for someone sparrow-sized. She said, "Pleased to meet you. I'm taking Ryan on a tour of Montreal."

He smiled. "I'm here with some buddies. I gave Lisa a call."

Well, that didn't sound too lovey-dovey. Neither did their stance, side by side but not touching. Not to mention him racing after me. My heart lifted, even as I scolded it. *No men. Not even ex-boyfriends.* Especially *not ex-boyfriends.*

"We're having a great time," she said.

He smiled. "Yeah, Lisa's an awesome tour guide. Listen, Hope, I'm here two more days. Maybe we could catch up sometime?"

I knew the mature, responsible, Lisa-friendly thing to do. Instead, I gave him my phone numbers, cell, land line, and pager, with my best smile. "Definitely. Call me."

4

Once I decided to kill her, I got pretty excited about it. There are so many ways to off someone. Think about it.

You could do it with your hands, like strangling, beating, or a karate chop. That one would be pretty funny, unless she knows karate too.

You could go totally hands-free and not be in the same room if you did poison or a fire.

I kinda like weapons like guns and knives. I even heard of using an ice pick.

Man, so many choices. It's like losing your virginity. You only get to do it for the first time once.

~

THE PHONE RANG TWICE that night, but both times, the caller hung up without leaving a message. I was too cheap to get caller ID, so all I could do was cross my fingers that Ryan would contact me before he left.

The next morning, I swung into the emerg nursing station and found a plain brown envelope propped against the printer.

DR. HOPE SZE. CONFIDENTIAL.

Mrs. Lee had written my name and her return address in indelible black marker.

I lifted the envelope. She'd chosen the padded kind, as if she needed to insulate the documents within. It felt surprisingly heavy for a bunch of paper.

"Mrs. Lee dropped that off last night," said Nancy, the psych emerg nurse. Psych patients need a lot of one-on-one that the regular emerg nurses are too busy to provide, so they get their own nurse. I'd vaguely noticed Nancy sitting next to the printer when I rotated through emerg last month, but I'd never registered what service she belonged to until I sat in her chair one day and a doctor told me the error of my ways. "That's the psych nurse's chair," he'd told me. "She always sits there." Now I sat there with her.

This envelope was the first concrete sign that Mrs. Lee meant business. Last chance to listen to Tucker.

Forget Tucker. I started to rip open the envelope flap.

Nancy shook her head and waved a clipboard at me. "Hot off the press."

I reached for the chart and laid the envelope on the table, both disappointed and relieved. "What've you got for me?"

"Reena Schuster. A twenty-nine year-old female who says she's depressed."

I was already scanning the triage note. Normal vitals, allergic to Haldol, nothing else remarkable. I hadn't done any psych-emerg before, but I'd done enough emerg last month to figure out the ER's no-nonsense approach to young, healthy, mildly depressed women: see if she's suicidal, and if she's not, give her the boot.

In a nice way.

I could give her a prescription or tell her to make an appointment with her doctor for a change in medication. If she didn't have an M.D., I'd hook her up with someone. And I'd make a "suicide pact." It sounds like something teenagers do with loaded shotguns under their arms, but actually, it boils down to, "Promise you'll come back if you feel like killing yourself."

So I already had vague plans for Reena Schuster before I even met her.

Room 14, the psych room, was a white box, usually empty except for the bed with restraining straps. Today its lights were off, which was kind of weird, but the surrounding emerg's fluorescent lights brightened the gloom of the room.

A heavy-set woman paced the room like a caged lion. Another woman, thin with bad blonde highlights visible even in dim light, sat on the bed and snapped her gum.

I knocked on the open door. The lion-pacer rounded the room to face me. She gasped and grabbed her chest so suddenly, her Medic Alert bracelet clinked against her watch.

Uh-oh. Ten-to-one, she was Reena Schuster, dramatic before we even started.

The skinny one narrowed her eyes at me without unfolding her legs from the bed. "Are you the doctor? You look way too young."

I forced a smile as I flicked on the light. We all blinked. "Hi, I'm Dr. Sze. I'm a medical doctor doing my residency training." I turned back to the lion-pacer. "Are you Reena Schuster?"

"Oh, God." she said instead of answering. "Oh. My. GOD." She threw herself on the bed and wrapped her head in her hands, rocking back and forth so hard on the edge, the gurney's wheels shifted. "It's fate. I know it is. I'm being punished."

"Reena. Chill," said the friend.

I cleared my throat. I'm not saying all patients love me, but was she really saying I was a punishment? Maybe it was the depression talking, although from what I've seen, truly depressed people don't have energy to pace or apply blue eyeliner like Reena. I tucked the clipboard under my arm, an uncertain smile pasted on my face.

Reena grabbed her own wavy brown hair with her hands and twisted it with her fingers until I saw her knuckles blanch. "Jodi? You see it too, don't you? We're coming full circle."

The friend, Jodi, put her arm around her. "Reena..."

"No. I know you think I'm nuts, but I'm serious. This is it. This is *it*!" Her voice rose to a scream. She dropped her hair and pounded her hands on her thighs.

I glanced at the door. I didn't dare close it. Rule number one: if you're worried, leave the door open.

Nancy stood behind the Plexiglas, frowning at us. So at least rule number two was covered: get help.

"Reena—"

"Don't say my name!"

Jodi drew Reena's head toward her chest and glared at me. "Could we get another doctor?"

It would look weak to go back without even asking one question. "I haven't done an assessment—"

Reena burst into noisy, messy tears.

"For God's sake, what do you want from her? She can't talk to you!" Jodi's voice was so hard, it cut through Reena's sobs.

Both Reena and I got very still.

I swallowed hard. Technically, I'm an M.D., but so many times, I didn't know what to do. My instinct was to flee. I steeled myself against it.

Reena's crying softened. I hovered in the doorway. Maybe I could wait her out. If, for some reason, I'd upset her, she could get over it and we could talk.

Still, I was relieved when Nancy's flats tapped into the room. "Is there a problem?"

"Her!" Reena said, pointing at me. Her red-rimmed, accusing eyes stabbed me from behind her curtain of hair.

"She hasn't even had a chance to talk to you yet, Reena. Would you rather come to the interview room? We've finished working in there, and you're welcome to come in." Nancy offered her a tissue.

Reena blew her nose loudly. "I can't. Not with *her*."

"She's the resident on today, Reena, and you've already talked with me—"

"So why does she have to go through it again?" demanded Jodi.

"This is a teaching hospital. You know how it works, don't you, Reena?" Nancy's body language, her comments, were all directed at

Reena. I realized part of my mistake was that I was trying to talk to both of them instead of concentrating on the patient. "We have medical students, residents, and staff physicians at St. Joseph's. It's part of the process."

"Yeah, but why *her*?" Reena's voice had turned more nasal, more whiny. My shoulders relaxed. I could handle brattiness, not hatred. Thank goodness for Nancy.

Jodi said, "Aren't we allowed to refuse?"

I gulped. Nancy said, "Yes, that's true, but we like there to be a reason. Do you have a reason?"

Silence. Jodi looked hard at Reena, who said finally, "I just can't."

Nancy glanced at me. "I'm sorry, Dr. Sze. Would you mind—?"

"No, no, that's all right." I handed her back the chart. Oops. I still had Mrs. Lee's envelope underneath. I tried to grab it back and flip it over, but it skittered off my fingers and landed on the floor, face up, with a bang.

I snatched it back, covering it with my body. "Excuse me."

Reena was already screaming, her hands welded into fists, her mouth one giant O, her body arched in misery, while Jodi yelled at me, "Get out, get out, get out!"

5

My hands were still shaking ten minutes later.

I paced the resident's room. It was smaller than Room 14. It was also dominated by a bed. But the door locked and I could be alone. So no one could see me gasping. The whites of my eyes. My heart throbbing in my throat, choking off my words.

Breathe.

I checked my watch. Twelve minutes. Long enough for them to subdue Reena. I should be back there. I should be running it.

Instead, I was alone with my panic attack.

"CODE WHITE. EMERGENCY ROOM. *CODE BLANC, SALLE D'URGENCE.*"

The words had echoed through the room. Men in white uniforms had descended. For one wild moment, I'd thought they were coming for me.

"Two of Ativan? She's allergic to Haldol," Nancy had said.

I'd nodded yes and bolted.

Some doctor I was, yelling at Tucker, telling him to respect me and my decision to return to work.

I couldn't even do psych.

Hell, I was too busy *being* psych.

Something about the room, the screaming, the *loathing* emanating from the two women threw me off.

Breathe.

I pressed my back against the white concrete wall and forced myself to take my own pulse, pressing my fingers against my carotid while I stared at my watch.

One hundred and twenty-four beats per minute.

Normal is usually between sixty and one hundred.

Breathe.

Well, at least pressing on my neck and providing some vagal stimulation might slow me down.

Lame medical humour.

Breathe.

I took my pulse again. One hundred and twenty-six.

Come on, Hope.

I glanced at my watch. Sixteen minutes away. Long enough for them to start asking, "What happened to the resident?" Nancy would have given the medication already.

Even though the emerg doctor was always in-house, and the psychiatrist was presumably on the way, I had to get back there.

On top of everything else, I felt terrible about dropping Mrs. Lee's envelope. I hadn't even realized I'd brought it into the room. It seemed like a violation of Mrs. Lee's privacy, although all it showed was her name and address. For all they knew, she could have been sending me Jehovah's Witness flyers.

Breathe.

Count: one twenty-two.

Better. Come on.

Even though I still felt sick, I unlocked the door leading back to emerg and stood inside it. The acid green walls of the room seemed to push in on me. I could hear someone flushing the toilet of the staff washroom across from me. The opposite side of the resident's room faced the main hospital hallway, so I could hear people talking in stereo, from the emergency department on one side and St. Joe's passers by on the other.

"—got to make a phone call—"

"I told him, no way. You want to, you do it."

"They're going to tap it under ultrasound. You might want to be there."

The key to the resident's room dangled from my hands. It was attached to a foot-long stick painted bright yellow, to prevent someone from accidentally walking away with it.

Footsteps approached the residents' room. "—think she's in here."

My breath hitched in my throat. I threw open the door and stepped into the hallway. My favourite emergency doc, Dr. Dupuis, gave me a quizzical look. He was pointing at the conference room beyond both the resident and staff room. It had nothing to do with me.

I smiled at him and, even though I still felt nauseous and clammy and like I wasn't in my own body, I pushed past him. Back to the salt mines.

First I took a good look at everyone to see if hell had truly fallen into a hand basket while I'd disappeared.

The unit clerk popped her gum as she sent a fax through. One nurse asked another, "Did you see the old chart?" as they both stepped aside for a janitor to empty the trash can. Someone had abandoned a chest X-ray. Even after a week away, I could spot the congestive heart failure at twenty paces.

I heard loud, angry women's voices from Room 14 before it went silent.

When Dr. Dupuis passed by me again, he said, "Don't worry about it," and kept walking with no other explanation. Still, I felt better, especially when Nancy emerged from Room 14 and said, "She's calmer now."

Forty minutes later, after Dr. Gatien had talked to Reena alone and signed off the chart, he called me into the psych office. I knew I was in trouble even before he tented his fingers and said, "Rapport is a very important part of psychiatry."

I nodded. The less talking I had to do, the better. I was grateful the med students weren't around to witness my humiliation.

"It is perhaps even the most important part. Rapport, through talk therapy, preceded the medications we rely on so heavily today."

I waited for him to get to the point. He was French. It might take a while.

"This is why I want you to consider very hard what you might have done to alienate this patient. This—" He picked up the chart and read off the name. "—Ms. Reena Schuster."

I squeezed my eyes shut. I wondered if beads of sweat had broken out on my forehead like in the movies. I resisted the urge to check. Better not draw attention to it.

"You may not have done anything, of course. It may have been a case of transference. However, it is unusual to get transference from the first moment. I'm not saying it's your fault."

Like hell you're not. But it was only a replay of what I was saying to myself.

"I am simply saying that some reflection is in order. She's calm now. She doesn't need to be admitted. Nancy told me a Code was necessary. Nancy is a woman who knows what she is doing."

Meaning that I didn't. That was certainly true. Tucker's voice rose in the back of my mind. *Grinding yourself to powder.*

"Dr. Sze?"

I jammed a smile on my face. "Yes. Thank you." I started to stand.

"About Mrs. Lee."

My heart dropped into my stomach. "Yes."

"It's natural to feel sympathy toward her. However, it is unwise to get *involved* with patients, if you understand my meaning."

I paused. "Yes. Thank you." He frowned at me, so I belatedly added, "Dr. Gatien."

This time, I managed to leave the psych office and close the door softly behind me.

A familiar brown envelope sat beside the printer in the psych corner of the nursing station. I'd abandoned it during my panic attack.

I flipped over the envelope. Mrs. Lee's handwriting stared at me again.

Nobody else wanted me to do this. And, for the first time, I seriously doubted I could do anything for Mrs. Lee, even offer basic words of comfort.

I could return the file to her unopened and say I was sorry. No can do. No harm, no foul.

Instead, I tucked the envelope under my arm so I could open it in private.

6

―――――――

They say psychopaths are born, not made.
      I don't know about that, but when I was a kid playing Clue,
      I wanted to do the crime, not solve it.
      Think about it. Colonel Mustard, creeping up behind the victim, trying not to let his tweed suit rustle before he whacks the guy with a candlestick in the conservatory.
      I went and looked up 'conservatory' in the dictionary so I could picture it better. In case you're interested, it's a glass room, like a greenhouse.
      Nice, huh? The blood would look so cool spraying against the glass.

I POPPED into the tiny St. Joe's library and cloistered myself at a study desk behind the journal stacks, away from the windows, with my back to the rest of the room. When I opened the envelope, photocopies of newspaper clippings topped the pile.

YOUNG DOCTOR SLAIN IN HIT-AND-RUN
      Montreal police are urging the driver who struck and killed Dr. Laura Lee on Île Ste-Hélène yesterday morning to surrender.

Lee, 27, was struck by a speeding vehicle believed to be a late-model, black Toyota, at approximately 5 a.m. as she walked the Concord Bridge to the Formula One track for her usual, early-morning in-line skate.

The motorist abandoned the scene, leaving Lee on the ground.

Lee was rushed to the University College Hospital, where she was pronounced dead from multiple injuries sustained at the scene.

The motorist was last seen on Pierre-Dupuy Avenue, heading toward Montreal.

Lee was a recently graduated emergency doctor at St. Joseph's hospital. "She will be missed," said Dr. David Dupuis, emergency department chief. "She's been part of the St. Joe's family for the past two years."

"I want to find who is responsible," said Regina Lee, the victim's mother, in a press statement. "If anyone has any information, if you might have seen anything at all, please tell the police."

Anyone with information about the accident is asked to call police at 514-555-1922, Crime Stoppers at 514-555-TIPS (8477), or online at www.555tips.com.

I SHIFTED my weight in the library chair. From the very beginning, Mrs. Lee had been determined to find the driver. I couldn't explain why, but it made me a touch uncomfortable. Even though I pride myself on speaking my mind and being goal-oriented, like Mrs. Lee, I did not know what to do with an actively grieving mother who was as fixated today as she was eight years ago.

The obituary didn't help.

LAURA LEE

Doctor, pianist, and most of all, beloved daughter, died tragically in a hit-and-run "accident" August eighth. Funeral August twelfth at

St. Gregory's Church at 10:00 a.m. In lieu of flowers, please contact police with any information regarding her death.

ONE MOTHER'S VIGIL FOR HIT-AND-RUN VICTIM

Montreal police are no closer to finding the driver who struck and killed Dr. Laura Lee, 27, on August eighth on the Concord Bridge from Île Notre-Dame to Île Ste-Hélène. Lee's mother will hold a vigil on the six-month anniversary of the investigation.

"This is unacceptable," says Regina Lee, a tiny woman whose strength belies her size. "They have no suspects, even though they found the car that hit her. Only a handful of witnesses have come forward, and their stories contradict each other."

Regina Lee is determined to do something about it. She has placed ads in the Montreal Gazette, *Le Devoir*, *La Presse*, and posted numerous blogs and posts, asking witnesses to come forward for a "substantial reward."

She will not answer specifics about the reward, except to say, "It is substantial in two ways. It is a considerable amount of money and the evidence must be substantiated." Crimestoppers has run a feature on Laura, but without obtaining any helpful leads. Mrs. Lee is determined to do it on her own: "Next week, I will hold a vigil on the bridge. I will be wearing a sign: 'WHO KILLED LAURA LEE?' I will hold a cross for her."

It is believed that Lee was heading toward the Formula One track for her customary morning exercise, in-line skating.

If anyone has information about Laura Lee's death, they are encouraged to contact the police.

WHEN I TYPED in a link she'd provided, I discovered a YouTube video interview with Mrs. Lee. A man held a microphone in her face and asked, "Do you really think the driver will turn himself in?"

Mrs. Lee was dressed completely in black, from shirt to shoes to purse. The camera zoomed in on her neatly made-up face. Even though the picture quality was crappy, I could tell her eyes were red. "Maybe. I can only ask. Maybe a friend will report them. Maybe the killer will at least feel shame and will know I have not forgotten."

"Some people say you're going too far."

She did not blink. "Some people's children are alive and breathing."

"Yes, but it's been said your own husband does not support your campaign."

She paused before answering, "I don't answer to anyone else except Laura, myself, and God."

The interviewer raised his eyebrows. "Does that mean you would consider vigilante action?"

She shook her head. "I want justice."

The interviewer paused and pointed at her black outfit. He asked, "It's been almost a year. Are you in mourning?"

She replied, "Always."

THAT GOT TO ME. *Always*. How do you survive that depth of sadness?

I tried to remember what Mrs. Lee had been wearing when we met. Something dark for sure. So she was still in mourning, if you hadn't already guessed.

I knew most people in the emerg probably thought she should mourn Laura and let her go. But how could you do that? How would you?

Which was why I had to help her. Even if I turned out to be just the five-hundredth opinion saying, "They did everything they could. I'm sorry."

I sifted through the police reports. It seemed like they'd interviewed a myriad of people, but only one woman said she'd been driving on Île Ste-Hélène on that Friday morning. She saw "a big black truck," wasn't sure of the make, model, or year, only that it was driving too fast, coming from Île Notre-Dame. She thought maybe there was a driver and a passenger in it. It was dented and the right headlight was broken, but it was raining and she hadn't gotten a good look at anything, including the license plate. Then, when she saw Laura's body, she'd pulled over on the island and called the police.

After the ambulance took Laura away, the police came and gathered what evidence they could, focusing on the blood spatter, a concrete rail imprinted with black paint imprints, headlight fragments, and skid marks.

They measured everything. They interviewed that witness, Lucinda McLaughlin, repeatedly. They put the word out through the media and through Crimestoppers.

I had copies of multiple reports, but mostly it was people saying, "Yeah, I saw a car driving weirdly that day." No one got a good view of the driver or the passenger. The main witness said it had been a black truck, but three others said navy, and someone else said beige.

Later that morning, at the corner of Embro and Saguenay, they found a Toyota 4Runner. Black. A man had called it in because of the blood and hair on the front left fender. Long, black hair. I swallowed hard and ran my hand over my own locks. I'd never been so relieved I'd cut them.

Of course, a Mr. Dwayne Richardson had reported the vehicle stolen the night before.

The identifying officers scoured the SUV and collected every hair, fingerprint, and cigarette butt from the ashtray. The cigarettes turned out to be Dwayne's, but the officers were thorough.

They ran it through the backlogged DNA sample system three years later. One blond hair, not belonging to the Richardson family, was found on the passenger seat. They documented the DNA results, but couldn't determine who it belonged to. Whoever it was wasn't in the criminal system's database.

It could have been anyone he'd given a ride to, but of course they were hoping it was the hit-and-run driver. They just didn't have any suspects to test.

The police also found red polyester fibers on the passenger seat and black ones on the driver's seat. These fibers, especially red ones, might have been from a wig, but it was hard to say. Certainly there was no longer any trace of a wig or anything more incriminating, like beer bottles that could have provided more DNA evidence.

The original owners were not under suspicion. Cars got stolen pretty often in Montreal.

The case was archived, which meant it was still open, but they had no leads at all. Only Mrs. Lee.

I put my head down on the library desk. It probably wasn't sanitary, but the wood felt cool under my cheek.

Some 'detective doctor.' I had no idea how to help her.

My pager went off. I leapt to my feet. Anything, anyone, even Reena Schuster, was preferable to my helplessness.

The pager number was unfamiliar.

When I called, the voice wasn't. Ryan wanted to take me out for lunch.

~

"MMM, PAKORAS," said Ryan, reaching for something that looked like deep-fried onions. "Want one?"

I stared at him. When he'd paged me and asked me out, I named an Indian restaurant around the corner from St. Joe's as a kind of test. Ryan and I ate mostly Chinese or Western food when we were together. I'd tried Indian once or twice on my own since moving to Montreal, so I figured I'd be pushing Ryan's boundaries. But here he was, more familiar with the menu than I was.

I gestured for Ryan to take a bite first. "How is it?"

He smiled and nodded. "Good. There's one in Ottawa that's better. I'll take you sometime, if you like."

I hesitated for a second, thinking of Tucker. But he was in my bad books, and it wasn't like Ryan was proposing. "Sure."

He cut the *pakora* with his fork and moved it to my plate. "Come on, Hope. We used to share everything."

That was true. I love food, and I used to insist we order different dishes so I could maximize my menu tasting. "Thanks." The tamarind sauce was tangy without being too strong. "Nice!"

"Thought you'd like it. Try the mint, too. One of my buddies at work is Indian. His mom is an awesome cook."

So that's how he'd gotten into it, not through Lisa. It was strange, seeing Ryan, so familiar, but different. Older, confident, more fearless. And still so freaking handsome. I'd met him at the table and hesitated because my first instinct had been to kiss him hello.

Now I tried the mint sauce to distract myself. Cool, creamy, but not as good as the tamarind. "So what's new and exciting with you?"

He laughed and leaned back in his chair. "Aw, same old. Work, playing squash, running. You know the drill."

Yes, but are you still drilling Lisa? "Yeah. How's Lisa?" I sipped my mango *lassi*. It's like a milkshake but with yoghurt and fresh fruit, and sinfully good.

"She seems to be doing all right." He grinned at me. "You gonna try the cilantro or not?"

I made a face. It's supposed to be the Chinese parsley, but I've never been crazy about it. Still, I could never resist a dare. I speared a tiny piece of *pakora* and swirled it around the cilantro sauce before popping it in my mouth. "Hey, not bad."

He smiled. Ryan had the best smile out of anyone I knew, boyish and charming but smouldering when he wanted it. He could have been in a toothpaste ad. Or an underwear ad. I crossed my ankles and pressed my knees together. What was wrong with me? *Remember Alex. Remember Tucker. Y chromosomes are bad.*

Ryan gestured with his fork. "See, you've got to try new things."

Mr. Conservative, now preaching novelty. "You're one to talk." Lisa flashed into my mind again. Miniature but spirited. Probably very athletic in bed.

He shrugged and sipped his water. "Yeah, I know. It's not like I'm a 'detective doctor' or anything."

I dropped my fork on the table and wiped my mouth. "I am getting so sick of that."

"I bet." He gave me a funny smile, quizzical and wondering at the same time. "Enough that you'll never do it again?"

My heart thumped in my chest. Oh, no. Don't let Ryan get down on me too. "Depends on the circumstances, I guess."

"I mean, I could kind of understand when you're working and you come across one of your own doctors, dead."

I flinched. That was what had happened in July.

Ryan squeezed my hand and dropped it before I could savour his warm skin on mine. "That would be harsh. But still, turning it into a whodunnit? You should have heard my grandmother."

"I'm glad I didn't." I wiped my mouth with my napkin.

He held up his hands. "Hey, it's your life."

Thank goodness he understood better than Tucker. I smiled at him.

"Anyway, I've got no complaints. I'm on summer vacation, eating good food with a beautiful woman."

I wasn't sure what to make of the compliment. The Ryan I remembered wasn't so smooth. He liked the way I looked, but he was usually too shy to say so unless I was all dressed up or we were naked in bed. I parried, "You're lucky you get a vacation. Must be nice."

He raised his eyebrow but didn't immediately leap to the bait the way he used to. *I warned you. Look at me, I'm an engineer. I only did four years of university and companies still headhunt me while you scrabble for quarters for the laundry.* Maybe him changing wasn't all bad.

"How's work, anyway?" I said.

"I'm still working at Norco, but I may go back to grad school. I haven't decided." He shrugged. "So what about you? Life's not too beige?"

I burst out laughing. I once wrote Ryan a letter in a red felt-tip pen and he'd said, "Why don't you write in blue or black, like everybody else?" Over lunch, I'd tried to explain that I wasn't like everybody else. "Most people want to join the herd of cattle. They wear the same clothes and say the same things and watch the same TV programs. If they were a colour, they'd be beige. I am *not* beige."

He'd given me a big smack on the lips, not caring if anyone else saw. "True. Your parents shouldn't have named you Hope. They should have named you Truth. Or Not-Beige."

We'd giggled in the sun, and it was good.

But when we'd started fighting, he'd said, "Do you really think you don't want to be like everyone else? You don't even like being Chinese."

I couldn't deny it. Nowadays, people might say "Yellow Power," with pride, but when I was growing up, I was the only non-white kid at my homogenized school. Kids called me squaw. An adult might yell, "*Konichiwa!*" as I walked down the street. A job interviewer once asked me when I'd moved from Vancouver, and told me he liked to make stir-fries at home. All of them were ignorant, some of them were assholes, most of them were painfully well-meaning when they assumed they knew everything about me because of my skin colour. *Oh, look, another annoyingly skinny girl who'll throw off the bell curve by day and cook bok choy for her Chinese grandmother by night.*

Sure, there were advantages to my culture. As a "banana," born yellow on the outside and bred white on the inside, I was barely starting to figure out how my academic achievement and family bond(age) had been shaped by my roots. But when I was growing up, all I wanted was to fit in. To be beige.

Anyway. So much had happened to me, but Ryan hadn't heard anything past my second year of medical school. I'd had patients die on me. I'd helped save other people's lives. I'd moved to another province. I'd solved a murder and almost gotten killed myself. "Uh...finished med school. Clerkship was really the best of times and the worst of times. Now I'm here."

He didn't look at me. "Are you seeing anyone?"

I shook my head. It was technically true.

"Did you?" He glanced at me, then away.

"Yeah. A guy in my class. It didn't work out."

Right away, he guessed, "My grandmother mentioned some guy. John. John Tucker?"

I half-laughed. "No. We're just friends." So far, anyway. "It was another guy, Alex. But that's over."

He raised his eyebrows. "You're over him?"

I shrugged. "Enough. What about you and Lisa?"

He looked straight ahead. "Nothing doing."

"Not even—" I wasn't sure exactly how to ask. Booty call? Or, more likely, yearning looks over hymnals?

But he said, flatly, "No."

"Okay." I swung my feet. Even though I hadn't had that much sun, my legs and feet were quite tanned. "I know it's none of my business, but I guess you didn't break up over religion."

"No, that part was good." He was silent so long, I thought he wasn't done, but finally, he added, "She didn't trust me."

It felt like a reprimand, however indirect. I stayed silent.

"Around other girls." He glanced at me sidelong, and suddenly I wanted to smile. Hope, 2, Lisa, 1.

The waitress brought us our main dishes, beef curry for him, *sag paneer* for me, *naan* and *basmati* rice for both of us. Steam rose from the dishes. My stomach growled.

Ryan laughed. "Did you get any breakfast?"

"Sort of." A pack of soda crackers from my lab coat pocket.

He made sure to serve me first. That's a Chinese thing. You show respect by serving the other person first, preferably starting with the eldest. I smiled.

I reached for the *naan*. Butter shone in the bread's dimpled pockets, a cholesterol sin, but I didn't care. Medicine makes you eat like you're at war. Not that psych was supposed to feel that way, but I was actually more stressed than when I'd been on emerg.

I tore off a piece of *naan* and watched Ryan's eyebrows come together as he spooned food on his own plate, careful not to let the different foods touch. I used to tease him about that kind of engineering precision. No wonder his hobbies included model airplanes and tinkering with solar car design. The guy was all about rulers and agendas. Except for me.

I started eating. The spinach in the *sag paneer* was mushy, but I liked the cheese. Ryan's beef curry was better. I mixed it with the rice.

He had a talent for ordering something better than me, no matter how I pondered and reasoned over the menu.

Ryan. Talent.

A light bulb lit up over my head.

Mrs. Lee's envelope was not as helpful as I'd imagined. Most of it was filled with police reports, dense with jargon, some information blacked out. Like I said, I knew that the team on the scene had measured tire tracks, gathered up pieces of a broken headlight, taken paint samples and measurements off the guard rail where Laura had been crushed.

Maybe, just maybe, Ryan could do something with that data.

But first, I had to talk to Mrs. Lee and get her permission.

7

The Mafia.
     The Crips.
     The Bloods.
The Yakuza.
They had it good.

That's what I wanted. An organization I headed, where I could throw a dart at someone's picture and say, bang. Take 'em out. And someone would. No fuss, no muss.

But part of me wants to know what it's like to kill someone myself.

I've seen dead people in the movies. They got their eyes blank and some nasty-looking makeup. But what does it really feel like to kill?

Say if you're strangling someone. You've got your hands around the neck. You're squeezing. She's fighting. She's clawing. She's choking. She's getting weaker. Limp. Unconscious.

Can you feel the second the life leaves the body? Or do you have to keep on squeezing until you're totally sure?

~

WHEN I ROLLED in at 8:36 a.m. for my morning psych ER shift, Nancy had already lined up an eighteen year-old sent by the CLSC (Quebec community health) clinic for "R/O (rule out) first psychotic break."

But Mrs. Lee waved to me from beside the psychiatry office, her face bright with expectation.

Although she smiled, her eyes tracked my every move. She wore a navy dress and beige sandals with a matching handbag, a perfect lady who was no longer in strict mourning, except she'd taken full advantage of my disclosure that I was in the emerg most days on this rotation.

She had hope. In more than one sense of the word.

I groaned to myself. The psych office door was open, and I couldn't see Nancy or the eighteen year-old, so I waved Mrs. Lee into the office. "Please sit down, Mrs. Lee."

"You read the file," she said, even as she tucked her skirt under her legs and drew her purse on to her lap. The woman did not waste time.

I nodded.

"You don't think I have a case."

My head jerked up.

The corners of her mouth turned up. "You think I haven't seen your expression before? I know it well."

That reminded me of a line in *Eat, Pray, Love* where Elizabeth Gilbert's ex says, "You have the opposite of a poker face. More like a...miniature golf face."

Mrs. Lee inclined her head regally. "I've read the file myself, many times. I know there isn't hard evidence, only hearsay. The police told me so. They felt sorry for me, but said they couldn't help me."

"Then why did you give me the file?"

She paused a long moment. "Did you see the picture?"

I nodded. They'd included her class photo in the news reports. "She was lovely." Clear brown eyes, delicate features, a touch of humour in her lips. Not to mention her *pièce de resistance*, a sweep of shiny black hair to mid-back, probably her one vanity.

Her eyelid flickered in acknowledgement. "Did you see the resemblance?"

I paused, unsure how much to let on. Who wants to admit that she looks like a dead woman? "Some."

"Not only in looks, but in how you act. She was very good at her work. She was always professional, always looking out for the patient, always studying." She paused. "She pretended to be tough."

I bit my tongue. Mrs. Lee was projecting Laura onto me, to use another psych term. How on earth would this woman know if I were tough or hard-working? I don't study enough.

I wouldn't argue with her. I didn't want to give her any more ammunition. I felt sorry for her, but Tucker was right. I'd gone far enough. Time to cut my ties. "Mrs. Lee."

"Yes." Her eyes were nearly black in the dim light, but extremely calm.

"I don't think I can help you."

"I admit the file doesn't give you a sense of Laura as a person. Her favourite colour was blue. She played soccer. We had a puppy who got run over when she was twelve, and she refused to have a dog ever again, because she loved him so much. She called me every week, even when she was terribly busy with her work."

I closed my eyes. I talk to my family every Sunday night, barring nights on call. The truth was, I could see myself in Laura and Laura in me.

"I know you're not a professional detective. But the professionals haven't helped me. I have to ask everywhere I can. Will you help me?"

I steeled myself. "Mrs. Lee, you asked me to read the file and I did."

"But there's more. In her room."

Going to a patient's house. Ixnay, ixnay. "No, thank you."

"She kept a filing cabinet that might contain more clues."

Clues to a hit-and-run?

"Please. I think that, as a medical professional, you might discover something the police passed over."

Why would a doctor make a better detective than a detective?

"Please, Dr. Sze."

I shook my head. "I'd be wasting your time."

She met my eyes. "Dr. Sze, as far as I'm concerned, my entire life has been a waste of time since she died. The only thing I can do is try and unearth the truth. I've been trying for eight years. I need a fresh pair of eyes."

It was illogical. It was false hope.

I opened my mouth to say no, but my heart answered instead of my brain. "All right. I'll think about going to your house." *After I decide if it's unethical or not.* "Actually, I was wondering something else."

"Yes?" Her fingers dented her bag.

"I know an engineer who does computer modeling in his spare time. I thought he might be able to use the measurements from the police report to simulate the...accident and prove that it was deliberate."

She nodded and cocked her head to one side. "The police thought it was an accident."

"Back then, they might not have done a computer simulation." If the Quebec police system is funded anything like the medical system, they'd be a good decade or two behind the rest of the civilized world. "R—I mean, my friend might be able to prove it. If it's true."

To my surprise, when I met her eyes, she was smiling. No tears. No argument. Just two words. "Thank you."

I licked my lips, more uncomfortable than if she'd argued with me. "But I don't want to give you false expectations. It probably won't prove anything."

"I know. But you're on my side. Thank you." She leaned over the desk to shake my hand. Her grasp was firm.

I glanced through the open door and spotted Nancy giving me the eye. Moments later, I ushered Walter Turrigan into the office. He looked like your average eighteen year-old who missed the golden days of heavy metal: a medium-built white guy with scraggly, shoulder-length hair, in a faded black Alice Cooper T-shirt and tight jeans ripped at the knees.

"Hello, Walter," I said after Nancy closed the door behind us. It seemed rude to read through the referral notes in front of him. I needed an ice breaker. "Do you go to school?" I'd never understood the Quebec school system. They do high school, some sort of pre-college thing called CÉGEP, and then college or university. At eighteen, I wasn't sure where he fit. "Or are you working?"

"I go to school. I might quit, though." He wasn't quite making eye contact. His gaze fell somewhere behind my left shoulder.

I glanced behind me. I saw nothing except some cabinets and a print of Van Gogh's sunflowers. I turned back to Walter. "Why might you quit?"

He paused. Shrugged. Brief eye contact. "I've got more important things to do."

The skin at the back of my neck prickled. "Like what?"

His eyes strayed to the sunflower print. No answer.

I repeated, "What more important things do you have to do?"

Another long pause, communion with the print.

I craned my neck around and took another look. Nice yellow sunflowers in a gold frame. We stared at it in silence together before I asked, "Does this picture mean something to you?"

His gaze flickered to me. "I can't tell you."

"Is somebody telling you not to?"

He shifted in his chair. "Maybe."

Bingo. This could be the moment to ask the most important questions. I needed to know if he heard voices and if they were dangerous. "Is this the same person who tells you to hurt yourself?"

His left eyelid twitched. "Who told you that?"

I had to move delicately and maintain our rapport but still gather the information. Once a psychiatrist told me his second choice of career was surgery. For the first time, I partially grasped the idea of slicing with words instead of with a scalpel. I parried, "Why don't you tell me about it? I want to help you."

He watched at the print for a long beat and seemed to ask it, instead of me, "Who are you?"

"I told you. Dr. Hope Sze. A resident doctor in psychiatry."

He paused. I waited. Silence is useful. But then he said, "I can't talk to you."

"Why not?" slipped out of my mouth. I'd rather have the scalpel. I'm way too blunt, too rushed, with words.

He raised his voice. "I can't."

Uh oh. I was losing him. "Would you rather talk to the psychiatrist?"

He stood up. "I have to get out of here."

"No. Please don't do that." I really couldn't let a psychotic patient leave, and the last thing I needed was a second Code White. "So, ah, tell me about yourself. Where do you live?"

"I live with my parents. I may move out, though."

There was a certain trend here. Whenever he gave me a little information, he immediately backtracked. "Okay. What school do you go to?"

"McGill."

Technically, we were enrolled at the same university, although the only time I saw the campus was when I got photographed for my student card and the few times I made it to aerobics class. "And what are you studying?"

"Engineering."

"That's a tough field," I said, meaning it. My dad was an electrical engineer. Ryan had a very heavy course load in mechanical.

"Yeah." I got a twitch of eye contact again.

"Do you think that's stressful? The work?"

He shrugged. "It's okay." He went back to staring at the sunflowers.

"How about staying at home? Do you get along with your parents?"

He glared at me for a second.

Ah. Houston, we have contact. "Are you mad at your mother for bringing you here? Or your father, for not coming?"

He burst out, "Leave me alone! My father—" His hands batted the air. "Shut up!"

I stayed silent.

His hand gripped the chair. The knuckles shone white under his skin, but his breathing slowed as he stared at the desk.

"Walter," I said quietly, "is someone besides me talking to you?"

He nodded, a tiny jerk of the chin.

It was enough. "Does he or she tell you to hurt yourself?"

An even smaller nod.

Geez. Poor guy. It was hard enough to battle through engineering and family feuds without the hallucinations. The stress might have triggered the psychotic break. "Did you hurt yourself?"

A curt shake of the head.

"No pills? Or, ah, weapons? A gun?" One of the suicide assessment scores specifically asks about firearms.

"No," he said to the ground.

"Do you take any drugs or alcohol?"

He lifted his chin and barked. "I said no!"

Damn it. I'd speeded ahead again and alienated him. But maybe I'd gotten enough. He'd admitted to voices in his head urging suicide. He needed to be admitted. I tried to remember what was left in the interview and realized I still needed to plow through everyone's favourite, the orientation questions. "I only have a few more questions left. They may sound stupid, but I have to ask everyone. Do you know where you are?"

He glared at me. "The hospital."

"Which one?" My voice was gentle.

"St. Joe's."

I asked him the date and what his mother's name was. Walter was looking more and more hostile as he answered correctly. I said, "I'm almost done, Walter, but I have to do a physical exam to make sure there aren't any problems. Is that okay?"

He checked the sunflower print. "I guess."

I was still getting a weird vibe off of him, so I opened the door. "This way, everyone can see that you're okay."

The psych nurse, Nancy, peered at me from behind the Plexiglas. Good. One of the med students, Robert, popped up beside her. I was covered.

I turned back to Walter's heart and lungs, finishing with a cursory neurological exam.

Next, Robert and I interviewed Walter's mother alone in the

family room, a little room with a stuffed green couch, two armchairs, and omnipresent boxes of tissues. Mrs. Turrigan licked her lips. "Walter's very tired. I need to take him home and let him rest."

"Yes, but you told the CLSC doctor that—" Nancy handed me some more notes. I checked them so I could get the exact wording —"Walter said that he could talk to the birds outside his window. They threatened to peck his eyes out. A voice in his head said that he could save them the trouble and pluck his own eyeballs out, one by one."

She shuddered. "Yes. Well. That's true, but I don't think he would do that if I were watching him. He's always liked birds. So if I could take my Walter home..." She had a round face with wide-set blue eyes, a combination that somehow made her seem younger and slightly unbalanced.

"Mrs. Turrigan. Is there a history of mental illness in your or your husband's family?"

She shook her head. "No. Nothing serious."

"Anything un-serious?" She looked blank, so I said, "Was anyone sad, or anxious? Did they see anything or hear anything other people couldn't?"

She paused to think before she waved her hand. "Oh, one of my aunts. My father's sister. She was very religious. She talked to Jesus. But wouldn't we all like to?" She forced a laugh. "We consider her lucky. Blessed, you know."

"And your husband's family?"

"Not that he told me." She gave a smile that was more like a flash of teeth. "We're separated."

Parents breaking up. One more stressor for Walter. "How did you think it was going for him at school?"

"He's always been the top of his class. He won lots of awards when he graduated, and he received a good scholarship at McGill. I've never worried about my Walter and school." She chuckled. "I don't understand what he talks about half the time. He's a bright boy."

"As far as you know, does he take any drugs or alcohol?"

She reared back in her seat. "No, no! Our family is very strict about that. We've always told him to say no. And he's been too busy. He raised money for children with AIDS when he was in CÉGEP. He plays guitar in a band. And now, of course, with engineering, it can be a bit much." She folded her hands in her lap. "Walter is fine, just overtired."

I felt bad for her. Robert and I exchanged a look. I wasn't sure if I should try and break the bad news to her or let the staff doctor earn his keep. "Mrs. Turrigan—"

Her cheeks flamed. "No! I don't know what I'm doing here. It's been a very long day. All I wanted was for his doctor to give him a few pills to calm him down. She made me come to the emergency room and now they're talking about making him stay here? It's ridiculous!"

"Mrs. Turrigan, I know it's hard." What could I say? She was in denial and I had no good idea how to comfort her. "I am going to talk to the psychiatrist, but Walter is probably going to have to...stay here." That was a good euphemism. "We're going to have to work together to do what's best for Walter."

She held herself rigid, but tears sprouted in her eyes.

Robert had been silent up 'til now. It was my case and he was there to observe. But he reached forward and touched her hand.

She stiffened.

We all held our breath.

Then she blinked and tears fell from her eyes, even as she kept perfectly still, her gaze fixed on the coat hook on the back of the door. In that moment, she reminded me of her son.

That made me think of Mrs. Lee. There's more than one way to lose your kid.

After admitting Walter, I felt exhausted. Instead of grabbing a coffee, I hit the gym.

St. Joe's has a little, staff-only gym beside its cafeteria that costs ten dollars per month. Whenever I have a few spare minutes, I put on my running shoes. Since it was before the lunch hour rush, I had the place nearly to myself. Now I only had to decide if I could go over to Mrs. Lee's house or not.

I sighed and lowered my stack of weights using my quads.

There are no fixed rules about interacting with patients, but we went over some guidelines in med school.

Don't hug. If they hug you, you can accept it, but never initiate. It's better if you pat them on the arm, at most.

Don't date.

But then the question always came up, what if you live in a small town where you're the only doctor and you don't have anyone but patients to hang out with?

So they made up some more rules:

Psychiatrists, never. Never date. Certainly don't screw. Nothing. Completely off-limits.

Emerg, where it's an in-and-out visit and you'll never see them again, wait six months.

Mrs. Lee couldn't wait six months.

I filled up my water bottle at the fountain while another guy blasted CNN and walked the treadmill. The door beeped, signaling another gym rat's entrance.

I sensed someone behind me and turned.

Tucker said, "Hey" and gave me a crooked smile. He'd combed his bangs down into his face, Brit-rocker style, and somehow it made him look more contrite.

My heart thawed. I was supposed to be mad at him for bossing me around, but it felt old. "Hey." For the first time, I noticed his nose was slightly deviated to the left. Born with it, or broken?

"What are you staring at?" He raised his voice to be heard over the news. *An armed robbery in Arlington, Virginia. The suspect is male, estimated to be in his early twenties...*

I lifted my water bottle and took a sip. It was a good excuse to break our gaze. "Nothing." I wiped my mouth with the back of my hand.

"Liar." He laughed softly and stepped toward me.

I felt trapped between him, the water fountain, and the trapezius pull machine. It wasn't a bad feeling, except I was totally confused about him. Weren't Tucker and I fighting? Sort of?

"You're calculating how to do my rhinoplasty, right?" He tapped the side of his nose.

"Yeah. How much it would cost to repair if I broke it again, if you start ordering me around."

He pretended to be shocked. "My mistake. Some girls like that sort of thing."

His last sentence rang out as the other guy suddenly cut the volume on the TV.

Ah. Masochism jokes. Way to undermine my physician image. I glanced over at the treadmill to see how the one guy was taking it. He was wiping it down and getting his access card out.

I swallowed hard. The tiny room smelled of old shoes and antiseptic spray. Not exactly romantic, but Tucker and I were going to be alone.

Always dangerous.

I tried to shift the mood and muttered, "Well, save your S&M moves for all your other girls."

Beep. The other guy passed his card over the reader. The door eased closed behind him.

When I looked up, Tucker was smiling. "I know. You're a tough nut."

Why was everyone calling me tough today? Mrs. Lee had said I was pretending to be tough, but still.

"Tori and I were talking about you."

I grimaced.

"—and if you can't beat 'em—" He paused slightly. I refused to meet his eyes. "—you join, 'em, right? So how can I help you help Mrs. Lee?"

I narrowed my eyes. "Are you serious?"

He shrugged and straddled the lat bench. I felt both relieved and disappointed he'd moved away. "Why not?"

I struggled to control a smile. "So you admit I'm right?"

"Never." He started pulling down the bar. I watched the muscles in his arms. Unfortunately, he was wearing a baggy T-shirt. I still admired his forearms. "But, as Tori pointed out, if my chief complaint is that you're working too hard, my job is to cut down your workload. So we're going to be your Scoobies."

"Huh?"

"Off *Buffy*. Her sidekicks are the Scoobies." He sighed. "*Buffy the Vampire Slayer*. You have no idea what I'm talking about, right? Let your education begin."

I laughed.

"I'm serious. Once upon a time, there was a blonde chick in Sunnydale, California, who discovered she had a special talent for kicking vampire butt. And demon butt. And, well, evil in general."

I started doing my triceps. I could see him through our weight stacks, since our machines were facing each other. Nice leg muscles. Hairy but not gross. When I glanced up at him, he was smiling, but he said, "There will be a test, Buffy."

If the test was on his legs, I'd probably pass. I cleared my throat. "There probably is something you can help me with." I glanced around one more time to make sure we were alone. "I've never been to Île Ste-Hélène. Do you want to check it out with me? Maybe this weekend?"

The smile spread across his face. "I was hoping you'd say that."

My pager went off. I checked the number. Emerg.

I sighed. Tucker just waved at me. "Later, Buffy."

NANCY SWIVELLED in her chair and pushed the chart toward me. "More business. Reena Schuster."

My heart fluttered in my chest. No. No more panic attacks. I took a deep breath. "Again?"

"We get a lot of repeat customers." She paused. "I already spoke with her. She said she doesn't want to talk to you."

I dropped into the chair beside her. It sank down to midget-height under my weight, reflecting my mood. "What happens then? Will the psychiatrist come in?" When I admitted Walter, Dr. Forbes had said he was in the middle of a case and would see him on the

ward. I couldn't see the psychiatrist rushing in to interview Reena
Schuster.

"I can give him my assessment. So can the medical student. But it's
not unusual for patients to be antagonistic. You could try talking to
her. Usually, they cooperate if you keep trying."

Of course I would try, but my stomach tightened. I felt light-
headed. I pinched my wrist to ground myself. I'd inserted tubes down
people's airways and shocked people's hearts. Why did I have so
much trouble on psych? "Sure. I wonder why she keeps coming back
here, though, if she refuses to see me."

She pointed to the address on the chart. "She's in our sector."

That made me think of Mrs. Lee. I rubbed my forehead.

Nancy gave me a strange look. "Headache," I said, trying to act as
normal as possible.

It was almost 11:30 a.m. I asked Robert to come with me. It would
be faster if we did it together, and he could take over if she
refused me.

I strode in the office. Reena was sitting in the corner with a coat
over her shoulders despite the heat outside. The same friend took the
chair closest to the door. "Hi, Reena—"

She put her hands to her mouth and almost screamed. "I don't
want to see you!"

My teeth clenched together so abruptly, I bit the skin inside my
lower lip. Why did she hate me so much?

Robert gasped, bumping into my back. "Sorry!"

I ignored him. I clutched her chart harder to my chest. I would
not drop anything this time. "I know you don't want to see me. I'm
sorry—"

Reena covered her eyes. "Oh, God, *you're* sorry!"

Jodi slid off her chair and put her hand on Reena's arm, her body
blocking me. "Chill."

Reena shoved her away. "I will *not* fucking chill, you bitch!" Her
face was blotchy, as if she'd been crying or sleeping face-down. Her
pupils were dilated and her lips were cracked. I wondered if she was
on something. I started to glance at her chart, to check her vital signs,

but Reena twisted her hair around her fists again, arresting my eye. Was she going to hit me next?

I stood frozen in the doorway, blocking the medical student, until I heard Nancy's heels tapping toward us.

I relaxed a smidgen and let her through. She said, "Now, now, Reena."

Reena pointed at me, her index finger trembling. "You want me to confess. You want me to go crazy. But I won't!"

Why would I want that? I shook my head.

"Of course you won't, Reena." Jodi threw her arm around her. "Everything is fine."

"*LIAR!*" She launched her head back. I could hear her gnashing her teeth. She was an animal.

I gulped. Jodi tried to draw her into her arms, but Reena shoved her away, shouting over her shoulder at me, "You should give me drugs! I'm not fucking talking to you! You can't make me! Do you want me to *get* suicidal? Is that what you want, bitch? Would that make everything even? Well, I won't!"

She pounded to the other side of the exam room and wrenched open the door to the hallway. Two people waiting for their X-rays looked up, startled, as she rushed toward them.

Reena veered sharply to the right, then burst out of the emergency department exit on to the street.

8

The hospital guards looked shell-shocked. They stared at Reena Schuster, disappearing down *Péloquin* Street, and then back at us for guidance.

"Oh, my God! Should we call a code?" I asked Nancy. With a Code White, they could've wrestled Reena down.

Nancy hesitated. "It would be the police now. She's off hospital property."

Jodi snapped, "Don't bother. She's fine." She raced after her, blasting past an old couple hobbling into the emerg. The woman with a cane stumbled. The old man steadied her elbow.

"Hey!" I called, but Jodi's dirty blonde hair vanished after Reena. At that pace, we'd lose both of them before I could dial 911. I backed into the psych room and reached for the phone.

Nancy laid her hand on mine. "Wait. She wasn't suicidal during my assessment this morning or when you saw her yesterday."

"Right, but—"

"She's off hospital property now," she repeated.

Robert shook his head and shoved his hands in his pocket. He wasn't getting involved.

"What are you saying?" All I could think was that my patients were literally running away from me. What was worse, two Code Whites in two days or one Code White and one taking off AMA (against medical advice)?

"I'll call Dr. Forbes," said Nancy.

I stepped back. She'd be better at breaking the bad news. She claimed the phone and spoke in muted tones.

"It's not your fault," muttered Robert.

I rubbed my hand against my forehead. Wasn't it? Should I have sent the medical student in solo, knowing she was unwilling to see me, instead of going in myself to try and hurry up the case?

And why did Reena hate me so much? I'd just met her.

I'd heard of projection and transference and vaguely understood the concept: patients had a lot of crap, and thought the therapist was doling it out, when in fact it was their own fears coming back at them. But I'd thought it only happened after long term therapy, especially Freudian. Reena had hated me on sight. Why did I make her so nuts?

She definitely seemed more unbalanced today. Why did she think I wanted her to go crazy or kill herself? I didn't even know her. I'd be happy if she stayed at home, eating Corn Flakes.

Nancy hung up the phone. "Dr. Forbes says there's nothing we can do. She's a borderline and a frequent flyer, and now she's off the premises. He's not going to send the police after her. She'll probably come back on her own."

Yes, probably tomorrow afternoon, when I was back on psych-emerg. My eyes ached with fatigue. This was supposed to be an easy rotation, but so far, it was worse than straight emerg. The ER was exciting. In, out. Boom, boom. Evening and night shifts took their mental and physical toll, but you got bragging rights and you had a set time to go home. At this rate, my next two months would be non-stop Reena Schuster refusing to see me and making everyone else think I was incompetent.

Nancy forced a smile. "You two should go eat. I'll call you when someone else comes in."

As we trudged up the stairs to the residents' room, Robert said, "Are you okay?"

Miniature golf face struck again. I shrugged. "I don't know why she bothers me so much."

"That's the borderlines' job, right? They make you nuts, too."

I hadn't even diagnosed her as a borderline. I had no instinct for psych. She told me she was depressed, so I went through the checklist for depression and thought about a few other diagnoses like bipolar disorder or substance abuse. That was it. But it was true, her chart was covered in borderline personality disorder.

Robert punched in the code for the resident's lounge and held the door open for me. "I knew someone who worked with borderlines. She said..." He hesitated and lowered his voice. "You can tell who they are because they make you so mad. If you want to strangle them, they're borderlines."

I half-laughed. "Yeah? The psychiatrist I worked with said to think of Glenn Close from *Fatal Attraction*." I passed through the door. "Thanks."

"That's good, too." He stood by the fridge door, obviously mulling over Reena, but more like he was interested instead of irritated. "I don't think she was typical, though. The scars on her arms were old. I doubt she's slashed herself for months, maybe years. Still, she was angry, and I think she had definite abandonment issues, so she does fit the profile."

He was going through the borderline diagnostic criteria. Anger, fear of abandonment, paranoid or suicidal under stress, a tendency to idealize or demonize people, and more often than not, wrist-cutting. Hey, that sounded exactly like Reena. And I shouldn't take all the hating personally—borderlines either loved you or hated you, and I happened to end up on the hate list.

For the first time, I stopped to look at Robert, not as a pudgy medical student in a white coat, but as a human being who was a lot more psych-savvy than I was or ever would be. "Are you planning on doing psych?"

He smiled, seemingly undisturbed by the rotting food smell emanating from both the garbage can and the refrigerator. "Does it show?"

They say there are two types of doctors, internists and surgeons. Internists like to pore over books and think deep thoughts; surgeons like to act. I'm obviously a surgeon. I'd classified Robert as an internist, but now I wasn't sure. Maybe psychiatrists are a breed of their own.

I threw open the fridge door to hunt for my bottle of water. Music videos blasted in the background. A med student I didn't recognize chewed lasagna with the remote in one hand and his fork in the other.

Tucker was nowhere to be seen. I glanced at my watch. Forty minutes had passed. No chance he was still in the gym.

I chugged from my bottle and chanted to myself, *I am not disappointed. I am not.*

My pager went off. Not emerg, but an outside number with an area code 514. Who would be calling me from outside the hospital but within Montreal?

"Is it Nancy?" asked Robert.

I shook my head. I could think of one possible candidate who'd take my mind off of Tucker. I walked to the wall-mounted phone and punched in the number, my pulse already accelerating.

A familiar male voice said, "Hey."

"Hi, Ryan," I said, aiming for calm instead of *eek.*

"Hard at work?"

"Yeah. I already admitted one patient."

"Geez. Is that why you're listening to Britney Spears?"

I laughed and glanced at the TV, where Britney managed to dance and flash her cleavage with equal abandon. "Something like that. I actually get a lunch break when I'm on psych."

"Amazing. Listen, I was calling about the thing you asked me." Mrs. Lee. Business before pleasure. "Could I use your computer to start on the modeling? I'm leaving on Thursday, but I've got some ideas."

I twisted the phone cord around my finger. Hmm. Ryan in my apartment, waiting for me to get home. Business *and* pleasure? "Aren't you supposed to be on vacation?"

"It's boring."

Ha. He'd rather do work for me than score with Lisa. "I should make you do downtime."

"But."

"If you come by now, you can pick up my keys."

"Sweet."

I wolfed down my sandwich, continually checking my watch. If Ryan was late, he'd interrupt my family medicine clinic. He usually had a good sense of direction, but what if he got lost in a strange city? Or got waylaid by a petite girl with claws?

Oh me of little faith. Not only did Ryan page me from the parking circle in front of the hospital half an hour later, but when I bounced up to him, he handed me a single dwarf sunflower.

"Oh, Ryan." I surveyed the orange-yellow petals and delicate stamens and wanted to kiss him in the sunflower, if you know what I mean. How did I ever let this man go?

Still, I had to laugh at the sheer impracticality of me carrying a sunflower, even a dwarf one, around the hospital for the rest of the day.

He shrugged and smiled. "Better than Britney, right?"

"Much." I sniffed it. No sweet smell, but still wonderful. I twirled it between my fingers while we stood in the drop-off circle, inhaling exhaust fumes and cigarette smoke and smiling like idiots.

Having Ryan here felt like I'd clicked back into my usual orbit. I knew those intelligent brown eyes, that straight nose, those well-chiselled cheekbones and gently pointed chin. Okay, he hadn't tucked his T-shirt into his khaki shorts the way he always used to do, and the shirt was a little more fitted than in days of yore, but moving up a point or two on the fashion scale was a good thing, right? I should probably try that someday myself.

He took a step closer, staring into my eyes like he was remembering things a lot hotter than my old T-shirts. I could feel the warmth of his body even though he hadn't touched me.

I started babbling. "We grew sunflowers in front of our house one year, but the birds ate all the seeds."

He didn't move any closer, but didn't move away, either. "I remember."

I frowned. "That was before I knew you. I think my dad planted them when I was, like, in grade eight."

"I remember you telling me about them."

That was the other thing about Ryan, his memory for details. Like once I pointed out a postcard of a Valentine in the sand on the beach. When V-Day came up half a year later, he stamped my name in the snow, surrounded by a giant heart. Oh. Ryan. The first, the great, the only love of my life. I opened my mouth. "I lov—"

Holy crap.

I turned scarlet and tried to swallow my tongue.

He stood and watched. He knew what I was going to say. I'd only told him a million times when we were together. Then he said, "It's okay, Hope."

No. Totally not okay to almost tell your ex-boyfriend you love him. Even if it was practically a reflex. I turned my head, swallowing hard, and crossed the pavement toward the grassy knoll across from the front entrance. A patient paused to stare at us, one hand steadying her IV. I glared at her.

Ryan kept pace with me. "Are you still all right with me borrowing your computer? My netbook is pretty basic, and if you've still got some of the programs I loaded up on yours—" He paused. "Unless you've upgraded computers? I should have asked."

He knew me so well. I hadn't upgraded or deleted anything. I stared at my scuffed sandals. "No, I still have same computer with the design programs and whatever else you put on it. It's all right. I'm sorry." *I'm sorry I almost said I love you. I'm sorry I lost you.* Wait, where did that come from? Did near-strangling make you lose your frontal lobe? "Don't listen to me. I'm—not myself."

I heard him shrug. "Who would be?" And when I opened my eyes again, he was looking at me with such compassion and something else, something so deep and familiar, I had to turn away before I could identify it as tenderness.

That was when I saw Tucker.

9

I leaped away from Ryan as if he'd given me *C. diff* which, if you don't know it, is not bacteria you want to get up close and personal with.

Not that Ryan and I were doing anything wrong, but guilt seared my gut anyway. Ryan reached for my arm. I stepped away and shook my head.

"Hope?" said Ryan.

"Not now."

Ryan turned his head to follow mine. We both watched Tucker push through the hospital doors and stride right over to us, his brown eyes narrowed and jaw clenched.

Tucker wasted no time. "Hey, Hope, how's it going?"

"Okay—"

"Hi, I'm Tucker, who are you?" His hand shot out between me and Ryan.

Ryan glanced at me. *Who is this guy?*

"John Tucker's one of the residents in my year and, um...a good friend."

Ryan nodded and shook the hand, stepping forward and forcing Tucker's arm back. "Ryan Wu." Both of them squeezed hard enough for their knuckles to blanch.

Ryan paused. I realized he was waiting to see if his name registered with Tucker, but of course, why would I mention my ex-boyfriend? Tucker already had enough problems with Alex, who fell more into the enemy with benefits category.

I felt obligated to add, "Ryan and I did undergrad together and, mm—" *We used to love each other, in every sense of the word.*

Tucker rocked back on his heels, surveying Ryan. "Oh, an ex-boyfriend?" He placed a slight emphasis on the *ex*.

I knew I should cut out the testosterone fest, but I was curious how Ryan would bury that one.

Ryan didn't disappoint. He looked straight at Tucker and said, "I'm not into labels."

Tucker's lips tightened, but before he could say anything, Ryan raised an eyebrow at me. Thanks to our old telepathy, I realized he was signaling me to give him the key to my apartment.

Yeah, right. I've heard of suicide by cop, where you want to die so you pull a move in front of a police officer, begging him or her to blow you away. But I had no desire to hand over my key to Ryan so we could commit suicide by potential lover.

I looked from one lickable guy to the other, and I'll tell you the truth, I wanted both of them. Ryan, who could represent my past, present and future; Tucker, who had only met me last month and had witnessed the worst of me, but somehow still understood me. Not to mention that I could happily spend the rest of my life underneath (or on top, or beside, or astride) either of them.

Both of them.

For the first time, I wondered why I had to choose.

I'd already picked the bad apple the last time with Alex. My judgment was obviously impaired, to use a psych term. So the best thing I could do was delay my decision.

I started to smile. Both guys looked at me like I was crazy, then edged closer, certain I would pick him.

Since I still wanted Ryan to help me with Mrs. Lee, I needed to give him my key without triggering either of them to think he was the master of my universe.

First, I turned to Tucker. "Hey, I'm glad you to see you." He looked smug until I said, "I wanted to talk to you about some psych stuff. If you have a minute, I'll join you in the bookstore." St. Joseph's has a teeny used bookstore where battered children's books can go for a quarter. Tucker usually poked around in the mystery section while I debated over Lois Duncan or *The Hunger Games*.

Tucker folded his arms. "That's okay, I'll wait."

I couldn't help admiring his forearms again. His skin was a bit pale for my tastes, but I liked his definition.

"If you'd just give us a minute," said Ryan, with a hard stare.

Damn. I'd never seen Ryan facing another guy down, and he did it well. I might have assumed he'd be all cheery and Christian about it, but he didn't give a millimetre. Also, I already knew the feel of Ryan's body, which could be classified as a lethal weapon. I liked that, too.

I had to bite my lip. For a girl who spent high school dances dreading the slow songs because guys almost never asked me to dance, revenge sure tasted sweet.

Tucker turned to me. "Are you ready, Hope?"

I waved my hand in front of my face in my best imitation of a Southern belle. "Fellas, I'm about to pass out from the testosterone."

Tucker snorted. Ryan looked confused, but my bad accent did break the tension a tad.

"T-man, I'll be with you in two shakes. Could you give us a sec? I'll bet they've got another Jeffrey Deaver in for you."

Tucker shook his head, but he sort of laughed. "I'll check on my bike." He stalked about two feet away, to the bike racks, and bent over a silver one. I hadn't known he biked to work. I had to give him points for that and for the fact that he knew how to give me some space without giving up.

Ryan grinned and held out his hand for the key.

I handed him the sunflower while I scribbled down my address and worked my key off its chain. I'd almost forgotten the flower, what with all the vying for my attention. "Thanks for helping Mrs. Lee.

Help yourself to whatever's in the fridge. Sorry, I haven't gone shopping lately."

"*De nada*," he said. He paused and leaned his face over me for a second. I knew he wanted to kiss me goodbye. In Montreal, it's normal to kiss both cheeks hello and goodbye, but in Ottawa, you usually wave or hug. Ryan was sending me a clear signal.

I ducked out from under him without trying to make it too obvious. "Thanks again."

Tucker called, "Ready?"

Ryan nodded slowly. "Ready." He wasn't talking about computer modeling.

I held my finger up at Tucker, signaling that I needed another minute. Neither of these guys were boy toys. This was going to be tougher than I thought.

"Want to grab dinner after?" Ryan asked.

I shook my head. "I'm on call. It's home call, so I'm not sleeping at the hospital, but I don't know when I'll be back."

Ryan squinted at me. "Sometime in the evening?"

"Probably."

He shrugged. "I'm not picky."

I almost laughed. Ryan wasn't a foodie like me. He could get wrapped up in a problem set and forget to eat until he ordered a pizza at two a.m.

"Let's play it by ear, okay?"

"Sure. I have to get this key back to you, anyway."

"Yeah. The concierge has an extra if I really need one, though."

Ryan frowned. "This whole thing doesn't sound very secure to me. Is there some sort of security code I need to get in? Do you have a guard?"

I burst out laughing. The residents' lounge had better locks than my place. "No and no. Wait 'til you see it."

The frown lines deepened. "Why, what sort of security do you have?"

"You'll see." I gave him a gentle shove at the small of his back. "Do you understand my map?"

He rolled his eyes. Engineering boy, naturally gifted at directions. "I'll manage." He handed me the sunflower again. I clenched it between my teeth and grinned at him. He shook his head, smiling, and waved goodbye.

When I walked over to Tucker, unsure of how to approach him, he rang his bike bell. The peal made everyone stare, from pedestrians to an idling taxi driver, even before he said, "'Detective doctor,' incoming!"

"Shh!" I hurried to his side, tucking the flower under my arm.

He smiled at me, looking more like a sunny, blond, surfer dude than a caveman fighting over a woman. "Just trying to help, Buffy."

"Don't call me that."

"Why not? It's a compliment."

"It sounds like I should be prancing around in a miniskirt carrying a dog in a matching outfit."

He pursed his lips. "I could go for that." He offered me the crook of his arm.

I shook my head. Ryan's dark head and lean body was nearly out of sight, but I didn't want to play too many games and lose both of them. Of course, maybe I'd lose both of them anyway. I pushed away that depressing thought and focused on Tucker, who shrugged and waved me ahead of him.

"Where to, Sherlock? You still want to go to the bookstore?"

I shook my head. "I want to talk to you about psych, Watson, but family medicine clinic starts in ten minutes."

His gaze turned from mild to piercing. "Confidential stuff?"

I nodded.

He smiled. "I'll walk you to the FMC."

We weaved through the parking lot, away from the *hoi polloi*, while I outlined my woes with Reena Schuster. "I guess what I'm wondering is, have you ever had a patient who seemed to hate you so much on spec? As far as I know, I've never done anything to her." I paused between a BMW convertible and a beat-up VW Golf. "Did you ever have her? It would make me feel so much better if she kicked your ass, too."

He shook his head. "The name is familiar, though. I wonder if I saw her as a med student."

"Did you do psych here?" Med students rotate through different teaching hospitals throughout Montreal, unlike residents, who spend most of their time at one "base hospital."

He shook his head. His gelled hair hardly moved, but that was part of his charm.

"Well, that's it, then. She belongs to our sector, so you wouldn't have seen her there, except maybe as a one-off." I'd heard that if you got another sector's patient, you did an assessment and then sent him or her right back to home base. It was unlikely Tucker would remember someone he saw so briefly, unless Reena raised hell back then, too.

"I could've seen her at the Douglas," said Tucker. "I did an elective there."

At a psych hospital? Hard core. "I didn't know that." I almost tripped over a Vespa.

"Yeah." He put his hand over mine and guided me into the next lane, confident and graceful, almost like we were ballroom dancing. I opened my mouth to ask him if he'd ever taken lessons, but his fingers trailed over the fine hairs of my arm.

That one stroke, so light I could barely feel it, electrified my skin and made me clench my teeth together. I pulled away from him.

His hand dropped back to his side, his face innocent.

He knew exactly what kind of effect he'd had on me. I tried to match his expression. I preferred him and Ryan duelling over me from a safe distance.

I stepped up my pace toward the concrete stairs of the Family Medicine Clinic, but he led me to the ramp sloping its way up off the side. "The scenic route," he explained.

I laughed. Tucker was such a weirdo, but I liked it.

He said from behind me, as we reached the FMC's front doors, "You might not think of it to look at me, but when I was a young grasshopper, I considered psych at one point. That was before I realized the big bucks were in family medicine."

I twisted around to goggle at him. He met my eye with a deadpan expression.

We both burst out laughing. The sun highlighted his jaw and slanted across his eyes, lightening them to golden brown.

He bent forward.

I hesitated, unsure whether to lift my lips toward his, or step aside like I had with Ryan.

He reached past me to grab the latch of the ornate front door and swing it open with a bow. "Milady."

There were so many things I wanted to say to Tucker and couldn't.

He kept talking like the undertow of lust wasn't dragging him under. "I still know some of the psychiatrists at the Douglas. I'll talk to them, tell them I'm on psych here, ask around a bit about your patient."

I stiffened. I couldn't explain why, but goose bumps rose on my arms. "Don't get into trouble."

His shoulders shook with suppressed laughter. "Pot. Kettle. Black."

"Still." I stepped through the door, into the cool, shadowed foyer of the FMC, away from him. "Thanks. 'Bye, Kettle."

As I walked toward the staircase, I felt conscious of his eyes following me. I spent the next four flights of stairs fantasizing about him. And Ryan. How about him *and* Ryan at the same time? Why should guys get all the threesomes?

Then I thought of how they'd practically slit each other's throats while saying hello.

That made for an unlikely *ménage à trois*. Too bad.

Still, I grinned to myself through my first two patient appointments, even while renewing reams of medications and enduring caustic comments from my supervising physician, Dr. Callendar ("You should check her renal function, Dr. Sze, if medical detective work still appeals to you").

Then Stan started booming on the phone in the conference room.

"No, I'm at my clinic this afternoon. Page Dr. Owens," said Stan. He rolled his eyes at me. I covered a smile. Locating is hopeless at St.

Joe's. Then his voice dropped to seriousness. "It is? Oh. Page him right now, then! Or call the ICU."

Stan Biedelman is not easily rattled, so I lifted my eyebrows at him while I edged past him to grab a bone density sheet from the dusty bookcase in the corner.

He hung up the phone. "It's your patient. Reena Schuster."

"What?"

"She's in a coma. Probably an overdose."

10

Reena.

Coma.

Dr. Callendar ignored me while he ragged on Omar, one of the other residents. Then he turned to me. On autopilot, I reviewed my eighty-two year-old lady with hypertension, osteoporosis, and a remote MI, here for a blood pressure check.

Dr. Callendar managed to slice his way through my haze. "You shouldn't be here."

I bit my lip. Dr. Callendar had hated me from the get-go, kind of like Reena, come to think of it. Still, I was surprised he was so abrupt with me, considering I'd been strangled and all, until he said, "You should take a month off. More if you need it."

Oh. He was actually trying to be nice to me in a screwed-up, Twilight kind of way. Right. Me. Post-traumatic stress. By this point, I had so much new stress, the almost-being-strangled stress felt like old news. But it was nice to know Dr. Callendar preferred me breathing rather than six feet under. I focused on his greying black crew cut and told it, "If I took a month off, I'd have to add an extra month to my training. I'm not willing to do that."

He shuffled through the files in front of him and coughed. "You might...there have been exceptions."

Curiouser and curiouser. I almost smiled at him. "I want to get back to work, too. I was going crazy sitting at home."

"You might go crazy here too, doing psych," Stan said.

Dr. Callendar shrugged. "It's your decision. But don't expect any special treatment."

Ah. The old Dr. C I knew and loathed. I met his eyes. "I never do."

"Good." A smile played around his thin lips as he handed me a manila file. "Meet Mrs. Valdez, your new thirty-nine year-old primip with gestational diabetes, in her thirty-sixth week."

In other words, a first-time mother with a strong chance of having a giant baby, and taking two days to deliver it vaginally.

Dr. Callendar continued, at higher volume for Tori and Stan, who'd joined us with their own cases to review: "Sometimes the CLSC gets patients who are late in their pregnancy. Some of them are refugees from other countries. Of course, the CLSC doctors don't deliver, but we do. I thought Hope would enjoy some obstetric experience, especially since she's on psychiatry, which only has home call." He nodded at the chart. "Why don't you take a minute to familiarize yourself with the patient, and then, if you have any questions, bring them up after the others have reviewed their patients."

Glumly, I opened the chart.

Dr. Callendar tapped a sheet of paper with his pen. "Oh, and Hope. Gestational diabetes is a fascinating subject. Why don't you do a presentation on that for us, at our next obstetrical meeting."

I tried not to show any emotion. As far as I could see, he'd pretended to care about my near-death encounter to provoke me more, like offering a massage before delivering a right cross. He'd feed off any sign of despair.

It was almost enough to make me look forward to psych call.

Reena.

Coma.

I RUSHED into the emerg at 4:55, hoping Reena hadn't made it to the ICU yet. On the psych desk, I found a copy of the psych consult: *29 y.o. F, known to you, OD, SVP assess for suicidality when medically clear.*

I covered my eyes.

I heard low-heeled shoes tap toward me and a heavy body lower into the chair beside me. "Don't blame yourself," said Brigitte, the evening psych nurse.

I looked into her plump, rosy face and asked, "How can I not?"

"We all blame ourselves when a patient comes in after we've sent them home. You didn't make her take those pills."

True. But, at the most fundamental level, she came to the emergency room asking for help. And I obviously didn't give it to her.

I tried to concentrate on the medical part. "Do we know what she took?"

Brigitte shook her head. "We're waiting for the tox screen. She's not on anything, and the paramedics didn't find any bottles at the scene."

I glanced at the resus room. "Is her friend Jodi with her?"

Brigitte shook her head. "No one but family. Her sister was the one who called 911."

Was Jodi actually her sister? They didn't look alike, not that it meant anything, but the vibe was not what I'd call sisterly. "Is her sister with her now?"

"Yes. I'm getting her papers together. They're about to move her up to the unit."

Once Reena left the emerg, I wasn't officially responsible for the psych consult anymore. Not that they'd probably want me to do it.

I walked over to resus. For the first time in my fledgling medical career, I cringed slightly as I drew back the curtain, afraid of what I might find.

Reena was intubated. I'd kind of expected that, since she was going to ICU, but it still shocked me to see the tube down her throat and taped to her face. Her eyes were slitted closed, and her chest moved up and down, hissing in time with the respirator. Two IV's, and an O2 monitor on her finger. Her face was pale but sweaty.

I would not have recognized her, behind all the equipment, except for her curly hair spilling over the pillow.

"Are you another nurse?" said the girl beside the bed, pocketing her cell phone. It wasn't Jodi. She had brown skin and long, shiny black hair. She was pretty except for slightly crooked teeth. She looked Native Canadian to me. Nothing like Reena, except they both had the same solid build.

"No. I'm Dr. Hope Sze, a resident in psychiatry."

Her eyebrows jerked upward. "Ha! I see." She paused. "Get it? It's funny because of your name."

I'd already heard all the jokes about my last name, from sze-sick to Great Big Sze. I faked a smile. I don't have a sister, but I doubt I'd joke around if mine were in a coma. "Yes. I'm sorry about your sister."

A peculiar expression crossed her face. "Is she going to be all right?" Her voice rose and trembled at the end. She was younger than she looked. Maybe this was her way of freaking out.

"I hope so. We're doing our best."

Her shoulders sagged as she surveyed the equipment. "I know."

We watched Reena's chest rise and fall with the respirator for a moment before a heavy-set woman in black burst in. "Oh, Wendy, Wendy, Wendy—" She wrapped her arms around the sister. "I can't stand it. It's too awful. I never got to talk to her. The last thing I told her was that she should get a better job, she'll never know that I love her—"

"It's okay, Mom," said Wendy, muffled, into her shoulder. "I know."

"I couldn't stand to lose both my girls, you know that."

"I know."

The respiratory therapist and an orderly entered the room, swiftly followed by an emerg nurse who unplugged Reena's equipment and re-plugged her into a portable monitor and ventilator. "Her bed's ready upstairs," explained the nurse, Véronique, as she scooped up the chart.

Reena's mother pulled a tissue out of her sleeve cuff and blew her nose. "I'm sorry. I'm sorry, I don't mean to break down. It's just the worst I've ever seen her."

Véronique patted her shoulder before she released the brake on the stretcher.

Mrs. Schuster wiped her eyes. "Thank you, you've all been so..." She saw me. Her eyes widened and her shoulders jerked. "Oh, my God." She put her hand to her chest.

"I know, Mom," said Wendy.

Mrs. Schuster gaped at me, still blocking the stretcher.

Was this because she'd seen the 'detective doctor' articles? What was the big deal, anyway?

"Mom?" called the RT.

Wendy steered her mother out of the way. "It's okay, Mom. That's just a resident. Her name's Dr. Zee or something."

Véronique said, "ICU's on the second floor. Can you follow us in the next elevator? It's going to be cramped."

"Sure," said Wendy, since Mrs. Schuster was rubbing her forehead like she had a headache.

I wanted to follow them up, but I had to give them some space. I'd check on her later. In the meantime, Brigitte was signaling me back to the psych corner. It was going to be a long night.

11

I hate groups. I'd rather be alone. So what the hell am I doing in group therapy, anyway?

The short answer is, it started as a joke. It's kind of a love-hate thing I've got with people. Can't stand them, but I like to poke and prod them when I'm in the mood. So I drift down to bars, slouch my way through the mall, drink coffee at the Second Cup, even throw the occasional ball at the dog park. Whatever. If people talk to me, I talk back. I figure it's good practice.

That summer, at the Second Cup, I noticed this girl watching me, but every time I looked at her, she'd look away. I know that game. I went along with it, keeping my gaze on her longer and longer until she caught my eye and smiled. She had a nice rack and good-enough legs. I figured, why not.

Only she didn't go out on Monday nights. I thought it was school or her mom or whatever. It turned out to be this group therapy. Turned out you can "self-refer," so I went along one night. She thought I was the greatest. I told her no, she was.

She'd just introduced me to the biggest group of suckers I'd ever met. I couldn't wait to play each and every one of them.

∾

By the time I finished my shift, it was almost 11 p.m. My eyes and tongue were dry with fatigue.

I'd fully expected Ryan to grab a bite and head to his hotel room when I called and told him I'd be late. Instead, he'd said, "Call me when you're done. I'll walk you home."

I stared at the receiver. I'd never had someone look out for me when I was on call. "It's okay. Côte-des-Neiges is supposed to be pretty safe."

"Is that why there are so many cops around?"

I had to laugh, despite the ripple of unease across the back of my neck. I'd asked the same question when I moved here. Montrealers were like, "Oh, yeah, that's no big deal," although one nurse said, "Gang activity." I'd noticed a lot of cop cars on Côte-Ste-Catherine Street, the main drag, but very few right around my apartment. I said to Ryan, "I guess the cops are supposed to make it safer."

"Why don't you drive when you're on call?"

Good question. A parking pass cost fifty dollars a month, plus gas. I was on call every other day for psych. That'd be a lot of driving. Walking only took me twenty minutes, biking half that. And in Montreal, people seemed to walk or bike or take public transpo. I sighed. "Because I'm cheap and I don't live in Texas?"

He paused. I think he understood what I meant. I walked because I could. Because I thought it was uncivilized for a woman to be too afraid to walk home alone at night. But Ryan said, "Call me when you're done. Or about to be done. I don't mind waiting."

It felt good to be looked after. "Okay."

And now, spotting Ryan playing with his phone in the waiting room, my spirits lifted. No matter how tough I act, it's wonderful to have someone else look after me once in a while.

Ryan smiled and stood, shoving his phone in his back pocket. He kissed my cheek, lingering for a second longer than necessary while his breath tickled my ear.

I held my breath. There was no denying it, the man was good.

Just as I noticed the few other patients staring at us, he reached for my backpack and unstrapped it with a practiced gesture. I'd almost forgotten he used to do this, literally taking the weight off my shoulders. "Thanks," I said.

"No problem." He pointed at the sunflower, nested in a juice bottle, which I'd set on a chair while we maneuvered the backpack. "Can you manage that?"

"Yep. I've been working out." We both laughed and stepped out of the ER.

I took a deep breath of night air, cool and less humid than during the daytime. Chalk up another reason to walk home. Ryan slipped his hand in mine. "How was your day?"

His hand was warm and his fingers slightly callused. I couldn't make myself release it. I ran my finger along his thumb. "Better, now. How 'bout yours?"

"Interesting. Do you want to hear the nitty gritty?"

"Okay."

He talked. I was too tired to grasp the details, but he'd done some preliminary work on the computer models and contacted some people for help. "I went through some websites. There are a few books at the U of O that I'd like to check out. I doubt they'll be too useful beyond the principles."

I tried to stifle a yawn as we stopped at a light. No cars in sight, but Ryan is very law-abiding. "Thanks for doing this."

"You're welcome." He squeezed my hand and led me across before the walk sign came on. A good idea in Montreal, where the lights go out so often, they often have little stop signs attached to the posts, to make it easier for the cops to handle traffic. "Now, about the apartment, Hope..."

His tone was a warning. I sighed. "I didn't have time to clean up."

"It's not that." We passed Ste. Justine's, the French children's hospital around the corner from my place. He said, "We've got to get you a better security system."

I had to laugh. "My landlord is so cheap that when I pointed out that the window in my screen door was cracked, he said he'd replace it. He came back two days later with a window that was probably older than both of us put together. He rammed and rammed it until it fit. Barely. I was surprised he didn't shatter it. There is no way he's paying for a security system."

"Yeah, but it's not safe. There's no lock on the outer building door, so anyone could walk in and buzz your apartment."

"Right, so they can get in the lobby to buzz me or deliver the mail, but there's a lock on the inner door to the building—"

"Don't make me laugh. This afternoon, I walked up and pushed it open. The last guy hadn't made sure it latched behind him."

"I locked my apartment door," I said.

"That's the only thing between you and the street? A kid with a credit card could jimmy those locks."

I stared at my toes as we walked. Even I'd noticed my wimpy security system.

"And you're only one storey up. Someone could jump up on your balcony and come in through your balcony door or the windows right beside it."

I shivered. "Ryan. I don't want to think about this right now, honestly. It's been a tough night."

He adjusted my backpack's straps. "Look. I know you don't like hearing it. But you have to take care of yourself."

"I know," I said in a low voice.

"Tomorrow, we can go to the hardware store and get some new locks, and at least put some wood braces in your windows so people can't force them open from the outside. I saw a big hardware store on Côte-des-Neiges. I'm sure they have everything."

He glanced across the street at the giant steel-columned building for HEC, the business school of *l'École Polytechnique*. That's the same school where Marc Lépine walked into a classroom with a loaded gun. He separated the guys from the girls and yelled, "You're all feminists!" before he shot and killed fourteen innocent women. That was over twenty years ago, but even so. There's a memorial garden a few blocks southeast of here.

I stepped up the pace and squeezed his hand so Ryan wouldn't notice the HEC signs and make the connection. "Okay."

My apartment security was lax, but it did have some Art Deco charm. I cleared my throat as we walked up the path. "You like the lanterns?"

He nodded. "Nice. I wish they were brighter, though."

True. I could hardly see my black shoes against the dirt path, let alone any potential intruders lurking behind the full-grown trees or hedges. Ryan grimaced at the street lamp, no doubt calculating its wattage.

Ryan opened the outer door for me. It was made of real, stained wood and there were nice frosted glass accents beside it, but after Ryan's worrying I felt acutely conscious of the single bolt holding the inner door closed. "At least it's locked this time," I said. I didn't tell him that it lay open half the time, what with people moving in and out of the building.

Ryan looked heavenward. "Probably because I was the last one out."

"Probably." I glanced at the mailboxes to my right. He turned around so I could dig the mail key out of my backpack. I didn't bother telling him that the lock on the mailbox was acting wonky. I used the key and shoved the flyers and bills under my arm without checking them.

"I hate to keep beating this horse, but you've got H. Sze right on that mailbox and buzzer. It has your apartment number, too. The least they could do is scramble the apartment and buzzer numbers."

I pinched my nose. "Yeah. Okay." These thoughts had flitted through my subconscious, especially after I almost died last month, but I hadn't wanted to deal with them. We lived in Canada. We were safe. Apartment hunting was such a pain in the ass, and since nearly all the leases in Montreal ran until July 1, I wouldn't have much choice if I started looking again now. "I don't know what I can do about that, though. Would you be happy if I only put my initials on the mailbox or something?"

He scowled. "Would that really make you feel safe?"

I knew he was right. I also knew that I sincerely could not deal with it tonight. I gave him a look.

His lips softened. He ran his hand through his hair.

I unlocked the inner building door and he opened it for me, following me up the stairs closer than a friend-only would. I was very conscious of his warm body behind me and, I had no doubt, his eyes checking out my rear view. Despite my exhaustion, my pulse leaped.

Ryan closed and locked the apartment door behind us, not only twisting the main latch but dropping the tiny bolt into the floor as I set down my sunflower and my mail.

He hung my backpack neatly on a peg in the closet. "I'm staying with you tonight."

I tried to laugh. "Don't be ridiculous."

He looked at me with those intelligent, gorgeous, and oh-so-stubborn brown eyes. "Hope."

"You came to Montreal to be with your friends."

"Yeah. You."

That stopped me for a second, but I plowed on. "I'm no more unsafe here tonight than I was last night or any other night. The only difference is that you've sussed it out and—"

"And I wouldn't leave a cat alone in this apartment, let alone you."

I knew that voice. He was not going to change his mind. It was a complete pain when we were in-fighting, but the truth was, I could use some company tonight. I sighed. "I won't be a barrel of laughs."

"That's okay. I like monkeys better anyway."

It took me a second to get it. I laughed. "You're awful."

"I know you. You want to take a shower, right? And eat. Why don't you get cleaned up while I get you some dinner?"

I eyed him suspiciously. Ryan always enjoyed taking advantage of me after (or during) a long, hot soapy shower.

He exhaled. "Your virtue is safe."

"Too bad." It slipped out of me. I hurried off to the shower before he could respond.

12

The girl turned out to be more complicated than I thought. No wonder she was in therapy. Needy, screamy, "Do you love me as much as I love you," "I'll die if you ever leave me," et-fucking-cetera.

I don't need that shit. There are easier ways to get laid.

But I stuck around a little longer because there was another woman in that therapy group. Long black hair, long brown legs, pretty, but stand-offish. As soon as she met my eyes, I recognized an intelligence and a will as strong as my own.

I was sick of easy marks.

Let the games begin, Dr. Laura.

~

FIRST, I checked my five voice mail messages. They were all hang-ups, which was strange enough to make me check my pager. Someone had paged me twice, but left only a single number: four.

Huh. That didn't seem like Tucker. Not that I was thinking of him or anything.

I paused before I deleted the nonsensical pages. They bothered me, but the incompetence of our "locating" team is legendary, especially at night, when the regular operators go home and leave the switchboard to the security guard.

Before I stripped down for my shower, I paused a long moment. Then I pinged the lock closed.

Ryan had raised a few more spectres in my mind.

Part of me wanted nothing more than to wind myself around his warm runner's body and forget the past few years had ever happened. I was almost certain he wouldn't turn me away. Almost.

But we weren't twenty years old anymore. I was a doctor. Tucker was...well, I had no real idea what Tucker was. Yet.

I turned up the hot water and glanced around the tiny bathroom. Not exactly romantic, what with the grimy grout and the slight gap in the blind in the window next to the tub. Well, at least the square mosaic tile floor was charming. And with any luck, Ryan would concentrate on me instead of the décor.

As I drew the translucent shower curtain closed and luxuriated under the spray, I grew fully conscious of the fact that I was naked with a thin wooden door between myself and Ryan. A man who knew my body extremely well and wasn't afraid to use it.

I ran my hand over my breasts.

I was on a man-moratorium. A *manbbatical*.

That made me want Ryan even more.

What about Tucker?

Tucker wasn't here. Although, frankly, the thought of him, too, made me arch toward the water.

I could hear Ryan in the kitchen on the other side of the bathroom. I had a teeny galley-style kitchen, so narrow that you could touch the fridge with your left hand and the oven with your right hand (and the broom closet with your right elbow). The counter top that ran in a U between the appliances met in a sink by the window at the base of the U. I could imagine Ryan boosting me up on that counter. Hmm.

On the other side of the kitchen doorway, I'd crammed a table, to make it an eat-in kitchen, and a metal shelf for my cereal boxes. The shelf barely fit between the built-in ironing board and the door to the interior fire escape stairs, so there wasn't as much room for shenanigans, but the table still had possibilities. I wondered if he'd ever done it on a kitchen table with Lisa.

Lisa.

I grimaced and lathered up my hair. I was a jealous woman. No denying that. But from all signals, she was now out of the picture.

For all I knew, Ryan only wanted my Wifi with a side order of apartment security. And Tucker might only want what he couldn't have.

But my entire body hummed the opposite tune. I bent from the waist, the water sluicing through my hair and flowing over my back. My skin was warm and wet.

Ryan and I had been virgins when we met. Because I had good girl hang-ups and he'd been indoctrinated by the church, we held off on the main event for almost a year. Which meant we specialized in foreplay. We could have taught a night course in kissing, a weekend lesson in massage, and given college credits in oral sex. And once we finally got around to full-blown sex, we'd read and talked and nearly done it so many times, we turned it into an honours degree, *summa cum laude*.

Now he was right outside my door, waiting for me.

Oh, God, I might not be able to wait for him. My hand drifted between my legs, dipping again and again. Maybe it was better this way, release myself so I could think more clearly...

"Jesus!"

Ryan's voice was so sharp and angry, it cut through the pounding of the shower and my libido. I froze. This guy did not take the Lord's name in vain. For him, it was a worse curse than the f-word.

I rinsed off the soap and conditioner, my heart thumping for a different reason. Something was wrong.

I climbed back into my used clothes and didn't bother to wrap my short hair in a towel. I threw open the door. "Ryan? What's wrong?"

He was standing in the doorway to the kitchen, frowning by the wall-mounted phone abandoned by the previous owners. "Hope. Sorry." Then he stopped and stared at me.

My cheeks were already flushed from the shower, but they would have heated anyway, under his gaze, raking me from messy, towel-dried hair to my still-intrigued breasts, right down to my slightly damp toes. I knew exactly what he was thinking. His brow furrowed. His nostrils flared. A muscle clenched in his jaw.

Just for a second. Then he shook himself. "Sorry," he said again. "Finish your shower."

"I'm okay." Maybe I'd misread his cues. I wished I'd wrapped myself in a towel instead. More classic. More prone to slipping to the floor.

He shook his head. "No, you relax. Really."

I cocked my head. "Ryan. What is it?"

He sighed and walked back to the front hall. "I knocked over your mail and found something."

He handed me a plain white piece of paper folded in half like a flyer. I unfolded a black and white photocopy of a picture of a tomb-stone. The name, prominently engraved in the rock:

HOPE.

13

Someone had photoshopped my name on a tombstone picture and left it in my mailbox.

I nearly dropped the piece of paper.

It could have been a coincidence. It could have been some mass mailing about the death of hope with a follow-up about the saviour who could save us. But somehow, I didn't think so.

After the near death thing, plus Ryan's paranoia, plus the weird phone calls, seeing my name on a tombstone made me really glad he was staying tonight. And it made me wonder what the hell was going on.

As Ryan pointed out, the name on my mailbox is H. Sze, not Hope Sze. So if this was personal, someone deduced my first name and where I lived in order to send me a picture of a tombstone with my name on it.

Who did it?

Only one way to find out. I walked to the kitchen for a Ziploc bag.

"What's going on?" said Ryan.

"I don't know, but I'll let the police figure it out," I said, sealing the bag. "They can check it for fingerprints. Where did you find this?"

He ran a hand through his hair, exasperated. "Tucked in your mail, with your phone bill and the KFC and Pizza Hut flyers. You can look for yourself. But the weird thing is, I swear I've seen that picture before."

I rifled through the flyers from Bell Canada, Videotron (my Net provider), and a notice from McGill. Everything else looked official, like it was from Canada Post, who has the contract to deliver junk mail. I was trying to remember if I'd seen the piece of paper tucked in with the rest when I took it out of my mailbox. I thought so, but I couldn't be sure.

"How the hell did someone do this? Break open your mailbox?" asked Ryan.

I sighed. "Actually..."

He snapped his head back to glare at me. "Don't tell me."

"My mailbox doesn't latch properly. The mailman left a note about it, but the *concièrge* didn't do anything to fix it, and I thought, well, it's just mail."

"So anyone could get into your mail."

I didn't answer.

"This place is a disaster."

I hadn't considered it paradise, but through Ryan's eyes, I had to admit it was appearing worse and worse. I tried to make a joke. "You should have seen the place I didn't take, with the two little dogs. The woman let the dogs poop on the balcony, and we almost tripped over a vegetable rolling in the middle of the hallway."

He reached for my shoulders. "Hope, this is not a joke."

I twisted away from him before he could make contact. "I know that! But I'm too pissed off to be scared." As soon as I said it, I realized it was true, and anger felt a lot better than a panic attack. My heart was still racing, but the fear was no longer crushing me. I almost smiled.

That made Ryan even madder. "What is wrong with you? You like getting strangled and having people sending you death threats in the mail?"

"You know I don't."

"Then, for heaven's sake, get out of here! You can transfer to Ottawa, right?"

My head jerked up. We stared at each other. We were both breathing hard. Somehow, I hadn't realized that was where he was going with this.

Ryan drew himself up, watching my face carefully. "I mean...that's home. You'd be safer around your family. And, well, I'd like to see you."

Not exactly the world's greatest declaration of love, but still much more than I'd expected from a random encounter with my ex-boyfriend. I didn't know what to say.

My ancient refrigerator began to buzz, breaking the silence. Then footsteps creaked in the apartment overhead.

Finally, I recovered my tongue. "Ryan. It's not that simple. I actually applied to Ottawa's family med program and didn't match there."

He waved his hand. "I bet that if you explained the circumstances, they'd let you in."

I wasn't so sure. An inter-provincial switch might be hard to manage. But home definitely had its appeal. My mom's cooking. Watching movies with my dad. Hanging out with my little brother, Kevin. And Ryan, whatever we had together. Past. Present. Future.

He touched my cheek. "You don't have to decide now. Just think about it, okay?"

I nodded mutely, leaning into his hand. Sometimes, I ached to be held. As if sensing this, he checked my eyes for permission, then folded me in his arms. I breathed him in. He smelled like sandalwood, clean laundry, and himself, that clean tang I had loved and lost. I buried my face in the crook between his neck and shoulder and blinked back tears. "Oh, Ryan."

"Hope." He stroked my hair, his voice low and sad. "You don't have to do this alone. You break my heart."

And then he kissed me. At first his lips were gentle, but as soon as mine parted, he pulled me closer. His tongue swept into my mouth. His arms tightened around me. I lifted myself on tip-toe to press my hips against him and he ground back against me, one hand raising to bury itself in my wet hair.

I lifted my left leg and hooked it around his. He groaned and lifted me up so I could wind both legs around his waist while we kissed and kissed and kissed, an extravagance of longing.

He pushed me against the wall. We were kissing so hard, I felt the moisture from my skin transfer to his cheeks and mouth, wherever we made contact. He ripped my shirt up and caressed my naked sides. When I arched away from him, my shoulders and head toward the wall and my pelvis against his, he slipped his hands around to my stomach. He nipped my ear, sliding his tongue around it and biting it again. I stifled a scream. "I could eat you alive," he muttered through gritted teeth.

One of the things I'd always loved about him was, no matter how buttoned-down and orderly and law-abiding he was on the surface, he was an animal in the bedroom.

In answer, I slid my hand down the neckline of his shirt, feeling his delectable brown skin and the few wiry black hairs sprinkled across his chest.

He tensed and slowly lowered me down to the ground, pressing every inch of his front against mine. I stared into his dilated eyes and ground my hips against his, silently laughing at his agony, until he shoved his hand under my bra and teased my breasts with his thumb and forefinger until I could hardly see.

He opened my bra one-handed. It made me laugh against his mouth, remembering how he'd practiced that move on me, until his lips descended to my collarbones and moved south.

If anything, he was better than I remembered. He was sublime.

Zero to one hundred in sixty seconds.

His lips moved from my left breast to my right.

One hundred and twenty.

BEEP! BEEP! BEEP! BEEP! BEEP!

I collapsed against Ryan and groaned.

"What is that?" he said, pulling me closer.

I rested my head against his shoulder. "My pager."

"You're still on call?"

"Yeah."

He checked his watch. "I thought you said home call usually ended after the evening shift. It's after midnight."

"Yeah, well." I didn't go into medicine for the lifestyle. Ryan's eyebrows drew together and his body tensed, but not in a good way. I shifted away from him. "Once in a while, it's a quick Tylenol order or something."

"Is that likely?"

For a guy I hadn't seen in over a year, he knew the system too well. Or maybe it was me he knew too well. I shrugged and tried not to look at my backpack.

He sighed and yanked it down for me. "Here."

"Thanks."

I don't think any other guy could have gotten me so heated so fast. But probably no one else could have me verging on a fight already, too.

I unzipped the front compartment and dug out my pager without meeting Ryan's eyes. He was standing too far away, arms crossed.

I checked the number and frowned. I'd almost rather see another number four or a hang-up. It was a hospital extension, but not emerg. "I'll just be a second."

I used the phone in my room after I closed the door. "Hi, this is Dr. Hope Sze, for psychiatry. Did someone page me?"

"This is Dr. See?" said a guy's voice, not butchering my name too badly, but still, a bad sign.

"Yes, that's right."

"Good. I'm glad I gotcha. Case room wants you. You got a woman in labour."

14

It's no fun if it's too easy. So I dropped a few hints in the next few sessions.

When the rest of them started talking about slashing and showing off their arms, criss-crossed with more stripes than a Bengal tiger, I made sure Dr. Laura saw my forearms. Scar-free. Muscular. Never seen the wrong end of a razor or even a ballpoint pen. I flexed them for her under the fluorescent light. I caught her frown and her glance at Dr. Ven, the dude who's heading up the therapy, but he was oblivious.

I winked at her. She frowned some more.

When they asked us about "abandonment issues," I listened to the rest of them. My dad left, my mom hated me, my friends think I suck, boo-hoo. Then we were supposed to write down all this shit and rip it up. "Take away its power," urged Dr. Ven. "Tear it up! Rend it! You are in control today!"

I left a blank sheet of paper intact.

I lingered in the hall after hours and heard her talking about me. "...not like the others...uncertain diagnosis..."

I smiled. You know it, darling.

Dr. Ven sighed. His lower voice was harder to make out, but I thought I heard, "...would probably benefit from individual therapy."

Bull's-eye. One-on-one with Dr. Laura, coming right up.

"SO THAT'S IT," said Ryan.

I zipped my bag closed. I'd grabbed a change of clothes and tossed in a banana and a thermos of water, but now I was ready to rock. "Pretty much."

"You have to go back and deliver a baby now."

"Yeah."

"And then you have to work in the morning?"

"Yes. Outpatient psychiatry."

"What if your patient's still in labour?"

I'd stay with the woman until she delivered and then I'd go back to work, but the fastest way to sum it up was, "I cancel everything."

"Like us," he said, under his breath, but I heard it. And, as usual, I wondered if we were ever going to make it. Back down to zero in another sixty seconds.

I stood and faced him. "I'm sorry."

He gave me a crooked smile that reminded me why I loved him. "But babies are like death and taxes, right? They don't wait for anyone."

"Right." I surveyed him for another millisecond. Was he really okay with this?

"This is crazy. You get paid, like, half of what I do. You're always running around. On top of that, you want to solve a hit-and-run from eight years ago. And you still love it."

I paused, my keys jangling in the air. "Yeah, actually." As far as I was concerned, there was no other reason to go into medicine.

He reached for his shoes.

"Ah, Ryan. I could be there all right and the rest of tomorrow and even the next night."

"I'm coming with you. I'll walk back from the hospital. You're driving this time, right?"

I nodded. "You sure?"

He kissed the top of my head. "Someone's gotta look out for you."

MRS. VALDEZ, my patient so recently assigned by Dr. Callendar, was waiting in the tiny triage room on the obstetrics floor. She sat in one of the padded chairs, her black hair loosely braided, her eyes glazed with fatigue. Her husband stood at her side, holding her shoulder.

"Took them long enough to find you," said the triage nurse, handing me the chart.

A volcano of anger erupted in my breast. How was that my fault? It took me a good five seconds to come up with a mild response. "Sometimes locating needs a little help." I took the chart. "Hello." I nodded at the couple while I refreshed my memory with the file notes. This was Mrs. Valdez's third pregnancy. Her contractions were eight to ten minutes apart. The nurse thought her cervix was closed and posterior. No blood or leaking fluids.

In other words, she wasn't in active labour. Yet.

"Doctor, we are very worried," said Mr. Valdez.

"I understand that. Hi, I'm Dr. Sze. I was supposed to meet you in my clinic, but looks like the baby wants to meet me now." I smiled at both of them, concentrating on Mrs. Valdez. She nodded at me and closed her eyes, leaning back in her chair and spreading her legs under her loose green skirt while I said, "I have a few questions. I know your regular doctor is Dr. Mackenzie. Is that right?"

She nodded. Her eyes tightened.

"Are you having a contraction now?"

She nodded again. Her husband squeezed her hand and said, "Can you help us, doctor?"

"I'll do my best." I glanced at my watch to monitor the time of contractions myself. "But first I want to know what happened to your other pregnancies. You had two miscarriages, one at six and one at twelve weeks?"

Mrs. Valdez said something in Spanish. Her husband translated and said, "Babies gone. All gone."

"So it's good this baby has made it this far. Let me examine you." Things weren't fancy at St. Joe's. The triage room consisted of one curtained examination bed, crammed right beside the nurse's desk, across from two padded chairs.

Although I'm no obstetrician, it took a lot longer for me to get her gowned, draw the curtain around her, and find the speculum in the second drawer and lube it up, than it did to check her and to agree that her cervix was nowhere near ready.

I explained that active labour meant contractions lasting at least sixty seconds, of strong intensity, every five minutes or less. The whole time, I was wishing I hadn't sent Ryan home.

It wasn't quite 1:30 a.m. when I slipped into the apartment, trying not to rattle my keys too much.

My heart in high gear and my brain was in about Mach-3, imagining what sinful situation Ryan had set up.

One fall, he planted tulip bulbs in a giant "H" on my lawn so that in the spring, I'd see my initial in bloom. He'd meant to do a giant HS&RW with a heart around it, but he ran out of bulbs. I was so overcome, I ended up doing him up against a tree, even though it was still pretty freaking chilly out.

Obviously, Ryan didn't have time for any great prep tonight. But he might be lurking in my bedroom, ready and waiting. Or he could have made me dinner with himself as the dessert.

I crept into my bedroom. He'd left the door open. The closed blinds filtered the street lamps into translucent moons.

The bed was empty.

I detoured into my living room/study, following his breathing. Here the shades were open. It was easy to find him crashed on the futon with his eyes closed, legs akimbo. As I stared at him, he rolled on his back and gave a slight snore.

Man.

No sex tonight for Dr. Sze.

I draped a fleece blanket over him, the one with a lion and a giraffe printed on it. Ryan muttered a bit.

I dropped a kiss on his lips.

He stirred and lifted his head.

I couldn't resist. I slipped my tongue against his lips.

He groaned.

My heart beat faster.

He slid back into sleep, and this time, I let him.

IN THE MORNING, my clock radio fired up and Smash Mouth sang "Daydream Believer," prodding me out of a dream that I was in an elevator. Before I'd fully processed that, I heard the door open and felt the mattress indent on the other side of the bed. Ryan sat beside me, balancing something in his arms.

I blinked and rubbed my eyes. He smiled, which only increased his gorgeousness to my grunginess factor. His hair was wet and combed back from a shower. He smelled like soap. He seemed to be holding my round cookie sheet draped in a red-and-white striped tea towel. Huh?

He whipped off the towel to display a big white bowl of Cheerios, a glass of milk, and one other item I couldn't decipher.

I had to laugh. "What is that?"

He handed it to me. "Your sunflower looked like it belonged in the kitchen, so I made you another one."

It was a piece of newspaper he'd folded into a tulip. My heart turned over. "Oh, Ryan."

"Hey, I gotta make it up to you for crashing last night. I wish you'd woken me up."

I wasn't sure how to answer. Part of me wanted to yell, Hey, why don't we make up for it right here, right now? Who needs Cheerios? The other part of me hesitated.

He saw that and patted my leg through the blanket. "I'll leave you to it. I've got to meet some guys for breakfast. Are you going to be okay?"

I nodded.

"I'll call you." He kissed my cheek. Ever the gentleman, he closed the door behind him.

So instead of wake-up sex, I ended up bolting down my cereal and calling the police.

I got a relaxed young constable, Donald Stewart, who told me that harassing phone calls are illegal under the Criminal Code. The first step is to figure out who's calling and the second is to prove they're harassing calls.

"How often do you get them? How many times a day?"

I tried to think. "Well, it's only been two days. If I include the hang-ups, up to five a day. I get weird pages too, but I don't know if that's a problem with the hospital operator or someone harassing me."

His silence told me he wasn't that impressed. Good thing neither of us had mentioned the 'detective doctor' thing. "What makes you think it's harassment?"

"I got this picture in the mailbox." I described it to him.

He said I could bring it to the station and they'd have a look, but no promises about the fingerprints. "It's not like in the movies. Now, for the phone calls. Press *57 right away, before anyone else calls. That's 'Call Trace.' You'll get a message saying if the call was successfully traced and you get charged five dollars per call up to ten dollars a month. The information gets sent to the police. But we have to get a warrant to access the information. It's not like the good old days when we could talk to Bell Canada and get the lowdown."

"Oh."

"It's not that big a deal to get a warrant. All you need is a few hours' typing and a JP on your side. But we need it to figure out what residence it's coming from. That's the best-case scenario. A cell phone server is a little trickier, but still possible."

"What about a phone booth?"

"Then you're pretty much Euchred. Oh, can you hang on a minute?" A male voice crackled in the background and Donald Stewart answered him before coming back to me. "Could I call you back?"

"Of course." I gave my name and phone numbers, but I already had my suspicions. If I were making phone calls like that, I'd use a phone booth. I wouldn't have a pattern. I wouldn't leave a trace.

"We encourage you to press charges. But I've only done that once in nine years. Most of the time, once we figure out where it's coming from, the person drops the charges. It's usually someone you know."

Great. I'd tell Ryan about it when he called, but he was going back to Ottawa in the next two days.

This was up to me. I activated Call Display online. I also decided to keep a phone log and make *57 my friend. When I had a chance, I'd bring the tombstone pic to the police. Now that I squinted at it, I could make out some of the original words on tombstone:

William.

Beloved husband and father.

1869-1911

Whoever made this picture wasn't even good at Photoshop. That comforted me a little.

I arrived uncharacteristically early for work so that I could visit Reena in the ICU. I hadn't rotated through the Unit yet, so I felt a little shy when I passed the small, dimly lit waiting room and pressed the button for the automatic doors.

I felt even more out of place when I saw the row of patients along one wall. What was I doing here? I wasn't on ICU. I wasn't responsible for the psych consult. And I'd decided to wear a miniskirt today, so even with the white coat, I looked like I'd taken a wrong turn.

A nurse looked up and frowned at me. Fortunately, Stan Biedelman hailed me from a large, square table by the window where he was reading charts and drinking coffee. "Dr. Sze! Are you bringing us more business?"

"Not if I can help it," I said, sliding beside him. "How's she doing?"

"You'll never guess what she has."

I pointed at an open chart, hoping it was Reena's. "Can I have a clue?"

"No, and you can't call a friend, either," he said in a bad "Who Wants to Be a Millionaire?" impersonation. "Try this on for size. She was unconscious. Her vitals were a little abnormal, temp of 38.0, heart rate 100 to 110, otherwise normal. Her first drug screen came back negative."

The ICU doctor arrived and nodded at Stan. I stood up to go, but Stan said, "This is Hope Sze. She's the psych resident who was looking after bed 4."

The doc held out his hand. "Hi, I'm Dr. Wharton." He had a British accent.

"Hi."

"I was asking her to guess the diagnosis," Stan said.

Dr. Wharton folded his hands and regarded us with some interest. "Don't let me stop you." The unit coordinator handed him a form, but he was still watching me.

Exactly what I needed, an impromptu audience. "Uh..." Fever. Unconscious. I mumbled to myself, "Dry as a bone, hot as a hare, blind as a bat..."

Dr. Wharton smiled. "The anticholinergic syndrome. But her pupils weren't dilated and her skin was sweaty, not dry. I'll give you another clue. Her tone was increased."

The problem is, you study syndromes, but patients present with symptoms, and you have to figure out what it is, under pressure, without sleep, without a textbook, and patients don't tend to follow the guidelines anyway.

"It's something you might consider with a psychiatric patient," Dr. Wharton added.

There are only a few reactions they emphasize with psych patients, so that narrowed it down. My brain clicked. Fever. Sweating. Rigid muscles. "Neuroleptic Malignant Syndrome."

"Right on," said Stan. "We figure she got some Haldol or something. She was allergic to it, you know."

Dr. Wharton nodded at me and took the paper from the unit nurse, ignoring us.

"That's right," I said slowly. I vaguely remembered that from her chart. "But how would she end up taking Haldol? We didn't prescribe it."

Stan shrugged. "Who knows?"

"Especially if she had a serious reaction in the past," I said to myself. None of it added up. Haloperidol was a relatively unusual allergy, not easily forgotten. And what about her Medic Alert bracelet? A nurse wasn't likely to ignore that and jab Reena with a syringe. Haldol is an antipsychotic, but Reena wasn't hallucinating. Sure, she'd been agitated, and we use it to calm down dangerously agitated patients. But Reena probably hadn't fled from our ER to another.

Stan said, "If you go through her chart, the first time she got Haldol, she got a bit spacey, temp of 37.9, that was it. Nothing like this." He waved his hand at her bed. From here, all I could see was the nurse, curved over a metallic cooling blanket.

"So is she going to be all right? How was her night?"

Stan said, "We haven't rounded on her yet, but I think she was stable. At least, she doesn't look like she's on dialysis."

I had to click through that. With NMS, the muscles seize up and start to break down. If the kidneys can't handle the protein load, you need dialysis. But twenty-nine year-old kidneys should be okay. I took a deep breath. I still felt responsible.

Stan said, "You know what the differential is?"

I shook my head. I'd blown my load with NMS.

"Serotonin syndrome. She's like a walking teaching case. We should bring the med students here."

I checked my watch. I was running out of time before my clinic. "Can I swing by her bed?"

Stan smirked. "Go crazy." He caught himself, glancing at Dr. Wharton. "I mean, good idea."

Reena looked even paler than the night before. Someone had smeared Vaseline on her closed eyelids, protecting her eyes from drying out, but rendering her even more unfamiliar. She was still on the respirator. Her breath condensed inside the translucent tube. The nurse clicked her pen closed and glanced at me questioningly. I explained, "I'm from psych."

"Thought so. She can't talk to you yet."

"I know."

I heard a bang from the doorway. The nurse and I both turned. Reena's sister, Wendy, had dropped a big box of Tim Horton's dough- nuts inside the automatic doors. She wailed, "I'm sorry, I'm sorry."

Another plump, middle-aged nurse hurried over to help her scoop them up. The box was still closed, but Wendy had stopped and folded her arms around herself like she was in pain.

The nurse managed to pick up the box and put her arm around Wendy, almost simultaneously. "Are you okay, hon? Who are you here to see?"

"Reena Schuster."

The nurse led her over while I debated staying at the bedside. I chewed the inside of my cheek while the nice nurse said, "Isn't she lucky to have a friend get up first thing in the morning to visit."

Wendy wiped her face with the back of her hand, muffling her word, but I caught it. "Sister."

"Oh, I'm sorry." The nurse paused at the central desk to hand her a tissue.

"It's okay. Everyone says that. We're f—f—foster..." She burst into tears.

I twitched. It felt wrong, me being here. "I'll come back later," I muttered to Reena's nurse, and fled.

The psychiatry department was located on the third floor of St. Joseph's hospital. No other specialty or patients came here, to what Stan called "the land of vomit carpet" (short orange shag carpet flecked with green). Between that, dirty cream walls and narrow hall- ways, and residual cigarette stink from "the smoking room," it was enough to make you run right back out again.

If you could. The ward was locked, meaning you had to press a buzzer and identify yourself before they let you in or out. So the suicidal and psychotic patients were kept in. For their own safety, but still.

I remembered my med school psych rotation in London, Ontario. I was assigned to the psychosis ward. The name alone made me laugh uneasily.

However, when they let me in, the nurse's station was filled with light from large windows. It seemed calm and bright and, as one, the nurses turned to smile at me and bid me welcome. Nothing like *One Flew Over the Cuckoo's Nest*. It was actually much more organized than the internal medicine wards I'd left. One thing I couldn't get used to, though, was that the psych patients kept wandering up and asking for things. Can I have a smoke break? Can I have my pills? Can Shirley have her pills? Is it lunch time yet? Can I have another cigarette? Did my brother come?

Here in Montreal, it wasn't only the ugly décor that bothered me. It was the silence.

The section where you get off the elevators and have to either turn left, towards the locked wards, or right, toward the outpatient hallway, the silence had a peculiar, heavy, muffled quality, as if the carpet had absorbed all sounds and signs of life.

If I were crazy, I'd go even crazier here.

I turned to the outpatient side. None of the staff or patients had arrived for the day. The metal cage at the appointment desk was closed, reminding me of a canteen after hours. Even with the stop at the ICU, I was still eager-beaver early for my first outpatient clinic with Dr. Ludovich.

I strode down the hallway. All the interview rooms were empty, even though the signs on some of the doors were turned to "occupied." I paused to drink at the water fountain, then walked back to the stairs, still uneasy. I'd rather leave and come back than hang around here.

In the hallway, outside the office, I paused to study the plaques arranged at eye-height. They were your usual variety, gold etched on black, mounted on a wood plank. One was for the St. Joseph's Residents' Award in Psychiatry. I was always on the lookout for awards, in case cash played a part, but I nearly choked when I saw the name from nine years ago.

Dr. Laura Lee.

My breath hissed out between my teeth. Maybe it was a coincidence, but it felt like a well-placed reminder from Mrs. Lee.

To calm myself, I scanned the other names, but the only other one I recognized was Omar. He was the second-year resident on my team, along with Stan, and had won the award last year.

I checked my watch. Five minutes until show time. Not enough time to go anywhere, but an eternity if I had to hang around this hall of creepiness.

The stair door banged open at the other end of the hallway. I jumped.

A young man with chestnut hair stood there. His face pointed away from me. His hair was haloed in the light from the windows at the end of the hall. His arms bent casually at his side.

My entire body seized up. Alex.

The last guy I slept with, and the last person in the world I needed to see.

The guy turned toward me. "Hey. Can you tell me where the cafeteria is?"

His voice was too high, his hair too curly, and his nose was too big. Just a random teenager. Not Alex. My heart still raged in my chest. I pressed a fist against it and said, "You're on the wrong floor. Go down one more."

"Thanks." He waved a hand at me and disappeared back down the stairs, the door banging shut behind him.

Alex was officially on a leave of absence. No one knew when, or if, he was coming back. I did hear he was going through counselling somewhere, but he obviously wouldn't choose to do it at St. Joe's.

I forced myself to take deep breaths.

I couldn't get used to the fact that you could fall for someone, make love with him, and, weeks later, have no idea where he was or what he was doing. Even if it was supposed to be Good for Both of You.

Right.

I'd lost touch with Ryan, but it wasn't the same. The Ottawa Chinese grapevine, i.e. my grandmother, kept me in the loop the whole time.

Alex could be incarcerated or incinerated, and I'd have no idea.

By the time I'd calmed myself down, it was one p.m. Time to amble toward Dr. Ludovich's office and pick up my first case.

Dr. Ludovich was a fifty-something blonde in a proper burgundy suit. She didn't waste much time on niceties. She said, "Welcome." Her accent sounded Eastern European or Russian. "Your first patient is a young man, Daniel Culpin. Here is his chart. He should be in the waiting room. You may pick either of the two interview rooms down this side of the hallway. Make sure you turn the sign to 'occupied' so that no one interrupts you. You should take a maximum of 45 minutes with each patient, so that we have time to review the case. You may go now."

Talk about getting to the point. Well, at least she didn't call me the 'detective doctor.' Also, organized doctors tend to start and end on time, instead of yammering away about hypertension for an extra hour while you try not to peek at your watch.

The "waiting room" was a bench near the elevators. St. Joseph's was not big on patient confidentiality. As I stood up to go there, my pager went off.

I didn't recognize the seven-digit number after the 514 area code. It looked like someone's phone number. It certainly wasn't St. Joe's. But what if they paged me to the pregnant patient's house or something?

"Excuse me," I said to Dr. Ludovich. "I'm going to answer this now so I don't interrupt my session."

Her lips compressed. "Very well. You may use my phone, line one."

I punched the number in.

A woman moaned at me.

15

I stopped breathing for a second and pulled the phone closer to my ear. Was someone in trouble?

Was I hearing right?

She moaned again, louder.

"Hello?" I ventured.

She spoke right over me. "*Ohhh, non. C'est pas vrai!*" She carried on, in French, groaning and gasping. *Oh, no, you can't do this to me. You're too big and so strong. Oh, I can't take all of you, oh, please...*

My eyes bugged out as I automatically translated it in my head, and then I burst out laughing. She carried on, asking me to call another number so I could hear the very juicy details.

Then she cried out, *Oh no! Not the two of you together!*

That was the end of the recording.

Dr. Ludovich tilted her head, unamused. "Are you friends sending you funny calls?"

I shook my head. "I think it was a wrong number. Sorry, I thought it might be my obstetric patient. She was in early labour last night."

Her lips softened a little, but not much. "I understand many of your colleagues use the pager as a contact for their friends."

Oh, great. Now she thought I was a slacker. "I don't. I don't like to be paged, so I ask my friends to call me at home. I know my patient is waiting, so I'll go get him, if you'll excuse me."

I stalked down the hall. It wasn't until I was halfway down to the waiting room that I remembered the creepy tombstone picture from last night. Was the sex line thing really a crank call? Or something more sinister?

Especially if someone happened to know about Ryan and Tucker.

Not the two of you at the same time...

How could anyone know about Ryan and Tucker? There wasn't anything to know yet. That was ludicrous.

Wasn't it?

There was one way to find out: see if anyone else got the crank page.

Work first. I saw the patient, a thirty-five year-old depressed man. Dr. Ludovich reviewed the patient with me, spending a lot of time on the fact that he owned five cats, but we agreed that he didn't seem at risk of hurting either himself or the cats. Then I waited for an anxious, nineteen year-old patient who never showed up.

Dr. Ludovich waved me away. "Why don't you finish your charting and research depression."

I skipped back to my interview room and paged Tucker.

He called back right away. "Hello, this is Dr. Tucker, returning a page."

I smiled and nestled the beige hospital phone closer to my ear. "Hello, Dr. Tucker."

"Hope." His voice dropped and softened, lingering over the O.

He could convey so much intimacy in a single syllable, it made me shy. "Hi." I almost whispered it back. Then I remembered Ryan and felt disloyal, which was ridiculous. All I was doing was paging a colleague.

"What can I do you for?"

I had to laugh. "Well, I got this weird page this afternoon. I've still got the number." I clicked through my pager and read it out to him. "Did you get it, too? Or anyone else at the FMC?"

"What's so special about this number?"

So he hadn't gotten it. I refused to dwell on it at the moment. "Call it and call me back. If you're not busy."

"I'm charting. Talk to you in five."

The phone rang again in about two. He burst out laughing, which was contagious. I laughed until my stomach hurt. Then he said, "That was the most creative come-on I've ever gotten in my life."

Heat flooded my cheeks. I wound the cord around my index finger. "Hello? It wasn't a come on. It was a crank call I got."

"Sure, sure. So what's the story?"

"Maybe I'm just being paranoid." I explained about the tombstone flyer. "If I hadn't gotten that, I probably wouldn't have thought twice about the call."

He sobered. "I don't like it."

I sighed. "Yeah, me neither."

"I mean the flyer. The call could be a coincidence. I'll ask around if anyone else got it. But the flyer—" He paused. "Are you in the phone book?"

"Yes."

"Under your full name?"

"No, H. Sze."

"But you're listed with your name and address?"

"Yes."

I heard him drum his fingers on the table. "I don't like it. Anyone could dig you up, especially with the whole 'detective doctor' thing."

"I'll go unlisted next time." I wondered how much damage that would do to my wallet. "But I'm already in this year's edition and that's not going to change."

Silence. "I have to think about this. Want to meet for lunch?"

I shook my head even though he couldn't see me. Ryan had mentioned meeting me at Rona, the hardware store. "Um, I don't think I'll have time. I've got a lot of charting."

"Dr. Ludovich, right?"

"Yeah."

He imitated her accent. "'Never mind what diagnoses the patient has. Did you ask what he does for a living?'"

I giggled. "Exactly. 'You can tell a lot from a patient's profession. And what about his living situation?'"

"Okay, you'll be stuck there forever. I'll finish up here and meet you in your counselling room."

"But—"

"On the third floor, right? Did you take one of the middle ones?"

I sighed. "Yes. The third one."

"See you soon."

I debated whether or not to open the door so Tucker could find me. But I prefer not to have passers-by gawk at me while I'm writing confidential notes, and I figured the sign turned to "occupied" was a pretty good signal. Everyone else would have cleared out by now. Like I said, I always end up bogged down, writing detailed charts while my *compadres* sail off for a *cinq à sept*. Gotta figure out how they do it.

Someone rapped on my door.

"Come in," I said.

Tucker stuck his head around. "*Oh, non, c'est pas vrai,*" he sighed, imitating the girl on the phone.

"Shut up." I was already laughing.

"You attract more trouble than anyone else I know. You have any leads you want me to chase down, Buffy?"

"Not yet."

He shut the door and perched on the edge of my table. "I'm ready and willing. And looking forward to checking out the island with you."

I frowned.

"You remember. You asked me to check out where Laura—" He hesitated.

"—died. Yes, I remember." That was before Ryan stayed the night. Ryan was going home soon, but I was sure he felt, as I did, we'd made an unspoken promise last night. He might well expect to come visit on the weekend, or even have me drive to Ottawa and visit him and my family.

Tucker was staring at me. "You're rescinding?"

I was charmed by his vocabulary even as I laid down my pen and tried to figure out what to do. "No." Not exactly.

He picked up my pen and my chart.

"Hey!"

He moved them behind his butt, so I'd have to reach around him to snatch them back, while his sharp brown eyes surveyed my face. "What's going on, Hope? At least have the decency to tell me."

Low blow. He knew I'd always prided myself on my honesty, and I was about to tell him. I was trying to be tactful as well as truthful, for once. "Well, you remember Ryan."

"Yes." One clipped syllable.

"He's—" Staying with me right now. No, too loaded. "He might have plans, but, well, nothing's fixed, so..." So then why was I bringing it up?

Tucker's eyebrows drew together. "You have got to be kidding me."

"Tucker."

"You asked me to give you space. I gave you space, I gave you a day, and now you're cancelling the plans you already made with me?"

"*No.*" My temples started to pound. "Forget it. I asked you to go to the island with me, let's do it."

He took a deep breath. Then he pushed my pen and chart back toward me. "Fine. Give me a call." He stood up and brushed off his pants.

I took a deep breath, too. My pride wanted to let him walk out the door and pretend I didn't care, but I knew I'd hurt his feelings. "Tucker, I just did, okay? Now you know about a 1-900 number you can call when you're lonely. It's a valuable service."

He shook his head and remembered. "Right." He flashed me a tiny grin. "Thanks."

"I'm sorry." I hesitated. "Ryan and I haven't gotten back together or anything. We just have a lot of history, and I felt like you had a right to know. But it's true, I already asked you and I was looking forward to it. I'm all yours on Saturday."

Tucker waggled his eyebrows up and down. "I can do a lot in 24 hours." He snagged the chair next to me and pulled it very close to mine.

A smile tugged at the corners of my mouth. "I'm supposed to be working."

He leaned over close enough that the warmth of his cheek seemed to transfer to mine. "I'll help. What is this. 'Lives alone with five cats (adopts strays), but says they are all vaccinated.'"

I yanked my papers away. "Dr. Ludovich really wanted that in there."

He threw his head back and laughed. "Why?"

"Oh, she said it showed how lonely he was, that he wanted companionship but had a hard time getting close to people. And I put the vaccinated part in, because I didn't want anyone to think he was living in an abandoned bus with a hundred starving, deformed cats, that the SPCA would have to put down. I like cats."

He shook his head, still smiling. "You are the nicest person."

I sighed and rubbed my forehead. "I wish. I used to be so innocent and sweet before medical school, but something about being up all night, patients swearing at you, I don't know..."

"You're still nice. You just act tough."

I didn't like that, like I was Rizzo from Grease or something. "What about you?"

"You tell me."

I tilted back in my chair so it balanced on two legs and I got a little further away from him. "I think you use charm instead. But, honestly, that works better from guys. Nurses walk all over gosh-darn-it, sweet, uncertain girls." I paused and tilted my chair back even further.

"Yeah, but women can use their looks to get ahead with the guy doctors."

I set my chair down with a thump. "Huh?"

"Sure. I see it all the time. They get away with 'I'll look it up later' because they're cute, whereas I can see my evaluation going south if I don't snap to it with the right answer."

"Bullshit."

He shrugged. "I call 'em like I see 'em. So do you."

I chewed my lip. "I'm always saying I don't know. Are you telling me I'm getting away with it by batting my eyelashes?"

He laughed. "God, no! You're always frowning in the emerg." At my expression, he added, "And you really do look things up."

Now I was afraid he thought I wasn't cute, even though all evidence so far was to the contrary. Plus, I like to think I'm enjoying myself in the emerg, not prepping myself for early Botox.

"That's a compliment, in case you didn't notice," he said.

"Right. I'm scowling my way through the articles."

"You take everything way too seriously."

He wasn't the first to say that to me ("Loosen up," "You're too sensitive," all riffs on the same theme), but Tucker particularly hurt my feelings. And, probably partly because I was tired, I suddenly wanted to cry. I closed my eyes.

"Hey." His voice softened again. "Are you okay?"

I couldn't answer right then. I concentrated on my breathing.

"Is it something I said? Hard to believe, because I'm always so charming."

I pinched my nose hard. "Yeah. You're a prince."

So he sat there and waited for me, which was exactly the right thing to do, until he said, "Psych can be pretty intense, especially when you're dealing with your own stuff."

Totally off-base. It wasn't psych, it was him, Ryan, Mrs. Lee, Reena —oh, wait, she *was* psych. Maybe Tucker wasn't completely off-base. But I wasn't diddling around with Oedipal or Electra complexes, I was freaked out over love, death, grief, and overwork.

He got up, but it was only to hand me the el-cheapo mauve-and-green box of hospital tissues, again, like I was a patient. I blew my nose. "Tucker..."

He put his head near mine and whispered in my ear. "I know what our problem is."

I drew back so I could look him in the eye, but also because I was both aroused and discomfited by his warm breath in my ear and against my cheek. "What's that?"

"We talk too much." His arm launched forward and tousled my

hair, making sure my bangs got in my eyes and generally rubbing hard enough to shock a cat with the static electricity.

I squealed. Girly to the max, but then I knocked his arm away and gave him a quelling look.

He laughed and lunged at me again.

I shot out of my chair so fast it fell over. "You're a dead man."

"Oh, I'm terrified!" He danced out of range. "What're you going to do, throw your pharmacopoeia at me?"

"Good idea." I yanked the little booklet out of my lab coat pocket. Cue cards and pens and slips of paper rained to the ground, but I ignored them as I fired the tiny book between his eyes.

He ducked.

I pitched the Sanford guide next. It was heavier and clipped his ear.

"Ow!" He scooped it up and threw it back at me, not trying too hard, but it bounced off my arm.

"*Ow!*" I jumped him and scrubbed both hands through his hair. In five seconds, I'd rearranged that spiky gel on top into something like a crop circle an alien might make, if the alien was drunk and joy-riding on an ATV almost out of gas.

"That's better than the gel look, okay?" I chortled, until Tucker stopped still and stared down at me, and I realized how close I'd ended up to him.

Close enough to touch much more than his hair. Close enough to feel dangerous. My fingers tingled from the friction, as if I were still touching him.

We stood there for a minute, breathing hard, eyes locked.

He slid his arms around me. Even through my white coat, I could feel his fingers flexing on my arms and then moving over to my back with exquisite slowness, never taking his eyes away from mine.

My heart beat in my throat. It felt wonderful and forbidden and most of all, inevitable.

So much so that I was the one to rise up on tiptoe, lean forward, and kiss him.

16

He hadn't shaved. I felt Tucker's bristles against my mouth and I liked it. It felt primal.

His lips were very warm against mine, but softer than I expected. Softer than Ryan's, I realized, and felt guilty, but not guilty enough to stop.

He kissed me back, hard, demanding, his tongue pressing against my own. He tasted like coffee and something deeper, his own taste. He slid his hands into my hair and pulled my close, smoothing my locks before running down my back and squeezing my ass.

I could feel the tension in his arms and his back. He'd been wanting this a long time. He was restraining himself.

The other feeling I got was: possessive. When he took me, he'd want all of me.

My tongue danced against his, teasing. He groaned low in his throat and pulled me even closer, his hands smoothing my thighs before moving up again. I smiled. I knew he could feel my mouth curve against his.

He pulled away and kissed the corner of my mouth, my cheek, my neck, my eyelids. "Oh, Hope. Hope." Then he came back to my lips and kissed me again, slower this time, deeper, but no less urgent.

When I kissed Ryan, it felt like coming home.

Kissing Tucker felt like an adventure. I tilted my head to one side and he followed me, lighter now, more playful, like we had all the time in the world instead of whatever seconds we could steal away in the conference room. He nibbled my bottom lip. I smiled again. He nipped me lightly in response before tracing his tongue along the delicate skin inside my lips.

And I knew then, if I had ever doubted, that he would be a wonderful lover. Skilled, but more importantly, playful and considerate.

Time for me to pay back. I broke away to inhale the skin at his neck. Heaven. I licked up to his jaw and dropped kisses alongside before moving on to his ear.

He chuckled low in his throat, but I was just getting started. I pushed him back into his chair, the one that had no arms. And then I straddled him, settling onto his lap. His eyes flared, dark with desire and approval.

The little voice inside my head, the one always calculating and doubting, was silent for once. I rubbed my nose against his, momentarily shy, and he rubbed back and settled his hands on either side of my waist. "You are fucking amazing."

That pulled me short. I inhaled deeply, my lips on his ear, trying to think beyond *Really? 'Cause I think you'd be an amazing fuck.*

He murmured low in my ear, "What's the matter, can't take a compliment?"

"I guess." I wasn't used to talking dirty. Not that I didn't like it, but the guilt was kicking in at long last. All my life, I'd been the nice girl, the good girl, the one with straight A's, voted most likely to attract a unicorn until marriage. And now...

My body stiffened up. I couldn't help it.

He sighed. It was a microscopic sigh. But still, enough to quell my libido. I started to swing my leg back around and stand up.

He dropped his hand on my thigh to block me. I squirmed. It felt too intimate, somehow even more so because he didn't move to stroke or caress me. He just waited.

The heat of his palm, the anticipation, the mystery of this new man made me bite my lip and settle my leg back down. Just for a moment.

Our eyes locked again.

He moved his hand higher.

Oh, God. Why did I wear a skirt today? I knew why. Because I was feeling sexy and strong and I'd wanted the entire world, including Tucker, to know it.

In this heat, I wasn't masochistic enough to wear panty hose. Which meant only the thin fabric of his pants and my panties stood between us. I could feel him and, from the look on his eyes, he knew it.

I licked my lips and did not move away.

His palm rested against my skin, mid-thigh and inching higher.

I closed my eyes. My legs were trembling. I was so wet. In fact, he might even be able to feel it. Was I crazy, straddling this man and potentially leaving a damp patch on his pants? I veered between freaking out and fucking his brains out. I slammed my hand down on his. "Tucker—"

He pressed the fingers of his opposite hand to my lips. "We always screw up by talking. Let's not talk."

I hesitated.

In that moment of weakness, he slid his hand up to the edge of my panties. His fingers brushed against the elastic. Teasing me.

This was madness. There was no lock on the door. I could hear someone's footsteps padding down the hallway. Dr. Ludovich, a patient, a janitor—anyone could barge in here any minute. I tensed my thighs to lift myself up.

He slid his finger inside the elastic to touch my skin.

I bit back a cry. It felt so good.

Then I leapt away from him.

He jumped up with me, kicking back the chair. "It's okay, Hope."

I was shaking with I don't know what. Lust? Self-disgust. I wanted him so badly. "I'm sorry."

He held up his hands, not daring to come closer but not leaving me, either. "I'm the one moving too fast. Sorry." He ran his hand through his hair, leaving it askew. "I just want you so much."

I could not help looking at his pants. There was a damp spot over a very prominent area. I closed my eyes. "I want you, too."

"I know. And I know you're—" He took a long, ragged breath. "You're vulnerable. I shouldn't have taken advantage of you."

Now, wait a minute. "You didn't. I knew what I was doing."

He shook his head and tried to smile.

I retreated into my anger. It was safer. "Look, this is what I was talking about when I said I was coming back to work, no matter what you think. I know you get off on me being a damaged maiden or whatever, but I make my own choices. Get over yourself."

In answer, he slid his finger down my chin, down my throat, to the V neckline of my shirt. I held my breath. My breasts were so close to his hand, I could weep.

"I'm already over myself, Hope. You just bring out the worst in me."

I felt my nostrils flare. But before I could object, he said, "I'm sorry. Not about this. If I had my way, I'd take you six ways 'til Sunday. But I'm sorry our timing always totally sucks. I'll let you make your own choice." He walked past me to the door and, with a deep breath, threw it open.

17

———————

S he's smarter than she looks. Today, at the group, she gives us a riddle, trying to be all casual about it. "Let's say a woman's mother dies and, at the funeral, she meets this guy she thinks is her soul mate."

Everyone starts hooting.

"That's fucked-up shit."

"You know what they say, someone dies and you get all horny."

"Who says that? Are you some kind of nagrophiliac or whatever?"

"Necrophiliac, you dumbass!"

"Language," says Dr. Ven, but he's looking at Dr. Laura like, what the heck are you doing?

I see the blush on Dr. Laura's neck, but she ignores it and raises her voice. "Here's the strange part. Three days later, she kills her sister. Why?"

I know the answer. It's obvious. The hairs on the back of my neck prickle. But I don't say anything. I breathe real quiet, in and out, and wait for everyone else.

There's silence, broken by: "Chicks, man. Who knows why they do anything?"

Now Dr. Laura's face is all red, too, but she waits out the laugh. "Anybody else?"

A curly-haired girl puts up her hand. "I don't get it. Is there, like, a right answer?"

"No. Say what you think. It's sort of a getting-to-know-you game."

Some game. Dr. Laura looks right at me. I look back at her, innocent.

The same girl chews her bottom lip. "I'm not good at tests."

Dr. Laura tries to smile, but it doesn't reach her eyes. "It's not a test. Is it a test if I ask you what your favourite colour is?"

"Everything here's a test."

That's it. The room's uneasy now.

"I plead the Fifth," says the Goth girl.

Another mini-laugh from the crowd. I give a fake smile, better than Dr. Laura's, and straighten out my legs like I've got all the time in the world.

Finally, someone bites. "My great-aunt's super into funerals. She's always reading the newspaper, looking for people who died. She's from PEI, right, where they got nothing better to do than broadcast people's obituaries on the radio. Twice a day. I'm not kidding."

Someone else snorts. "What does that have to do with the soul mate guy?"

"The guy's a red herring."

"Nah. I bet he told her some shit about her sister, and she offed her because of it."

Dr. Laura's eyes flicker and her hands tense up. She'd make a lousy poker player. "What kind of information would that be?"

We stare at her blankly. Dr. Laura purses her lips. "Or, as you might say, what kind of shit would make someone off her sister?"

Even I got to laugh at that one. She's not that much older than us, but she acts like she's two hundred and two.

The little black girl says, "Oh, Dr. Lee, you said a bad word! Now you're gonna get it!" She pretends to shave her finger at her, like it's a carrot she's peeling. I remember doing that in grade three. We're all cracking up.

Dr. Ven clears his throat, but Dr. Laura ignores him. She is bent on this. "I'm interested. Come on. Have you guys ever thought about killing someone?"

I almost laugh out loud. Sweet Jesus. Seems like I can't stop thinking about it.

Dr. Laura says, "It's important to be open about our feelings. That's what this group is all about." Her eyes flash on me again. "How about you?"

Even Dr. Ven perks up a bit. My lips feel stiff, all of a sudden. I got to tread carefully here. "Yeah, okay."

"Okay what?" Dr. Laura can't wait.

"Okay, we should be open about our feelings." The group chuckles. Dr. Laura's nostrils flare, so I give a bit more. "Yeah, I've gotten mad at people. But I've never killed anyone."

Yet.

I feel like she can read that from my head. She's breathing faster, eyes narrowed. God, I love leading her on. I add, "If your mom dies, though, you might go kinda nuts."

And, like I knew he would, Dr. Ven jumps right on that like a flea on a dog. "Let's talk about that. Have any of you ever experienced a loss? It doesn't have to be your mother. A grandparent, a friend, even a pet. Hold up your hand."

Out of the corner of my eyes, I can see Dr. Laura gritting her teeth.

I know exactly why that woman in the riddle offed her sister. She's hoping the soul mate guy will show up to this funeral, too. Seems obvious. But since no one else seems to get it, I'm keeping my mouth shut.

I'm impressed, though. All these fancy degrees and Dr. Ven couldn't figure out how to lick his own ass if that was his only ticket out of hell. But this resident, this nothing, parachutes in, and like that, she's on to me. Or at least she's got her suspicions.

Right on, Dr. Laura. Keep playing.

BACK HOME, I changed into a short sundress, bolted down a glass of water, and asked Ryan, "You sure you want to go to Mrs. Lee's?" It might make the weirdest non-date in history.

Ryan nodded and laced up his shoes. "I want to talk to her and get an idea of what she's looking for."

"I know it's your last night here. I'm sorry. She said the date was auspicious." Ah, Chinese superstition. At least with Ryan, I didn't have to explain lucky numbers while we trotted down the stairs to the indoor garage, accessible through the apartment's basement. "You sure you're okay with this?" I asked one more time, even as I climbed in the car and fastened my seatbelt.

He kissed my cheek. "Absolutely." He looked at me, and his forehead crinkled. "Are you okay?"

I adjusted the rear view mirror instead of meeting his eyes. What he didn't know about Tucker would not hurt him. At least, not right away. "Okay," I repeated brightly, and threw the Ford Focus into reverse while I hit the garage door opener attached to my visor.

While the door oozed open, a cyclist wheeled her bike into the bike rack near the washing machine. There wasn't that much room to maneuver in the garage, so I waited instead of risking running her over. Obviously, I wasn't from Montreal. She waved her thanks as she threw open the door to the apartment basement.

"Did you see what I did at your apartment?" said Ryan.

"Sort of," I hedged, trying not to think about how he'd beefed up my security while I'd straddled another man. "I know you changed the front door lock, so I'll have to give the new key to the concierge." I accelerated out of the garage.

"I cut sticks to prop the windows closed and stop anyone from forcing them open from the outside. There's a lot more I could do, but I had to get the tools."

"You mean you couldn't get by with my screwdriver and Ikea Allan wrenches?" I braked at the red light and signalled left on Côte-Ste-Catherine.

"You needed them anyway. I'll leave them at your apartment."

"What did you get?"

"Just the basics. A saw, a drill with multiple bits, a hammer and nails. Oh, and some hinges and nuts and bolts."

"I'll pay you back." Thank God Tucker and I hadn't done more. I felt so guilty, my chest was practically concave.

"No, it's my present to you. I wanted you to be safe. Ever since..." Two lines appeared between his eyes again, the glabellar lines, as they say in derm.

The light changed. I squeezed my car into the right-hand lane despite an oncoming taxi. "Since what?"

"You know," he said.

I did know. He meant ever since I almost got killed last month. Tucker's reaction was to make me take time off work. Ryan's was to shore up my security. If I had to pick between their approaches, I'd go with Ryan's. At least that was practical.

For the first time, I wondered if it was a coincidence that my ex took a vacation in Montreal and just happened to run into me. I rubbed my eyes.

"Tired?" said Ryan.

I nodded. And foolhardy, going to a patient's house. But she insisted, and somehow, visiting her seemed more kosher with company. Ryan could testify that I didn't cross any limits.

Ryan touched the back of my neck. "You're tense."

I nodded again and gave him a pained smile.

He started massaging my neck as best he could from the passenger's seat. He hit a trigger point on my levator scapulae and I yelped.

"You want me to stop?" Ryan glanced at the bus that was trying to merge into my rear bumper.

I shook my head and hit the gas, before braking suddenly for the Lincoln in front of me. "Just go lighter."

He did his best in the stop and start traffic. Ryan's never been the best masseur, but I felt myself relax into his fingers. It was so good to have someone to care about me. It made a big difference to come home to him instead of an empty apartment.

Mrs. Lee lived in Montreal West, an area I didn't know well, but was only about 15 minutes' drive from mine. I managed to park right across from her building. "It's an omen," I muttered to myself.

A grey duplex apartment door popped opened. Mrs. Lee appeared on the front stoop, waving.

She greeted us and put the kettle on. Ryan answered in Cantonese and whipped out his laptop, so they were already best buds by the time she took us on a tour of her home, culminating in Laura's small, neat bedroom.

"I moved her things here after," Mrs. Lee said, and stopped. She forced herself to continue. "She had her own apartment."

"I understand." It must have been so painful to go through Laura's possessions and move them back to her childhood room. I didn't want to cross the threshold, but my dread was nothing compared to what she'd been through.

Ryan touched her arm and said something. Mrs. Lee paused, nodded at me, and allowed him to lead her back toward the kitchen. Since my Chinese is limited to hello, thank you, and the names of especially tasty restaurant dishes, I was grateful to Ryan for putting her at ease and giving me some privacy.

Mrs. Lee called over her shoulder, "You're the detective. Look at anything you want. Open it up. I trust you."

I nodded and smiled, but it felt more like a wince.

I've read a lot of books where they say the dead person's room is kept as a shrine. Probably that was true here. At least, I didn't get the feeling a whole lot of moving and shaking went on here, aside from regular dusting. But there was a clear division between Laura's child-hood and adulthood in this small, square space.

The décor was the most obvious blast from the past. One book-shelf was dedicated to school photos, awards, and stuffed animals, but an older Laura had hung a U2 poster above her bed and suspended some CD's on fishing wire from the ceiling in front of the window. The evening light made them sparkle like rainbows.

I swallowed hard and scanned for the newer, less emotional stuff. The most obvious sources of information were the two black filing cabinets pushed against the wall and a bulky old computer squatting on the desk alongside a freshly-dusted box of 3 1/2 inch floppy disks. I wasn't one hundred percent sure how to use those, so it was good that Ryan had come along.

The bookshelf wedged next to the door was crammed with medical books and neatly-labelled binders.

I sighed to myself. Needle. Haystack. Meet the twenty-first centu-ry's lust for paperwork and gigabytes. What was I looking for again? What kind of clue?

Mrs. Lee had specifically asked me to look at Laura's files, so that's what I would start with and, more than likely, end with.

Ryan's voice carried from the kitchen, talking faster than usual, and Mrs. Lee laughed in reply.

It was the first time I'd heard her laugh, and she surprised me with a deep chuckle.

I couldn't abandon her now. I yanked the first filing cabinet's drawer open.

Within a minute, I could see that the similarity between me and Laura ran only skin deep. I sighed with relief. I hadn't consciously realized it, but the whole "you look like Laura" thing had been getting to me.

Fortunately, we were entirely different animals.

She'd been very organized. She'd made file folders according to clinical specialty—oncology, say, or rheumatology—and kept filing articles until at least the week before she died. I couldn't get over her alphabetized and colour-coded files. She even used those stick-on dots, I guess so she could tell at a glance, "Oh, it's yellow, must be family medicine."

I'd made up a less complicated system, but gave up after a week, when I decided, "If I need it, the Internet is my friend. If I don't print it out, I can save a few trees." Plus I was lazy.

I wasn't sure how research articles were going to clue me in to any potential murderer, but at least I knew how to sift through this stuff better than the police. And since everyone said Laura was into psych and emerg, that's where I'd find any money.

I started with the specialty I liked and missed: emerg. I recognized two of the same articles they passed out to me last month. Geez, didn't they update their teaching files in eight years? But I agreed with the topics she'd kept, like intubation, toxicology, Coumadin. All keepers.

I flipped through a few hand-outs she'd made, including all the PowerPoint slides for her presentations on sepsis and ectopic pregnancy.

There was nothing personal except four reference letters, which I read.

"Laura is extremely organized, punctual, and knowledgeable."

"Laura has excellent clinical acumen."

"I would not hesitate to recommend Dr. Lee."

"One of the best residents in recent memory."

Wow. I could only hope they'd speak half so well of me when I graduated. Two were doctors I didn't know, Dr. P.K. Kumar and Dr. Charles Ouimet. One was from Dr. Valerie Chia, an ER doctor. The last and warmest was from Dr. Kurt Radshaw, the doctor whose murder I had solved. I paused and blinked. He'd been a good man.

Otherwise, the emerg file was pretty much business and not very useful.

The psych file was a lot fatter. I flipped through the articles quickly. The topics were the same then as now: suicide risk assessment, determining patient competence, depression and bipolar disorder, etc. But then I found a whole stack of papers on antisocial personality disorder.

That was unusual. It's the medical term for sociopaths, psychopaths, whatever you want to call Robert Pickton, Jeffrey Dahmer, Paul Bernardo, Hannibal Lecter, and other personifications of evil.

I've never diagnosed a patient as antisocial. Not even on the advice of the attending staff. You can imagine how it wouldn't exactly be a popular label.

Maybe Laura had done a presentation on it. But for her emerg presentations, she'd kept copies of the overheads. No such animal here. And again, I couldn't imagine the staff saying, "Let's teach the medical students about something useful like antisocial personality!"

I did attend a forensic psych lecture in med school. I thought I'd hear about cool cases, but it turned out to be an hour or two of legalese and disappointment.

I scanned the articles themselves to learn more about the disorder. I already knew a little bit. The classic triad—the "watch out for this kid" trio of symptoms—is fire-setting, cruelty to animals, and bedwetting.

We all laughed about the last one in med school because it seems so incongruous, but here it was again in black and white. If you dig into their childhood, they often tortured pets and set fires by day and required rubber sheets at night.

The other thing I remembered, the biggie, was lack of remorse. Usually, if you hurt someone, you feel bad about it, even if you quickly justify it to yourself.

But psychopaths really and truly don't care beyond their own needs. It's mine, I want it. You're in my way, too bad. Steal from the collection plate. Boot the dog out of the way. Just a hop, skip, and a jump away from adultery, embezzlement, and yes, murder.

Fellow people and creatures are obstacles in their way.

They may be charming. They may sleep around. In other words, they'd probably out-play and out-last on *Survivor*.

A few more nuggets from Dr. Hare, a Ph.D. and the research main man: a lot of them work in the entertainment industry, which kind of makes sense. Law and politics are an even more natural fit. And once he mentioned it, I could imagine them fitting in as cult leaders, mercenaries, and (ugh) military personnel. But he also found them in medicine and the clergy.

Yikes. They were everywhere. All cunning. Hostile. Treacherous. Cruel.

I shivered. It makes you wonder how many people are wearing a mask.

Arguably, the job of a psychiatrist is to take that mask off.

Had Laura encountered someone who fit this picture? And instead of blowing the whistle, had she tried to diagnose and treat him herself?

Because if there was one flaw in this golden girl, I suspected it was her pride. She wanted the A plus-plus-plus. What better way to do it than to capture a criminal herself?

Then I almost smiled. Okay, I still saw some similarities between us.

But back to the more pressing question. If I went out on a limb and said, Yes, there is a psychopath who killed Laura on purpose, who was it?

I ran through the rest of the file and found two oddities. One was an orthopedic review article on bone age, focusing on the closure of epiphyseal (growth) plates in adolescents. She should have filed that under ortho, or possibly emerg, not psych. I flipped through it. I already knew that long bones lengthen through little growth plates on either end of the bones, turning cartilage into bone. The growth plates look like black lines on X-rays.

When I show teenagers the film, they occasionally get excited because those black lines mean they're still growing. Once the growth plate closes and the black line disappears, that bone's as long as it's going to get. But since most of them are already taller than me, I can't get too excited. I only want to know if they've fractured right through the growth plate because that's the weakest link.

Laura had made a note:

Humerus ossification:

Upper end ~20 y.o. , lower end ~16 y.o.

Radius:

Upper end ~18 y.o., lower end ~20 y.o.

That was hard core. Orthopods need to know that kind of information, but not most emergency doctors. Well, more evidence that Laura deserved a gold star.

The other weird thing was a pamphlet for gay-lesbian-bi-transgendered teens. That made me wonder if Laura had been gay.

I skimmed the remainder of the filing cabinets, trying to avoid sustaining any paper cuts, while Mrs. Lee started up some heavy duty opera in the other room. A soprano filled the apartment, further setting my teeth on edge.

Finally, I shut the cabinet with a bang. As I'd suspected, Laura was far too ethical to bring patient notes home. Even if she had, there was no way I could pull the charts on all the patients she'd seen.

The psychopath might not have been a patient anyway.

I tapped my pencil on my teeth while Ryan hummed along to the music. I grinned to myself. Mr. Culture.

There might be a faster way of cutting through the chaos. I flipped through Laura's old Day Timer. It was all work, no play, but it did tell me that when she died, she was running Monday evening group therapy at the Douglas Hospital. A truly antisocial personality might be memorable eight years later.

Tucker knew the doctors at the Douglas. It was time to talk to Tucker again. *Oy vey.*

A baritone joined the soprano, their voices duelling for supremacy on the recording. My stomach rumbled at the smell and sizzle of food from the kitchen.

At long last, I stood to join Ryan and Mrs. Lee, wondering how, even if a sociopath existed, I might manage to catch him nearly a decade later.

18

There are real bad guys and there are posers.

A guy in our borderline group fooled me at first.

I earmarked him early. I figured he could come in handy. He came on to Reena's little foster sister.

Reena tried to warn Wendy off. "He's older than me. He's nineteen. And he's got a record, okay? As in criminal? Leave him alone."

"I like bad boys," she said, flaunting her tiny tits as best she could.

Wendy was one-hundred percent poser.

So Reena started on the guy next. "She's underage."

"She sure doesn't act it." Mike drained his beer.

"I mean it. She's only thirteen."

"No shit." But I saw his eyes dart from side to side. He was thinking about easier pussy. Naw, this guy didn't play in my league.

Still, when Wendy crooked her finger and yelled, "Hey, this is my new song!", he got up. They thrashed to Demerit and she practically gave him a lap dance before she puked up her beer.

Reena burst into tears and locked herself in the bathroom to do some serious slashing.

I knocked on the door. I told her what she wanted to hear. But all the *while, I was thinking about how to make this soap opera work for me. I couldn't figure it out then, but it would come to me.*

MRS. LEE'S dumplings were not quite as good as my mother's, but I wasn't about to complain. I added more hot chili-garlic sauce and said, "I read some of Laura's files, but I'll have to think about them. Could you tell me a little about her?" I wanted to know what she was really like, warts and all.

First, I got all the saintly stuff. Laura went to church regularly (big smile from Ryan, carefully neutral expression from me). Laura volunteered for the local food bank. Laura went rollerblading almost every day, barring ice and on-call duties, even if she had to get up at four a.m. on surgical rotations. Laura'd had a grand total of three boyfriends in twenty-seven years, all of them serious, one of them a fiancé named Brendan Ho, but supposedly they all ended as friends.

"So why did they break up?" I asked.

Mrs. Lee pursed her lips. "None of them were good enough for her."

I had to laugh.

Mrs. Lee didn't. "She was too picky, even when she was a little girl. She would practice the piano again and again until she had it right, even when her teacher said it was good enough. She graduated from high school with the highest marks. She was the class valedictorian, but she was angry because another boy had higher grades at another school."

I made a face. Another guy edged me out for valedictorian, but otherwise, I could relate.

"She loved Brendan, but she was always complaining that he didn't work hard enough. I told her, 'he is good, he loves you, he has a good job'." Mrs. Lee shook her head. "Nothing was good enough. Her father said she got that from me."

"If she did, I know she got other, good qualities from you," I said.

She laughed. "Hope, you're too good to me."

That surprised me. "I haven't done anything."

She patted my hand. "Don't you understand yet? You believe in me." She turned to Ryan. "You, too. Thank you for coming. Eat more."

Obediently, I picked up another *she jau* and swirled it in the sauce. Nothing beats homemade cooking.

"No problem," said Ryan, sipping his tea. He paused. "I don't suppose those ex-boyfriends...there might be a link there?"

We both looked at him. He grinned and shook his head. "Maybe I've been watching too much *CSI* or whatever, but you know the whole 'If I can't have you, no one's going to' angle?"

"That's true." It had flitted across my mind, but I wasn't sure if I should bring it up to her mom. Ryan probably already knew her better than I did.

Mrs. Lee said slowly, "Brendan married another girl. They have twin boys. I know his mother. I would be very surprised if he had ever hurt Laura."

"Maybe I can look into it. Do you have contact information for her other boyfriends?" I asked.

She shook her head. "I only know their names."

"I have her day planner," I said. "And her old computer might have some contact information, if we get into it next time."

"We can try and track them down," said Ryan with a firmness that surprised and gratified me. He took my hand.

"I wish she had found a good man like you," Mrs. Lee told him.

I shifted uncomfortably in my chair, but Ryan's hand tightened on mine. I knew he was warning me to keep mum about our status. It was true, Ryan was a good man. Just not officially mine.

Ryan kissed the back of my hand before letting it dangle back down between us. I glanced up under my eyelashes, afraid Mrs. Lee would disapprove at his public display of affection, but if anything, she looked wistful. To change the subject, I said, "Did you get any leads from running an ad in the paper, asking for witnesses to the accident?"

"I've run them every year since she died."

Ryan and I exchanged a look. No fooling around with Mrs. Lee.

I took a deep breath. "Any leads?"

She shook her head. "I turned everything over to the police. Of course, who knows if they actually bother to do anything about it." She snorted and swirled her tea in her cup. She'd eaten the least of the three of us.

"Did you do it this year?"

She nodded and gestured for me to have more. As I obediently picked up another dumpling with my chopsticks, she said, "Yes. No answer so far."

"Maybe we could try on Craigslist or something." My last word got cut off when Ryan rubbed his thumb over the skin of my wrist. It felt so good, I sucked my breath in.

Mrs. Lee cast me a sharp glance.

I tried to wriggle my hand away, but Ryan held firm while he asked in a perfectly normal voice, "Do you have any ideas what might have happened?"

"Of course." Mrs. Lee's eyebrows lifted. "She didn't want to worry me, but I think maybe she was getting threatening letters or telephone calls."

I tensed, thinking of my own graveyard letter. "Why do you say that?"

"She was jumpy when she answered the phone. She started using her answering machine all the time. She started paying for Call Display. She said it was because she was so busy, but I knew she wasn't telling the whole truth."

Okay, now maybe we were getting somewhere. I shoved aside my own uneasiness. "Did you ever overhear any calls or intercept any letters?"

She shook her head. "I was hoping she gave them to the police, but they said they never received anything."

Damn. Dead end. "Did you check her phone records?"

"Yes. I only have records of her long-distance calls. She was a good girl. She called her grandmothers every weekend and a few friends once a month. There was nothing suspicious."

I sat forward in my chair, squeezing Ryan's hand. "If you think someone was after her, do you have any idea who it might be? Through work, or socially—"

"Work." Her chin swung downward.

"Why do you say that?"

"My daughter was a good girl."

I'm sure there are perfectly angelic girls around, but most of them aren't twenty-seven. Your halo gets at least a teensy bit tarnished by then.

"We didn't want her to go into medicine. I told her to become a dentist. You have a nice private office, an assistant for you, start work at nine, out at five so you can have babies. But no." Mrs. Lee shook her head and tightened her lips.

"Why did she want to do medicine?"

"She said she didn't like teeth!"

Ryan and I both laughed. Traditionally, all parents want doctor kids. Dentistry is kind of an also-ran. Laura Lee may have been one of two kids in history, rebelling against her parents by donning the other kind of white coat.

Mrs. Lee rubbed her forehead. "I told her, if you want to do medicine, you specialize. But she wanted to do general practice. I said, okay, you can still have a clinic, you can still have nice hours, but then she did emergency medicine."

I suddenly wanted to laugh, even though I understood her anxiety. Emerg means working around the clock, taking on all the drunks and druggies, the bloody traumas, the screaming children and broken limbs. It's not very glamorous or well-paying or just plain tidy, the way Mrs. Lee would like it.

I wondered if my parents felt the same way. Probably. The difference was, they didn't know enough about it to object.

"And the psychiatry!" Mrs. Lee threw up her hands.

I understood that, too. Asian people don't believe in talking about their problems. But I was starting to like Laura, that crazy revolutionary. I could see how she'd thwarted her mother by becoming a doctor and picking disciplines her mother didn't understand or value. But that didn't mean she'd been murdered because of it.

Mrs. Lee rapped her teacup down on the table. "I bet it was a psychiatric patient. So unstable."

I sighed. Psych patients are always fighting such a bad rap.

She bristled. I actually imagined little bristles popping out of her skin, like porcupine quills.

For the first time, I found myself disliking her, or at least her prejudices. "Do you have any evidence?"

"If I did, do you think I would be asking you?"

I bit my lip. No pay, no respect. Why was I doing this again?

She took a deep breath. "I'm sorry, Hope. Sometimes you remind me of my daughter."

From the way she said it, I knew it wasn't the Hallmark version.

Ryan stayed silent, but he swung our clasped hands back and forth, soothing me.

I opened my mouth, glanced at Ryan, and shut it again. I was committed to Mrs. Lee, and to Laura's memory. As soon as I had a chance, I would call Tucker and arrange our excursion to Île Ste-Hélène to keep investigating.

But before that, it was Ryan's last night here and he was outlining the delicate skin between each of my fingers.

IT WAS A BIT AWKWARD, opening the apartment door one-handed, but I didn't want to let go of Ryan. From his crooked grin, he didn't, either. He slid his arm around me and bent his lips to the back of my neck. I jerked to attention and he laughed, low and deep, as his lips parted.

I pressed my back against the wooden door and squeaked as his mouth made contact. Part of me couldn't believe he'd make a scene in my own hallway, seconds away from privacy.

The other part of me said bring it on, big boy.

Inside the apartment, my phone rang.

We both stiffened.

Damn you, hospital.

Ryan spoke first, slowly raising his warm lips off my skin. "You're not on call, right?"

"Not for psych. But my pregnant patient..."

He pretended to bang his head against the door.

"I know." But I didn't know what to do except twist the key and push open the door. By the time I picked up the phone, it had switched over to voice mail, but the person hung up.

I checked my pager. Still blank.

Ryan exhaled, lower lip curled upward as if to ruffle his bangs, only he didn't have bangs anymore. His crew cut didn't stir.

I tried to pretend the mood was salvageable. "Usually the hospital would page first and leave a message, instead of calling my house. So I don't think it's them."

He just looked at me.

On cue, the phone rang again. It was easier to pick it up than to talk to Ryan. "Hello?"

No answer.

For some reason, my Caller ID was blank. Shouldn't it have kicked in by now? I drummed my fingers on the desk, waiting in case it was a telemarketing company with a long pause before it clicked on to a person. I always let them spiel away for a minute before I ask them to remove my name from their calling list. It was awfully late for telemarketing, but with my luck, I might have attracted an extra-devoted employee. Plus it was another delaying tactic. Ryan watched me with his arms crossed.

"Hello?" I repeated, but only got silence. I hung up.

"Why don't you have Caller ID?" he asked.

"I signed up for it. They must have lost my order. Or maybe they didn't have time to process it? I'm not sure."

"You need to check on that. Now."

"I thought there was other stuff you'd rather do." I'm not good at being a femme fatale, but I tried for coy.

He didn't smile or reach for me. "Look. If nothing else, I want you to be safe. You're getting weird letters and phone calls—"

"I know." I'd rushed home to Ryan and Mrs. Lee instead of stopping at the police station with my graveyard pic, so as penance, I dropped into my desk chair and logged on to bell.ca. While I clicked, I said, "Did you come to Montreal looking for me?"

He started before his lips thinned. "Yes. Well, not completely."

I waited. He didn't explain, so I prompted. "You mean Lisa, right?"

He rubbed his hand across his forehead, a gesture of irritation I knew so well. "What does this have to do with Caller ID? Or are you changing the subject again?"

I scooped up my Bell bill and entered my account number while still trying to maintain some eye contact. "Humour me."

He shrugged. "I was going to take a few days off anyway. She invited me, said Montreal's a great city. Which it is. So we took the train down—"

I figured that was so all of them could drink. Ryan doesn't hang out with other teetotalers at work. I always liked that he could be friends with everyone, instead of only sticking to his church group.

I clicked "I accept" on the website. It didn't seem to have a record of this morning's order.

"—and I thought I'd look you up while you were here."

"I'm glad you came," I said, which was true. "Do you have Lisa's phone number?"

"Why?"

"Is it unlisted?"

"No, she's in the book. But why?"

I shrugged. No sense getting him more worked up. But our old nemesis, the phone, rang again. Ryan grimaced while I picked it up.

This time, I thought I heard a soft breath before a click.

If I'd been alone, I might have been spooked. As it was, I tried to look on the bright side. "Well, I definitely don't think it's the hospital."

Ryan stood up. "Hope. This is not a joke."

"I know. I'm going to keep a phone log for the police."

"How about for yourself?"

"Yeah, that too."

"If this steps up, will you call the police again? 'Cause I'm not going to be here to look out for you. I guess I could change my ticket—"

"No, Ryan. You've done enough for me." I gestured at the barred windows. "This has probably been the world's worst vacation for you."

"Oh, I don't know. It had its benefits." He grinned.

But guilt had finally kicked in for me, punching through my fatigue and Mrs. Lee mission and panic attacks and lust attacks. I jumped to my feet. "I'm serious. You hardly saw Lisa or your friends, you cloistered yourself here doing a computer model and changing my locks, and every time we, uh, try to get down, I get called away." I paused. "I officially suck. You are free to go."

Ryan threw his head back and burst out laughing. "Yeah, right."

I grabbed his hands and held them like I could transmit my determination to him. "Ryan, I am so serious. Get out of here. There are a thousand better women here for you. You know the T-shirt, 'Good girls go to heaven, bad girls go to Montreal.' I'm toxic to you. I bet you could find a good girl who'd marry—"

He silenced me with a kiss. A kiss hard enough to stop my brain, tender enough to stop my breath for a second. Then he broke it off. "Hope."

My lips were still turned upward for more. I had to reprogram myself for speech. "Yes?"

He smiled. "I wanted to do all that for you. I mean, yeah, you get called away more often than Superman and it's annoying. But when I heard you almost died..." He shook his hands loose, then fiddled with the mouse, drawing zig-zags across the screen before he spoke again. "It made a lot of things clear to me. I'm glad I got to do your windows and locks. I'd rather do that than go fry on a beach somewhere. And even this thing with Mrs. Lee, I got an idea why you do this stuff. I just want you to be safe."

I had to swallow the lump in my throat. I still thought he was too good for me.

"I don't know about the people you hang around with. Especially that Tucker guy."

My eyebrows jerked upward, not to mention my stomach. "What about him?"

"Well, he seemed pretty mad you were hanging around with me." He shrugged but met my eye steadily. "Do you think he might hold a grudge about it? He knows where you live, right? He's got your number."

"Uh huh." In my best "Your point is?" voice.

He shrugged again. "I don't know. I think he might be the one leaving you those messages and hanging up and whatever."

I didn't know whether to laugh or choke. I ended up sounding like a rooster being strangled. "I don't think so."

"Just keep an eye on him. That's all I'm saying."

"Will do." Oh, God. Now I was close to cracking up. I mean, the thought of Tucker spying on me, that was hysterical.

The right side of his mouth cocked up in a grin. "Awright. That's enough talk. So can we get busy?"

19

I laughed, like I was meant to, and we both relaxed. But instead of reaching for me, Ryan perched on the edge of my desk and said, "You still have Henry!" He pointed to the wooden artist's model to his left. Henry lounged on his back with his head between his hands and his knees bent. "Is he doing sit-ups?"

I swatted Ryan. "He's supposed to be relaxing, since everyone tells me I'm so uptight."

"He could be relaxing while doing sit-ups. Sounds like you." Ryan smiled. He already knew the back-story. I didn't have to explain how I bought Henry for a drawing class years ago, only I sucked at it, so I turned him into a kind of emotional barometer and procrastination tool.

Ryan picked Henry up and straightened him into a standing position, keeping one arm folded. It looked like Henry was scratching his head. "What do you think?"

"He has lice?"

Ryan grinned. "Yeah, right. He's supposed to be thinking of how to put you in the mood."

I was embarrassed, but refused to admit it. Instead, I reached for Henry. I'd never used him as foreplay before. "Well, this is a start." I twitched the bent arm so the ball hand was more where the ear would be, if there'd been an ear.

Ryan's brow crinkled, but he poked my left ear with his fingertip.

I giggled. "No, I meant that you should listen to me."

"I'm listening." He kissed my earlobe. Then he licked his tongue along the edge of my ear.

I was starting to forget what I wanted to say. With the functional part of my brain, I extended Henry's arms at shoulder height and raised him so Ryan could see.

Ryan got it and slipped his arms around me.

I pushed Henry back on to my desk without checking where he landed.

Ryan and I could take it from here.

Then my conscience prodded me one more time. I had to tell him about Tucker. "Ryan—"

He shook his head and kissed me until neither of us could speak. Then he lifted me on to the desk. It creaked slightly. I lifted my eyes to the glow of the lamp light on the ceiling. The heat and humidity of the day had dissipated, leaving only cool, lovely night air. This felt so right. His hands dropped on either side of my hips, blocking me in. He bent to kiss me again.

I'd missed him. This man. These lips, warm and smooth and firm, and the way he moved them, both tender and knowing.

He tasted a little spicy, like his favourite cinnamon gum, as well as his own familiar tang. His fingers trailed along the back of my neck, making me shiver. He chuckled a little and pulled me closer, exploring my mouth while his fingers followed along my dress strap, brushing my exposed shoulder and back. I wrapped my hands in his thick hair as his palms swept across my back. He chuckled again.

I drew back, trying to break myself out of the mood. "What's so funny?"

He dropped slow kisses down my neck in answer. I quivered and closed my eyes.

He murmured, against my skin, "Hope." I could hear the smile in his voice.

My heart beat so hard, I was sure he could feel it in my throat.

He slipped a hand down the back of my dress. "I didn't *think* you were wearing a bra." Since I was small-built, I skipped the bra if my top was skimpy. His palm pressed against the bare flesh of my back. I arched my body toward his.

He smiled down toward me, his hips nudging between my legs. I tried to press them back together, but he refused to budge, and after a minute, I relaxed and tilted my head back for another kiss. When he reached for the buttons on my cap-sleeved top, I helped slip it off. I was still wearing my black spaghetti-strapped dress underneath.

He gave a low whistle. I grinned and kissed him some more. Flatterer.

I felt his hand move up to my shoulder, stroking my collarbone and the line of my neck. Exquisite. I slid my arms down his back, remembering his slim, muscular build with my hands.

He slipped the left strap of my dress off my shoulder.

I shook my head.

Ryan quirked an eyebrow and paused. When I didn't move, he flicked the right strap off my shoulder.

I clutched my elbows in to my sides to keep my dress up, still mute, still torn between *hell, yes* and *no way*.

Ryan grinned and looped his index finger in the front of my dress. He was touching the fabric, not my skin, but he was so close to both my breasts, I held my breath so I wouldn't accidentally brush them against him.

Our eyes met. Oh, yes, he was enjoying this, too.

I teased him by taking a deep breath myself, increasing the gap. I chuckled at the way his eyes were instantly drawn south.

In retaliation, Ryan hooked the front of my dress down, thoroughly exposing my cleavage and probably eighty percent of my breasts.

I yelped and jumped backward, which inadvertently flashed all of my goods before he let go.

We were both breathing hard and laughing at ourselves when he rubbed his forehead and said, "Hope, there's just this one thing."

20

I immediately pulled up my straps, crossed my arms, and leaned away from him. "What."

He tried to reach for me. "It's not that bad."

"Just tell me, Ryan."

He ran his hands through his hair. "Bad timing, I know."

I was the master (mistress?) of bad timing. I waited.

"I want you to know I'm very..." He exhaled. "...interested in you. I didn't want to get carried away."

"Uh huh."

"Because I'm not—I mean, this time I really am waiting for marriage."

It took a second for my lust fog to dissipate, but from the look in his dark brown eyes, he meant it. I stopped to calculate what this meant.

He was saying no.

He was *saving himself.*

Holy crap.

"It's a decision I made in the last two years. It's not personal."

They say that when you do a guy and he turns gay, it has nothing to do with you. That's never happened to me. (Yet. With an n of two, which is a very small sample size.)

So what does it mean if you do a guy and he swears off premarital sex? I couldn't see it as a compliment, but I struggled to act mature about it. I twisted my legs to the side, away from him, and said, "Thank you for telling me."

He looked up at me from under his eyebrows. "Should've kept my mouth shut, right?"

I sighed and shook my head. "I'd rather know."

He touched my hair. I tensed, but let him. He said, "The last thing I want to do is hurt you. I just couldn't figure out how to tell you before."

I exhaled. I couldn't fault him on that one. It seemed like I was always running off. Still, it's kind of presumptuous to tug on your ex's sleeve and say, Guess what? I'm a born-again virgin!

I tried to smile while I adjusted my top and repeated, "Thanks for telling me."

"Nah. I screwed the pooch on this one."

I had to laugh. Sometimes he surprised me.

"Because I really did want to see you and, uh..." His eyes flickered, but he didn't look away. "Take it from there."

I nodded. In his own way, Ryan was as confused as I was.

"Do you want me to go?"

I thought about it and shook my head.

"We could play Cranium or something."

I managed to laugh.

TWO HOURS LATER, I awoke on the futon, my legs tangled with his, my head tucked under his shoulder, breathing his skin, with my contact lenses cemented to my eyeballs.

I blinked, trying to force tears into my eyes, and turned my chin to look at Ryan. We'd forgotten to pull the blind. The streetlamp light, filtered through the leaves of the trees in the front yard, spilled over both of us.

He wasn't sleeping. He was wide awake and looking back at me. He stroked my hair.

I kissed the tender skin under his arm and closed my eyes again.

THE NEXT MORNING, I was running late, but I stopped when I caught the eye of a patient smoking in the front circle outside the hospital. She waved at me, shaking out her long, dark hair.

Wait. That wasn't a patient. That was Reena Schuster's sister, Wendy.

"Hi," I said. "How are you doing?"

She shrugged. "Been better."

"Yeah." I held my breath against the smoke.

Her eyes laughed at me while she held her cigarette in the air. "You going to give me a lecture?"

I shook my head. "You know the drill. And now's not an easy time to quit. How's Reena doing?"

Her chin jerked away from me. She took a quick, angry puff. "They don't tell you anything."

Automatically, I reached for her arm, but stopped before I made contact. "I'll drop by and see if I can translate for you."

She sucked on the smoke and shrugged, but after a minute, she nodded. "Thanks."

So before lunch, instead of hitting the resident's lounge or the library, I hustled back to the ICU.

Good timing. Stan was clicking through an online article from the New England Journal. I dropped in the chair beside him.

He barely glanced away from the screen. "Have you picked out your article for journal club? You're presenting soon."

"Um, no."

"This is a good one on hypertension in pregnancy. I suggest

avoiding the one on horse-versus-rabbit antithymocyte globulin, unless you want to confuse everybody."

"Good call." I cleared my throat. "I was wondering how Reena Schuster was doing."

He clicked on the print icon. "So what else is new."

Dr. Wharton passed behind Stan's left shoulder with an old chart tucked under his arm. Dr. Wharton said, "I've never seen such a dedicated envoy from psychiatry."

I forced a smile. Wendy and her mother were watching from Reena's bedside. "Just call me an army of one."

"Your timing is fortuitous," said Dr. Wharton, sitting down with his chart. His beeper went off.

I looked at Stan. He shrugged and said, "You're welcome to check her out yourself. Her vitals are almost normal. She doesn't have a fever anymore, her renal function is down to one-ninety, and her tone isn't as rigid."

"She has inconsistent tone, it seems," Dr. Wharton put in as he stabbed a number into the telephone.

I raised my eyebrows.

Stan said, "Check her neuro vitals. Sometimes the nurses still find her rigid, and sometimes they don't. Basically, if you sneak up on her and bend her ankle, it's flexible, but then it stiffens up, and so does the rest of her body."

"O-kay. I assume she's not in a coma anymore?" I craned my neck, but from where I sat, Reena was a bundle under the blankets.

"I suspect her EEG will prove that her state is psychogenic," said Dr. Wharton, before turning to the phone. "Joe? Have you seen the patient on 5 South?"

I lowered my voice to Stan. "You think she's faking NMS?"

"No. She has it, or had it. But we think she's exaggerating the symptoms. She doesn't want to come out of the ICU." He rolled his eyes. "So, back to you, buckaroo."

"You're putting her on the ward anyway?"

"As soon as they free up a bed. Which better be soon, because there's a GI bleed in emerg."

"But you already got your a psych consult, right? What did they say?"

"Not a hell of a lot. You can read the consult."

Officially, Reena wasn't mine anymore. They keep the residents in the emerg and the medical students on the psych ward as well as the emerg. The staff psychiatrists do the consults on other services during the day. But I couldn't let this one pass. "Could you get her old psych charts?"

"Why would we do that?"

"Humour me. You've got a unit coordinator to help you, and I bet her mom would sign the consent."

Stan narrowed his eyes. "How far back do you want me to go?"

"Say, spring, eight years ago?"

"And why would I do that for a patient who's about fifteen seconds away from leaving my service?"

I paused to think. "I'll bring you a bagel."

"A real one. Not one of those soft, puffy ones from the grocery store. We call those Christian bagels."

I laughed. We shook on it. And I went to see Reena.

Her eyes were closed, but she was breathing on her own. Her colour was better, in that she was pale, but not morbidly so. Her IV bag was half-full. No more O2 sat. She was even wearing socks, red argyle ones. Funny how real clothes or a bedspread from home makes a difference. She was definitely being suited-up for the ward.

"Hi," I said to Wendy and her foster mom.

Wendy nodded. Mrs. Schuster said, "Hello, Doctor."

"Hi, Reena." Did her eyelids tighten for a moment before deliberately smoothing out? Or was that only Stan and Dr. Wharton in my head? I decided to talk as if she could hear me. "You seem to be getting better."

Reena's breath hitched for a second. I didn't imagine that.

I turned to page through the chart at her bedside. As described, her vitals and creatinine had improved. Then I asked Wendy. "Could you tell me again what happened? How did she end up here?"

She looked at her mom. Mrs. Schuster said, "She took pills, doctor. I don't know why. Everything was going so well."

So well that she came to the emergency room twice before fleeing me? I eyeballed Wendy, who avoided my gaze. I asked, "Who called 911?"

"My daughter." Mrs. Schuster wrapped her arm around Wendy's waist. "Thank God. I don't know what I would have done otherwise. Losing one of my girls..."

"You're not going to lose us, Ma," Wendy muttered, her mouth now safely tucked into her mom's shoulder.

"Maybe not now. But you never know. She's not out of the woods yet." Mrs. Schuster released her and yanked some tissues out of her purse, carefully dabbing her eyes. She'd taken the time to apply mascara and eyeliner today.

"How did you find her?" I asked Wendy.

Another pause. I glanced at Reena. She appeared motionless, but Wendy drew back from her mother, followed my gaze and wrapped her arms around her own waist without answering.

Mrs. Schuster said, "Thank goodness they were both home. I think Wendy heard her hit the floor. Isn't that right, love? I wish I'd been the one to find her. I'd rather walk through hell than put one of my girls through it. I've already been through hell so many times, what's one more?"

I smiled sympathetically and tried to steer the conversation back. "Yes, I can see how that—"

"You have no idea. I can see it from your face. You're young. Maybe even as young as Wendy, here, I don't know. It's hard to tell." She scanned my face. I braced myself for the "with you Orientals" part, but she managed to bite that back. "I hope you never have to go through what I've gone through. Reena, here, in and out of hospitals since she was thirteen. My husband died of a heart attack in my arms. Not one, but both my girls telling me they're gay! What are the chances! Is it contagious?"

"*Ma.*" Wendy's fists bunched up.

Mrs. Schuster barely paused, but she turned her head and waved at her daughter's bed. "And now Reena here, on the brink of death. I tell you, sometimes I wonder how much I need to be tested."

"I think we all feel like that sometimes." I was thinking of Mrs. Lee. Two different mothers, two different women grieving.

Mrs. Schuster looked right at me. "Can you help my daughter?"

"I'd like to. She, ah, didn't feel comfortable seeing me." To my surprise, I saw Wendy's neck flush as she averted her eyes from me yet again. What did she have to be embarrassed about?

Maybe she knew why Reena hated me. That put me off my game for a second, but I steeled myself. Mrs. Schuster was asking me for help, even if her two daughters were not. "I'm only rotating through psychiatry. I wonder, though, if we could do some family counselling in one of my outpatient clinics." Even as I spoke, my brain was shrieking, what are you doing? Your plate is so full, it's already toppled to the floor! Reena hates you! Her foster sister hates you! Why would you counsel them?

Wendy's eyes widened, but Mrs. Schuster was already saying, "Thank you, doctor. I like you a lot better than that other head-shrinker. Give me your card."

21

I traded some favours and dug up Mike's criminal record. Stealing cars, theft under a thousand, big fucking deal.

But I like to keep my hands clean.

I called Mike up and met him in a parking lot behind a Couche-Tard downtown, where no one could hear us. "I want you to get me a car."

"Yeah?" He shook a cigarette out of his pack and lit it.

"A big one. Something easy to drive. An automatic."

He sucked on his stick for a while. "Why?"

"Does it matter?"

He shrugged and looked me in the eye. "I don't do that shit anymore."

I laughed in his face. "Yeah, right."

He shrugged again and got up to go. "Anyways..."

Before the word was out of his mouth, I sighed. "It's too bad about Wendy."

He carefully straightened his spine. "What about her?"

"You guys breaking up and all. She told me what you did to her. Kind of sick, dude. Especially with her being only thirteen."

He stopped breathing for a second.

"She was thinking of talking to someone about it."

"I never—"

"She recorded you with her phone. She showed it to me. Not smart, Mike."

He stood there with his cigarette burning in his hand, too stunned to flick the ash off. I waited for a minute. I was enjoying this. Not only did his face go a weird, pale grey, but he even smelled funny. Can someone smell like fear?

I relented. "But I talked to her. I told her to hang on. Don't back that up. Don't upload it anywhere. I told her you were a good guy. You were even doing a favour for me." I paused. "She sent me a copy and destroyed hers."

I watched his Adam's apple bob in his throat. He glanced up and down the lot, but we were alone except for an old Geo and a GMC truck in the corner. He muttered out of the corner of his mouth, "All you want is a car? For the video?"

I nodded. What can I say? I'm really a soft touch sometimes.

WHEN I UNLOCKED my bike at the end of the day, I saw a heavy-set woman out of the corner of my eye. She turned, and her lustrous black hair caught the sun. It was Wendy, pacing on a small rectangle of lawn in front of human resources, across from the emerg entrance.

She didn't see me. She was too busy yelling into her cell phone.

"Where are you? Why didn't you come?" Pause. "Don't give me that. You couldn't leave her alone before, and now that she's in a coma, you...No. That's *bull*shit. I did everything you—*everything*. And what...oh, yeah, you're doing it all for me. You are sick." Pause. "Don't you dare hang up on me. Don't you—goddammit!"

Slowly, I wound the chain around the seat of my bike. It clanged on the frame. Wendy's head jerked up.

Uh oh. I nodded at her and secured the lock on the chain. Better to pretend blissful ignorance. Hear no evil.

She advanced on me like a bull. The only thing missing was the cartoon smoke rising from her nostrils. "You spying on me?"

I pulled my bike out of the rack, keeping it between us. "Nope."

"You're always around. Watching. Listening. Giving everyone the creeps."

I unhooked the helmet from my backpack and snapped it on my head, never taking my eyes off her. "Thanks." I backed up, wheeling my bike away.

"Don't you walk away from me." She walked around the rack.

I wasn't walking, I was biking, but something told me she wouldn't appreciate the joke.

She planted her hands on the handlebars. Or she would have if I hadn't backed up fast enough to scuff up a bit of sand on the pavement. I switched from defence to offense. "Why don't you call back whoever it was on the phone? That's who you're really mad at."

Her eyebrows soared before she slitted her eyes. "You playing with me?"

"Not at all." I glanced around, catching the eye of the parking guard lurking in the front entrance, but he was immediately distracted by someone holding a bill in his hand.

"Stay out of our business, okay? We don't need your *counselling*." She made sarcastic quotes in the air. "We don't need your help. We just need you to fuck off."

I mentally flipped through a few responses. I try not to get riled up with patients or their families. It was only five p.m., so there were plenty of people around. I didn't need to feel threatened. I opened my mouth to defuse the situation, but instead, I said, "Is that why you're harassing me?"

Her head snapped to the side, but her eyes never wavered. "What?"

"I don't know what you'd call it. A picture of a gravestone in my mailbox. Calling me at home. You were trying to scare me off?"

"I have no clue what you're talking about." But her gaze dropped to the ground before she rallied. "Pretty scary, though, right?"

"Yeah. Petrifying."

She shook herself. "Anyway, the point's the same. Leave us alone." Her voice rang hollow.

I waited. We both knew her mother was going to call me and

schedule an appointment with me, if she hadn't already. We were going to see each other, showdown or no showdown. "Look, Wendy. Who are you trying to protect?"

Her eyes widened. "No one."

She was lying. We both knew it. My tired brain clicked like it was trying, and failing, to make a connection.

Her turn to go on the attack. "I was wondering if your supervisors know you're asking all these questions instead of doing your real work."

My stomach dropped, but I tried on a poker face. "What do you mean? I think they'd be pleased I'm showing such an interest in my patients."

She bent in close enough that I had to lean away, but I did it slowly, striving not to show fear.

"Yeah, an 'interest,' is that what you call it? Accusing me of sending you letters and calling you? You think because I'm gay, I'm that hard up? As a matter of fact, I've got—" She bit back the rest.

I stared at her. I'd accused her of being my poison pen pal without any evidence or even a clue about her motivation. No homophobia intended. But was she really admitting to harassing me, or shooting off her mouth?

"Oh, forget it!" Wendy waved her hand at me and stormed away.

I took irrational pleasure in watching her thighs jiggle as she walked. It was easier than trying to figure out why she was trying to scare me, and if it had any connection to Laura's death.

It was easier than admitting I was freaked out.

Ryan was gone. Wendy was psycho. I'd have to figure this out alone.

Or almost alone.

After that, I really needed a treat, so before I started call, I hit our local Japanese resto for some takeout and paged Tucker from the residents' lounge while the steam still rose from one of the Styrofoam boxes.

"Back already?" he said.

"Yeah. There weren't any consults yet, so I bought me some

teriyaki and you a bento box." If he was anything like me, supper was an excellent suck-up/make-up/thank you/are we still friends? gift. Plus I wanted to talk to him about Wendy. "Anyway, I'm in the residents' lounge, if you want to pick it up." When he didn't respond, I said into the micro-silence, "Or I'll leave it in the fridge. Whatever's good for you."

"They haven't gotten back to me yet," said Tucker

"Who?"

"The staff at the Douglas. You wanted me to ask about antisocial patients."

"Yes, I know. That's not why I was calling, though."

"Wasn't it?"

"Well. Only partly," I admitted.

He barked with laughter. "That's what I love about you, Hope. If nothing else, you're honest. So here's the million dollar question. Why else were you calling?"

"To talk about Saturday?"

"Sounds good. Anything else?"

I thought of what we'd done and crossed my legs. It sounded nuts, throwing handbooks at each other and then nearly getting it on, but he was so hot. "Maybe."

"And you're playing it safe by meeting me in the residents' lounge, where medical students will be our chaperones and romance will be held in check by the smell of rotting garbage?"

"Well..." I glanced around. Two medical students hypnotized by the TV, a third by Facebook. "Yeah, that pretty much sums it up. But my food smells a lot better than garbage."

"No dice."

"Huh?"

"The residents' lounge stinks, Hope. I try to avoid it. Meet me outside somewhere. It's August and you're on psych call. Live a little."

My idea of living dangerously was leaving the premises to grab supper even though I was on home call and had 20 minutes to respond. He was probably right, but it annoyed me. "You want your bento box or not, Tucker?"

His laugh crackled back at me through the line. "Yeah. At the picnic tables outside HR. See you in five?"

I hung up on him. We both knew I'd be there.

Seven minutes later, while I unsnapped my wooden chopsticks for teriyaki chicken, Tucker sampled some sushi. "Not bad. How've you been?"

"Uh, busy." I blushed and dug into my chicken to hide it.

"I'll bet. Well, me too. I talked to one of the psychiatrists, Dr. Ven."

"But you said—"

"Yeah." His brown eyes turned serious for a second. "Just wanted to make sure you wanted me and not just my skillz. Happens too often."

I pushed my Styrofoam container aside. "So what did you find out?"

"He has a great memory and he's really a nice guy. He's going to get out some of his notes, but he still remembered that group of borderlines. It disbanded a decade ago, something about funding, before they restarted it the following year."

I suspected the history lesson was to keep me in suspense as long as possible, so I bit my tongue.

"They thought it would be a good idea to have group therapy for borderlines, same as for everyone else. They have issues of anger and abandonment, as you know, so the idea was that they could work on those together. But he said there were problems. Some of the girls got together for 'slasher parties' afterward, where they brought out the razor blades and cut their own arms, egging each other on. Two of the girls had to be stitched up in the emerg." Tucker shook his head. "He did remember one guy, though, he thought might have antisocial personality. Michael Martinez."

"A guy," I repeated.

"Yeah. He was the only man in the group. That's probably why Dr. Ven remembers him so well. He was also the only one to have serious trouble with the law. Breaking and entering, theft under a thousand dollars——not hard stuff, but enough to get him a record. He was nineteen at the time, so it didn't get all wiped out the way it would have if he'd been underage. Actually, most of the borderlines were over eighteen. It started with eighteen and under, but got expanded, plus they didn't want to kick out the patients once they turned nineteen..."

Tucker was way too interested in the mechanics of the psych group. "Okay, so this Michael Martinez. What else do you know about him?"

"Dr. Ven was going to look it up, but he remembered him as very charming. Always had a girlfriend. We laughed about that. I said there's less worry about abandonment issues if he's always stringing them along, but Dr. Ven said actually borderlines get screwed up sometimes when the partner dumps them and it becomes a self-fulfilling prophecy. Plus Dr. Ven remembers that Martinez kind of changed around the time of Laura's death. He became a lot more secretive and defensive, and then stopped coming altogether. Dr. Ven tried to track him down and get him to come back, but his phone number was a pizza place he used to work at. He kind of slipped away."

"Okay. And Dr. Ven never said anything about that to the police?"

"He said it was all circumstantial. As a matter of fact, a lot of the patients acted peculiar when Laura died. He thought they were uneasy about the reminder of their own mortality. He thought it might be part of the reason so many of them dropped out."

"Who else dropped out?"

"Like I said, he's getting back to me."

"I'd like to talk to him."

Tucker stretched his legs out and ate the last piece of sashimi. "I know you would."

I whipped out my phone. "Do you have his number?"

"Uh huh." He made no move to give it.

I waited with my finger poised in the air. "Tucker?"

"I know you'd like it, but this is my part of the 'investigation.' I'm covering it, Hope."

"But—"

He shook his head and closed his eyes. I reached across the table, stopping short of his hand. "Come on, Tucker, what difference would it make if I talked to him?"

"He doesn't like to break patient confidentiality, for one," he replied without opening his eyes.

Damn. "Well, what about—"

"It's different. We used to work together. But you're the 'detective doctor' parachuting in from Ontario, you know what I'm saying?"

I grimaced.

He put his legs down and laughed openly. "Anyway, I lured you here to talk to you about something else."

The look in his eye made my heart pound all of a sudden. "Saturday?"

"And beyond. Don't worry, it's not about jumping your bones."

"How disappointing."

He clucked his tongue. "That's my girl. Can I try some of your chicken?"

I held the box toward him. "You're trying to draw it out and torture me."

"You know it." He was deft with the chopsticks. Good with his hands. It made me wonder how he'd be in bed. Again. He caught me looking at him and laughed. "Good, huh?"

I pretended he was talking about the food. "Yeah, I like their sauce."

"Right." He lifted his eyebrows. He seemed a lot more confident and playful than the last time we'd seen each other. I wondered what had changed. Maybe it was the lure of being a 'detective doctor' himself. Well, I could live with that.

But then Tucker smiled, and I thought it was more likely our dalliance in the conference room had recharged him somehow.

"Well, you've been kind of torturing me, Hope." Despite his light tone, I tensed and waited. I had an idea what was coming.

He surveyed me. He and Ryan both had brown eyes, but Ryan's were dark brown, black in some lights, intelligent and deep. Tucker's were lighter, with some gold in the iris, and usually more playful. Except now they were intent. I waited for the Ryan-guilt. I deserved it.

But he surprised me again. "My parents are college sweethearts. Did you know that?"

I shook my head.

"You never asked. But they've been together since he asked her to dance to the Police's *'Every Breath You Take.'* They play it on their anniversary every year." He grinned and rolled his eyes. "They probably would've gotten together before except he threw spit balls at her in grade seven, and she wouldn't have anything to do with him for years after. But they both said they 'knew' the other one was the right one. All our lives, they've been telling me and my sisters that, and we've been like, okay, whatever, hippies."

I had to laugh. "I didn't know you had sisters."

"Two younger ones. We quoted the divorce rate at them, we told them life was a lot more complicated, new millennium, yadda yadda. And then I saw you at the resident orientation." His mobile face turned serious. I found myself holding my breath.

"Everyone else was on time, serious, and I'd known almost all of them for years. You burst in late with this huge smile on your face. You were wearing shorts when everyone else was in dress pants. You had so much *energy*, like a hummingbird or something."

I had to laugh at that.

"And right off the bat, you didn't take shit from anyone, including me. And I knew." He looked me straight in the eye and repeated, "I just knew."

Holy macaroni. He was serious. A small, secret part of me was amazed and touched while the rest of me was scared. I never knew Tucker saw me that way. Cute, sure. He'd always been interested. But he was talking *coup de foudre*, or as the English say, love at first sight.

"I can't explain it. I could hardly believe it myself. Still can't." He shook his head, too. "Sometimes, I think it's a masochism thing." He didn't say, but we were both thinking of Alex and now Ryan. I winced. He waved it away. "You drive me crazy. But other times..." He looked at me, tilting his head to the side. "I know what I'm doing. So I'm waiting for you. Not passively. And not forever. I'm not a saint. But you're the one, Hope."

My mouth went dry. My heart started drumming like another panic attack, but in a semi-good way. He wasn't exactly saying he loved me, but it was pretty close. He was calling me his destiny. And I had no freaking clue what to say back.

He shrugged and smiled. "You don't have to say anything. I just wanted you to know. Thanks for the bento box." He stood up, untangling his legs from the picnic table.

I found my tongue again. "Now, wait a minute. You can't say that I'm 'the one' and leave."

"Actually, I can do whatever I want."

"Yes, I know, but..."

"And if someone had laid that on me, I'd want some time to think about it."

"Yes, but—"

"Unless it was you." He frowned before he gave me a lopsided grin. "I'm looking forward to that."

I exhaled. "Tucker."

"I'm impossible. I know." He saluted me and started walking away, bento box between two fingers, his head held in a jaunty way. Faintly, on a breeze, I heard him whistle but couldn't quite make out the tune.

Before I could decide what to do, my pager went off for a consult in emerg.

22

The next time I saw Tucker, we were riding the rails to Île Ste-Hélène on a gorgeous Saturday morning in August. I'd been trying not to think about what he'd said about me being the one, but it was kind of like the elephant in the room, or in this case, on the subway. I admit I was wearing the same board shorts he'd admired at the resident orientation meeting, dark red with red and white hibiscus inset along the waist and outer thighs. They showed a lot of leg. He'd smiled when he saw them. I blushed.

"I like the notebook," he said as the metro clattered against its tracks.

I rested said spiral-bound notebook on my lap. "Well, as a 'detective doctor,' it behooves me to take notes." I tried not to notice his thigh, which he kept a careful two inches away from mine. It felt sort of like a date with Tucker, but we were on our way to see where Laura Lee had died and perhaps been murdered.

"What's wrong with your smart phone?"

I exhaled and looked at him. He knew my current cell was a crappy pay-as-you-go phone. It works, but it takes ages to text on the number pad, let alone take notes.

"You should get a new one."

"Look who's talking." Tucker had gone swimming and drenched his pretty little Blackberry while he was horsing around with his friends.

"Hey, I took the battery out and put it in rice. It should be okay after five days."

I rolled my eyes. "My old-school phone is better than no phone. But even if I could afford a tablet, I like pen and ink. I might do some drawing today." I'd tucked my camera in my purse, but sketching the scene seemed like something a detective might do. I worked my pen into the spiral of the notebook.

"Can you draw?" he asked.

I laughed and shook my head. "Nah. I even tried lessons."

"Maybe that could be my department, then. I'm not bad."

I raised my left eyebrow.

"Seriously. Can I have your book?"

I handed it over. He pulled the pen out of the spiral ring, narrowed his eyes at my face, and started sketching on the first page.

"Wait a minute!"

"Shh. The *artiste* is at work."

I subsided, trying to catch glimpses of the work-in-progress.

"Quit moving around. Can't you read the metro ads or something?"

"Sure, I'm dying to know about hair loss."

"Good."

I never realized how excruciating it could be to pose for a drawing. He wasn't even making me sit still, but I was curious and impatient, and couldn't figure out how to hold my face, let alone my body. Why was I wearing shorts again? What if, with his artist's eye, he dappled in cellulite on my thighs or sketched the stretch marks on my knees?

But I was flattered, too. No one had ever drawn me before. How did he see me?

Maybe it all was a big joke and he was putting the finishing touches on a smiley face.

Basically, I was torturing myself. In a nifty writing book, *Writing*

Down the Bones, Natalie Goldberg talked about "fighting the tofu," this sort of useless struggle against yourself. Hello, tofu. So I crossed my arms, tapped my foot, and stared at everyone else on the metro. Much better than the ads.

It was relatively empty on a Saturday morning, but there was a mom with an infant. The kid was babbling to himself, "Ar ar ar ar ar, ayaaaaaa," and trying to stand up in her lap and leave greasy finger-prints on the window, all at the same time. The mom smiled, but she looked tired.

The electronic sign flashed and the recorded woman's voice said, *"PROCHAIN ARRÊT, BERRI-UQAM."*

Tucker shut the notebook. "That's us."

"Yeah." I knew that we had to switch over to the yellow line and hit the island, but there was a question in my voice. I reached for the notebook.

He gave me a slash of a smile. "I'll show you later."

"When you're done?"

"Kind of."

What kind of answer was that? But he was already gesturing me to the door and grabbing my hand to lead me to the Longueil line. He rubbed his thumb along the back of my hand as if he'd done it before, many times.

When we stepped out of the station, my hand tightened on Tucker's. He squeezed back, but he didn't say anything as he pushed open the Plexiglas door for us.

Sunlight met my eyes. I squinted and shielded them. I hadn't understood why she'd come all the way here for a morning constitutional, but now I had an inkling. Since the metro stopped on Île Ste-Hélène, one of two islands in the channel of the St. Lawrence River, we were across from the old port. We could see mighty old ships as long as a city block or two, rusted, but still awe-inspiring for landlubbers like me. That was a whole world in itself.

Beyond the port, I saw the brick and concrete-and-glass buildings of downtown Montreal. A hop on the subway and you could admire the hustle from a distance, while surrounded by grass, trees, and some cool structures unto themselves.

My favourite was the Biosphere. I like round things, and here was a giant sphere built out of metal struts, for no purpose I could tell; but if I rollerbladed past it every day, it would make me smile.

Then my gaze fell on the benches outside the station. Laura probably donned her blades here, tightening the straps, testing them out on the grey paving stones. I imagined her tucking her shoes into a backpack and tightening the elastic on her pony tail before setting off for her usual a.m. exercise, on an August morning like any other.

Except it had been raining. So there were probably even fewer people about at 5:30 a.m. And the paving stones would have been a little more slippery, so maybe she bent her head against the rain, or her vision was slightly obscured by her hood.

As we stepped off Île Ste-Hélène, I saw a beige, rectangular contemporary art statue with indentations that made me think of grinning teeth.

Tucker snorted. "It looks like a dentist's model."

"I think so, too." Then I fell silent. It seemed sacrilegious to joke around and today that statue felt more creepy than funny.

We crossed a road with a 30 km/h sign. We could have followed it toward *La Ronde*, an amusement park, or probably a dozen other attractions, but we were headed to Île Notre-Dame, a kind of sister island connected by a bridge. The bridge where Laura was killed.

We had to pause for a car. I let go of Tucker's hand. From here, I could see where she had died. My teeth clenched. I took a deep breath and inhaled exhaust fumes. Then I marched toward the bridge.

Tucker kept stride with me. "She was heading to Île Notre-Dame, right? So she could blade on the Formula One track?" Montreal hosts the international race car circuit in July, but for the rest of the year, bladers and walkers and whoever else take over the track.

I shook my head. "That's what some of the media said, but she was hit from behind. The police thought she was coming back across the bridge between the islands after she'd already bladed. Whoever hit her was coming from Notre-Dame. She didn't see them coming."

I paused at our end of the bridge, the north side. There was a little booth where a guard could sit, as well as a wrought-iron gate rolled back to let cars through. My heart lifted. "Hey. Look. Was a guard here?"

Tucker shook his head. "I think they only have guards when there's an event, so they can charge fifty bucks for parking."

"Right." So that was why police report hadn't mentioned a guard. Not too much call for parking in the early morning hours. "I wonder why she took the metro instead of driving?"

Tucker shrugged. "She may not even have had a car. A lot of residents don't."

Another thing I found odd, although endearing, about Montreal is that many people don't own the ubiquitous four-wheeled machines the rest of us are addicted to. So many people talk the talk about the environment. Not many do anything about it.

And then I did what I'd been dreading. I set foot on the bridge.

There wasn't much to see. Two lanes, one each way for cars, with a pedestrian lane on the west side. No proper barrier between cars and people, only black posts circled with reflective tape. I shook the first post. It was a rolled plastic tube barely bolted down. Any adult could rip this off, let alone a car. I bit my lip and raised my eyes to the bridge itself.

The sides were made out of concrete Jersey barriers, the same as on construction sites, but lined up with no gap between them. They were topped by some sort of vertical-barred metal railing. Altogether, the bridge was at least as high as my shoulder, with no easy way to climb up and escape.

If I'd been on blades, with a car coming at me, I'd have to see it, reach up, try and drag myself above car height by the strength of my arms alone while my wheels slipped on the concrete—no deal.

I could try and blade away from the car, but again, not likely.

"Back then, they didn't have these barriers," said Tucker, pointing at the plastic poles. They only put these in since Laura died and Mrs. Lee, uh, insisted."

It wasn't much of a barrier, but it was certainly better than nothing.

The bridge wasn't long, maybe 40 feet across. Around the midpoint, someone had drawn a small black cross on the concrete. I raised my finger to it, but dropped my hand before I made contact.

Instead, I peered over the edge into the St. Lawrence River. It was muddy brown today, even though the current was flowing swiftly. I'd say it was a thirty-foot drop, although I'm not good at estimating distances. Jumping into the river was probably better than being hit by a car, but I wasn't sure how deep or cold it was in August, and it would be damn hard to swim in rollerblades.

I heard a couple arguing in French behind us. We moved aside for them and their little dog. I pretended to read the plaque describing river vegetation adapting to changing water levels, but I couldn't concentrate.

A pack of cyclists passed us, so we stepped up our pace to the other side of the bridge, onto Île Notre-Dame. There was an empty guard house here, too, as well as a matching gate. Some mounted signs described the many events scheduled over the summer, from concerts to cross-country races.

Tucker gestured at the smoothly paved track which stretched far in the distance. We fell into step, breathing the fresh air. He took my hand again and I let him. I felt a little better experiencing where she had lived instead of where she had died.

Still, I said, "I wonder why they didn't put up a plaque for her."

"Couldn't tell you."

"I wonder if it was because Mrs. Lee was such a pain in the ass. Did you know she held a one-woman vigil here, holding a sign saying, 'Who killed my daughter?' in both official languages?"

Tucker smiled and shook his head.

We kept walking. The sun beat down on our heads. Uh oh. Black hair absorbs a lot of heat, and I don't need face wrinkles. I tugged

Tucker off to the side and pulled a navy Tilley hat out of my bag while some cyclists passed us. Tucker burst out laughing.

"Why, you like skin cancer?" I asked.

"Yeah, love it. By the way, most of the damage is done before you're 18."

"Actually, that's a myth. Only about a quarter of your sun exposure is done as a minor. I'll send you the reference. And by the way, I need my book back to make notes." I held out my hand.

He tucked it under his arm. "You'll cheat."

"Trrrrust me, I'm a doctor," I drawled, channelling the creepy doc from the Simpsons.

"Well, as long as you're a *doc*tor, I'll count on your ethics to stay away from the first section for now."

"What, you're going to claim a third of my book?"

"Uh huh. You can take notes and I'll sketch here and there. Not just you. I can draw the bridge, the track, the Olympic basin. Whatever you want."

I gazed at him with new respect. "Thanks." As a non-artist, it hadn't occurred to me.

"You're welcome."

"I brought a camera, but you can do the diagrams. Do you mind sketching the bridge?"

While he did that, I took some pictures, including one of him. The sun turned his hair into a near-white halo. He'd left out the gel this morning, for once. He was wearing a blue dress shirt with the sleeves rolled up, and light khaki pants, despite the heat. He looked how I'd imagine JFK Jr. (alive, natch)—a preppy, well-tailored young man, handsome enough to break your heart and make you think it was worth it.

Tucker closed his book and beckoned over a tubby guy. "Excuse me, sir. Would you mind taking our picture? No, facing the Formula One track, if that's okay. Yeah. Awesome."

And so our day was immortalized in a photo, him looking gorgeous and casual, me smiling despite my acute awareness of his hand burning my hip through my board shorts.

23

I'm not from Montreal.

Most people here don't care. They're not too big on outside geography.

When the richer Anglos go on vacation, they head to Vermont, Ottawa, or the Eastern Townships for day trips. They fly out to L.A., the Caribbean, or Europe for long trips. They don't give much of a shit about the rest of the country unless it's Toronto or Vancouver.

That made it easy for me to disappear and reappear in Montreal. They have no idea where I'm from and it makes no difference to them. I'm white, I'm clean, I'm educated, I speak English and okay French. Good enough.

I needed a new I.D., though. So I stole a few until I hit the jackpot. The age was off by a few years, but the picture looked close enough. I scored a driver's license, Medicare card, social insurance card, two credit cards, Interac, even some shit like the auto club and a hospital card. All nice and easy to reroute to my new address.

Plus I was legal to drink, 'cause the drinking age was only eighteen here. Not that I ever let it stop me before, but it was cute to have real, legal ID—even if wasn't actually mine.

I met a lot of interesting people.

I made up a lot of good stories that even I started to believe.

It rocked until—well, I never thought I'd get fucking busted by Dr. Laura.

That was when I really started up the death-row plan for the good doctor.

It wasn't that hard to convince people to help. My new ID paved the way for some good friends. You just have to know how to ask.

~

AFTER I MENTIONED I liked round things, Tucker took me inside the Biosphere. That is, *la Biosphère.* As we approached, I asked, "Are we allowed? Is it actually another ecosystem in there?"

He laughed. "That's the *real* Biosphere. This is a water museum."

It was indeed a museum dedicated to water. A fountain trickled to the right of the entrance. I paused to read a sign inside the door. "Hey, Buckminster Fuller built this."

"Makes sense. He was the sphere guy."

"Yeah, but I did a science project on the molecule Buckminster Fullerene. They call it the bucky ball."

His forehead crinkled.

"You know what I'm talking about? A spherical carbon molecule? It was in—oh, now I can't remember the journal. I'm sure we could look it up. They even make a desk toy based on it."

He slid his arm around my waist and rested his chin on my head. I stiffened a little, noting the feel of his chest against my back and his breath ruffling my hair, but we both pretended not to notice.

He said, "Actually, I'm kidding you. I do remember that."

"Really?" I craned my neck to see him behind me.

He dropped a kiss on the top of my head. "Yeah. Obviously we were meant to be together." And then, before I could react, he let go first, theoretically to pay admission into the museum, but I had my suspicions.

I could hardly concentrate on the museum displays, even though I liked the outfits made out of recycled materials, from batteries to salmon skins. Tucker pointed at a dress made out of light bulbs and copper wire and said, "I could see you in that."

"It's transparent," I said. Wire doesn't leave too much to the imagination.

He grinned.

They say women are the ones who play games, but some guys know exactly what they're doing to keep you in suspense. When we ended up back at the gift shop in the lobby, I decided to take control. "I'm going to buy you a present."

"Not necessary."

"Just a little something." I held up the world's ugliest belt, made out of woven tetra-pack strips. This one was white, and polka-dotted by pictures of miniature oranges.

Tucker backed up a step like the belt hurt his eyes. "You don't have to."

"Hey, you paid the admission."

"My pleasure. You don't owe me anything, including this—" His eyes darted to the two museum guides at the front desk, well within earshot, with no other customers to serve—"fine belt."

I cackled to myself. I couldn't imagine any guy looking hot in this thing except maybe RuPaul. "Prove to me that a Montreal guy can carry it off."

"It'd look better on you."

"After you show me how it's done." I slapped the belt down on the counter and one of the girls rang it up before Tucker could open his mouth again. I think they were ecstatic to sell the first one in this millennium.

Tucker wrapped the belt around his forehead like it was a bandanna. "You like?"

"I like," I purred and kissed his cheek. His skin was slightly rough against my lips.

He turned to look at me. His brown eyes were so close and intense that somehow it turned the joke on me.

I drew back. He let me, but he looped the belt around my waist as if it were another arm holding me.

"I'm not into S&M," I said, trying to make a joke.

"That's what all the girls say," he answered, pulling the belt back and pretending to whip it against his palm.

I retreated to a safe distance and averted my eyes. Time to make another joke. "You could call Rihanna."

"You know, she keeps texting me. Good idea." He looped the belt through his shorts. "Think this will get her going?"

I giggled. "Definitely." That belt was about as sexy as dentures and beige loafers.

We fell into step on the way to the metro. While we waited for the next train, he said, "Not only am I a fashionisto—is that a word?"

"It is now."

"But I can cook. Did you know that, Buffy?"

"I did not."

"I'm going to make you dinner next week. Wednesday okay with you?"

A train screeched into the station. I raised my voice. "Why Wednesday?" Part of me hoped today's non-date would keep on rolling after dark.

His brown eyes were shrewd. "Neither of us are on call and I can't wait 'til the weekend."

We hopped on to the metro car. I didn't have to look at him while I asked, "How about tonight?"

"Prior engagement."

"Oh." I sank into the nearest seat and pretended to study an ad for the Montreal Botanical Gardens. I said to it, "Well, I was sick of you anyway."

"It was the belt, wasn't it?"

I nodded glumly. "All part of my devious plan."

"I'll walk you home anyway."

We walked in awkward silence. Tucker whistled "Who's That Chick?" while I unlocked my apartment door. The notes echoed down my hallway. I paused with the door open, wondering if I should invite him in or if he had to hustle off to "Rihanna."

He gestured me through the door. "My journey ends here. I had a wonderful time, Hope."

Me too. So why did I suddenly feel choked up? I must have PTSD or something. I tried to smile. "Yeah, that was fun. Have a good time tonight."

He pulled me into his arms. I closed my eyes and raised my chin. He brushed his lips against mine. His lips were warm, firm, and soft. He lingered for a second, long enough for my lips to part, but he turned his head. "Any more and I'll never leave." Even as he spoke, his arms showed no sign of loosening.

"So don't."

"It's business. You'll respect me in the morning."

Before I could object, he kissed me again and stepped away, pointing at the bag. "Feel free to check out my drawrings." He faked an English accent.

All of a sudden, I was sick of his 'Man of Mystery' tease routine. "I'd better thank you, then." I grabbed his face and kissed him, hard enough that his emerging stubble abraded the skin around my mouth. Our tongues danced and I wrapped one leg around his. When he half-groaned and dove deeper into the kiss, weaving his hands through my hair, I responded for a minute before tearing my lips away. His hands slid down to my ass, trying to keep me there, but I stepped back forcefully.

With any luck, he'd follow me in.

We eyed each other. We were both breathing hard and fast. Even in the dim light of my hallway, I could see his pupils were dilated.

I raised my eyebrow in a challenge. Should he stay or should he go now?

He tipped an imaginary hat to me. "You're good."

I nodded. I felt good.

"I'll call you tonight."

Obviously not good enough. "Sure." I smiled sweetly, but I had to stop myself from slamming the door. I did throw the bolt with unnecessary force and even bolt the tiny latch into the floor. His loss.

To distract myself, I opened the backpack and pulled out my notebook.

Inside the front cover, I found the sketch of me. Two things struck me right away. One, I wished my thighs were thinner. Two, I recognized how my eyebrows were drawn together in a slight frown.

Ugh. It was like a train wreck. But the more I examined his drawing, the more I stared at my own eyes. They were intense, almost hypnotic with suppressed emotion. Slowly, I noted the sweetness in the curve of my cheek, the positively sexy bow to my lip and the grace in my neck. My hands were clasped and my legs crossed, superficially ladylike, but my shoulders were open and a mischievous smile lurked in my lips.

I'm no art expert, but somehow, Tucker had transmitted his feelings for me through the drawing.

I didn't feel as abandoned anymore.

I touched the corner of the paper softly, almost reverently.

24

I sat down at my desk and pulled Henry on his feet, his arms raised in victory over his head. I could not stop staring at that drawing.

Did I deserve a guy like that? A guy who could draw, a doctor who spent his spare time teaching himself different languages and who would work his old psych contacts to help me out?

What about Ryan spending his vacation and his hard-earned cash armouring my apartment and building a computer model for Mrs. Lee? I'd bought him a thank you present online, some cuff links made out of Lego men, but it seemed so inadequate.

Too much thinking. I got myself a huge glass of water and checked my voice mail messages.

"Hi, it's Mom. Dad is back from his trip to Toronto, but Kevin has a cold and I'm not feeling so good. I don't know if you want us to come visit or not—"

I forwarded to the next message. Only my mother would ask if it was okay to visit me with a cold, when every day I usually saw about a billion colds, flu, stomach viruses, and other infectious diseases.

"Hi, it's Mom. Dad has a cough, too, maybe from the airplane. You remember, he flew to Chicago the week before? I don't know why, such a funny time to get a cold, I hope it's not anything. You know, with global warming, I worry sometimes."

That explained why my family wasn't all over me, the way they had been for my week off recuperating. The little-girl part of me wished they could have stayed here longer. My mom would make *congee* like I was the one with a cold. My father would pat the couch and ask me to watch TV. Kevin would offer to play the violin or to do math homework with me to cheer me up.

On the other hand, by the end of last week, I was more than ready to escape my tiny apartment and get back to work.

My mother was still talking. "...Grandma was saying you saw Ryan this week. His grandmother told her." Pause. "I don't know if you want to say anything about that."

My father's voice rumbled in the background. I couldn't make out the words, but his chiding tone was obvious.

"Okay, okay, Dad. It's none of our business. I'm just saying, if you wanted to talk."

My father murmured again.

"Okay, never mind, forget I said anything. Are we still talking tomorrow, or are you on call? Wait, Kevin wants to talk, even though he's sick. Okay, pick up the phone, Kevin."

Kevin's cough exploded into the recording. "I'm sick. My head hurts. My nose is all runny, mostly clear, but yellow, too. I can't wait until I start coughing up stuff. That's pretty cool. But Mom's been making me take lots of cough medicine, so maybe I won't."

I touched my hand to my temple. Sometimes I missed them so much, especially Kevin.

Two hang-ups. I refused to speculate, only noting down the date and time. Caller ID had finally kicked in, but both of the hang-ups were from unknown callers and it was too late to trace them because I'd gotten one more call after both of them. I'd send my data to the police.

The last recording held Ryan's low voice. "Hello, Hope."

I closed my eyes. Hearing from him felt like a tonic. I needed him. I shouldn't, but I did.

"I wanted to come up this weekend. I wanted to show you and Mrs. Lee the model, which is going pretty well. Work has been crazy, but I spent some time on it. I think I can show they ran Laura over on purpose."

Hallelujah. That was one reason I loved that guy. I could count on him. I seized a pen in case he was going to deliver any details. He could e-mail me the rest later. Mrs. Lee would be ecstatic.

"The only thing is..." He sighed. "Something's come up. Well, actually, Lisa came up. The Chinese grapevine probably already told you. It's no big deal, she caught a ride with a friend, but she's staying until Sunday."

Slap down.

I started hyperventilating. I knew it was too good to be true. Two guys wanting me. Now Tucker was off doing God knows what, and Lisa was working her charms on Ryan.

Did I have any right to be jealous? No.

Was I?

Hell, yeah.

Ryan's voice penetrated my consciousness again. "Did Tucker ever find that Martinez guy? He never answered my message. Anyway. Like I said, about this weekend, no big deal. I'll be up next weekend. I'll call you later, okay?"

No big deal.

No big *deal*.

No big deal, my sweet brown ass.

And why was he talking about Mike Martinez with Tucker?

After that, I abandoned my tentative plans of R&R with water, ice, a fan, and a well-read copy of *Sarah, Plain and Tall.* I got up and paced. I did not want to brood. I did not want to weigh my own hypocrisy. I could not bring myself to study psychiatry.

Ryan said his preliminary model showed it was murder. I assumed he wanted to demo it for me and Mrs. Lee, and troubleshoot any problems before we took it to the police, but we'd better have our act together when we hit the station.

Ergo, I reviewed the facts that I knew about Laura Lee.

Someone ran her down on August eighth, eight years ago.

They found the vehicle, but no fingerprints except members of the owner's family, and a single blond hair that wasn't in their criminal database.

We had no suspects, although Tucker was suspicious of Michael Martinez from Laura's borderline group.

How could we track down this Martinez guy?

I flipped through the white pages and found three listings for M. Martinez, no Michael. That was a start. I'd have to come up with a good story, though. Maybe pose as a telemarketer?

While I was thinking, I Googled Michael Martinez in Montreal. The online white pages were the same as the print listing and the name was so common, I found listings on everything from a baseball player to a music teacher.

I wanted to talk this over with someone. Tucker and Ryan were both out. I hesitated with my hand on the phone for a minute. I'd been really bad about calling back my med school friends, and it was a bit weird to start ringing them up and saying, "How you doing? Crack any chests? Cool. Listen, I'm pretending to be a detective now...."

Suddenly, I remembered Tori Yamamoto, my bestest Montreal girlfriend. Duh. I'd been overdosing on testosterone lately, and she'd been working off-site. Time to give her a call. She could apply her meticulous intellect and give me another, much-needed perspective.

The phone rang and rang. I waited for her machine to kick in, but suddenly I heard a click and she said, "Hello?"

"Hey Tori, it's Hope."

"Oh, Hope!"

She sounded surprised. I forced a laugh. "Yeah. Sorry I haven't been in touch since Tuesday. How've you been?"

"I'm good."

I remembered Tori was not a big chatter. It was always kind of a shock after my other, motor-mouthed friends. I came to the point. "Great. Listen, I don't know what you're up to tonight, but I was wondering if we could hang out."

She paused long enough that I knew it would be a 'no.' I doodled on my phone pad, a monster of curlicues and googly-eyes with hooked eyebrows, while I waited for her to frame her response. At last, she said, "Well, I would like that, but...please hold on a second." She covered the receiver, but I heard her light voice and then a man respond.

A baritone, actually. One that was strangely familiar.

No. It couldn't be.

My gut said otherwise.

Tori came back on again. "I'm sorry, Hope, I don't think tonight is—"

"Is that *Tucker?*" I burst out.

"Well." For the first time, she sounded flustered. "Actually, yes. But it's not, ah..."

I waited for her to explain herself. Themselves.

His voice rumbled in the background again.

"I would like to see you," she said finally. "Maybe tomorrow?"

I could not believe it. He'd only left my place a little over an hour ago. He must have gone straight to Tori's.

Did the guy have yellow fever or what?

The walls of my little apartment seemed to fold in on me.

I thought I was so special, but I wasn't. I was just another prospective notch on Tucker's bedpost. I was just Ryan's ex-girlfriend. I was just another resident grinding my way through the medical system. I was just another sucker Mrs. Lee had prodded into helping to dig up ancient history.

I wanted to scream. I wanted to smash the phone. I wanted to kick in Ryan's computer screen and tear Tucker's drawing up with my teeth.

No. I would never tear up that drawing.

What I really, really wanted to do curl up and cry my eyelashes off.

"Hope?" said Tori. "I'm sorry, I really should go. I'll call you tomorrow, if that's all right. Maybe after breakfast?"

Sure. After you have breakfast in bed with Tucker. I could hardly speak through my clogged throat. "All right. 'Bye," I managed.

And then I did cry. I was so exhausted. I sobbed until my nose and throat were raw and my head ached.

I knew I should drop off into sleep.

I knew I was not firing on all cylinders, what with the previous case, the psych stress, the man-madness, and the patient potentially about to deliver.

Instead, I called the one person I was sure would be healthy, home on a Saturday night and happy to talk to me.

25

I felt better even before Mrs. Lee put the kettle on. I took the thick white china cup in both hands and blew on the tea. It held the faintest aroma, although I could see small bits of leaves on the bottom of the cup.

"Thanks for having me over," I said softly. "I couldn't stand sitting at home doing nothing."

Mrs. Lee set out homemade oatmeal cookies without replying. I realized that I'd probably summed up her past eight years. We sipped and munched while I gave my painfully thin summary.

"I want to find this Michael Martinez," she said, setting her cup down.

"I guess Tucker and Ryan are working on it, although they haven't told me much."

"It's not enough." Her eyes were nearly black in the dim kitchen light.

I understood. "What were you thinking of doing?"

"Tracking him down myself," she said immediately, before grimacing. She picked up a cloth and wiped down the table. "Do you have any ideas?"

"I think they're covering the usual leads. I was thinking about your file, though. You put an ad in the papers."

"Every year." She nodded and sat down again, the cloth still crumpled in her hand.

"What if we put an ad out for Michael Martinez, offering a reward? Someone might come forward. From the borderline group, or someone who knew him."

Her brow creased in thought. "That's a good idea. I've been asking for information about the accident, but if we could track down the perpetrator, I'd like that even more."

"We don't know if he's the perpetrator."

She scrubbed at the table with new zeal.

My usual guilt kicked in. "Of course, a newspaper ad may be a waste of money. Let me put up some free ads online and post a few flyers around McGill. He'd be twenty-seven now, a bit old for college, but—"

"I will pay for it," said Mrs. Lee. "All of it. The advertisements and the reward for information. I want to do it in every city paper and the Internet, too."

I shook my head. "I think that would be pretty expensive. I could probably pay for two ads, one in English and one in French."

Her barely-there eyebrows arched in amusement. "How would you afford it? You know you hardly get paid as it is."

I'm the first to complain about our meager residency salaries, especially when I get ten grand less than my Ontario classmates, pay higher taxes, and have to cough up tuition fees, rent, and food to boot, but I was not about to take advantage of Mrs. Lee. "I don't know that this'll turn up any information. It's a stab in the dark. I can't take your grocery money for that."

She threw back her head and laughed, but her laughter had an edge. "Laura had a life insurance policy."

"She did?" I don't have one. You never expect to kick the bucket below age thirty, minimum.

"All this time, I've been investing the money, unwilling to touch it, hoping that..." She shook her head. "Never mind. I can afford a few hundred dollars better than you can. If I can spend the money on anything that has to do with my daughter, so much the better. In fact, I would like to give you an honorarium."

I held up my hand. "No way."

"But you've been spending all your spare time on Laura."

"It's the least I could do for you." I sipped the tea and changed the subject. "We never talked about money before, though, Mrs. Lee. Is it possible someone else wanted Laura's inheritance?"

She sucked her bottom lip. "I don't see how. She had no will and the money came back to me and my husband."

"What happened to your husband?"

"He died of a heart attack two years after Laura died. He was only 62 years old. I like to say he died of a broken heart." She managed to smile. "She was always his little girl."

My dad said the same thing about me. I shoved the pain behind my heart, where it could haunt me later. "What do you want the ad to say? I could put it up online tonight."

SUNDAY MORNING, still furious and restless after zero calls or messages from Tucker or Tori, despite their promises, I decided to do something unprecedented: go to the hospital on my weekend off.

I marched over to St. Joe's instead of biking. I wanted to feel the sidewalk under my sandals. I wanted to glare at the people suntanning bare-chested on their balconies with their feet planted on the railing and a phone cradled against their ears. I wanted to stomp past the soft-bellied middle-aged women who tended their gardens. I wanted to shake my head at the drivers blocking the road, four-way flashers going, so they could dash into someone's apartment.

Oh, and I wanted to put up some signs asking for information on Michael Martinez. Mrs. Lee might be shelling out the bucks, but I had a computer and a printer and packing tape aplenty.

I crossed through HEC, *l'École des hautes études commerciales.* I'd kind of avoided the *Université de Montréal's* business school because of the whole aforementioned massacre deal, but now I needed to affix notices, and it was possible that Michael Martinez was a business dude. I added a poster to the closest lamp post. As an environmentalist, I wasn't about to plaster them everywhere, but with every sticky-kiss of packing tape, my mood lifted.

I hadn't gotten any more mysterious phone calls or letters overnight. Maybe I'd scared Wendy off.

Fifteen minutes later, I cut through St. Joe's emerg, wondering if I might run into Tucker. Neither of us was on, but you never knew. I put up two posters in the waiting room before the fluorescent lights and the smell of iodine made me reconsider my folly. Before I could back out into the sunshine, Nancy beckoned me over to the psych corner. "What are you doing here? You're not on call."

"Yeah, I know."

"Get out of here. It'll still be waiting for your tomorrow."

"Yeah." Now I felt silly. "Well, I hope you have a good day." In emerg, it's bad luck to say the word "quiet," because it seems to guarantee the opposite. Of course, some people, like me, crave the excitement and say it on purpose, but I wasn't working today.

"So far, so good. Nothing much going on. I thought I'd rearrange the office and check over some old charts that finally came in." A peculiar smile plucked the corner of her mouth, so I had to ask.

"Like what?"

"Like Reena Schuster's old chart from the Douglas. They sent it here instead of to the floor."

"Maybe I could take a look," I said quietly.

She shrugged and pointed at the psych office. "It's on the desk."

I licked my suddenly dry lips, paging through Reena's chart. I noticed something very interesting about the dates of her visits. The rest of her records were on the internal medicine floor with her, so I took the elevator to 5 South and skimmed through the complete box set of Reena's charts from St. Joe's. Finally, I walked over to see the woman herself, in room 5312.

It took me a minute to realize that on the H-shaped internal medicine floor, odd numbers were on one side of the hallway and even on the other. I cut through the middle of the ward, the horizontal bar in the H, past the nurses' lounge, and only spotted 5312 because of the woman coming out of it.

She was wearing sunglasses and a short-sleeved taupe blouse with an A-line skirt. Her highlighted blond hair was drawn back in a sleek ponytail. I assumed she was a social worker or something, but a woman yelled from down the hall, near the nursing station, "Jodi! Hey, Jodi!"

Right, Reena's old emerg friend, Jodi. Now I recognized her, but she'd come a long way from chomping gum. Like the surgical residents said about colleagues who went from greens to gorgeous, she sure cleaned up well.

Jodi swept into the horizontal hallway in the middle of the H without turning to look at me or the woman calling her.

Wendy, red-faced, stormed after her. "Wait!"

I ignored them both and slipped into Reena's room. With any luck, I'd be gone before Wendy or anyone else returned.

Reena lay alone in bed in her private room. She looked much the same as the last time, except her lips had cracked and, on closer inspection, she breathed a little too evenly and seemed to wear a purposefully blank expression on her face. I couldn't put my finger on why, but I bought the coma act even less this time around.

I glanced around the room, at the bedside tray pushed along the wall and the telephone resting on a bedside table, reflecting how useless most of the stuff was for someone in a coma, even a fake one. They hadn't bothered to hook up the TV. I pulled the one padded armchair up to the side of the bed, making sure to scrape it along the tile floor.

She didn't wince at the screeching or crack open her eyelids. Not bad.

"Hi, Reena," I said in a friendly way. "It's Dr. Hope Sze."

No reaction.

"That's a better reception than you gave me in the emergency room. Remember, I'm the resident on psychiatry." My voice crept up as if in a question. I paused to tame it. "I understand you've been in a coma."

Stillness. Really, she was pretty good at it. I darted forward and lifted her arm up over her head. She let me. I released her arm pointed straight up in the air, at ninety degrees from her body. Slowly, her arm fell down the same path it had come up.

A truly comatose patient would have let it fall down and hit her face.

"That's a pretty good act, but not good enough. I heard they're transferring you to psych."

Her lips tightened a fraction before relaxing again.

"What are you so afraid of, Reena? What makes you rather stay here, in the hospital, with your eyes closed, not talking or moving 24/7? That's the 'life' you want?"

Her left eyelid twitched. Maybe she was getting tired of faking it.

"Talk to me, Reena. Tell me what it is."

I sat in silence, watching her, for five minutes. It doesn't sound like long, but if you've ever tried to meditate or otherwise remain completely silent and still for that long, it feels like eternity.

I was pretty comfortable in the armchair, of course. I wasn't the one faking the coma. But I didn't particularly want to run into Wendy, either.

So I leaned forward to whisper in her ear. "I have an idea why you might be doing this. I read your old chart from the Douglas."

Her nostrils flared. Her breath caught up short before it restarted.

"In the chart here, it says you seriously attempted suicide five times in the past eight years. Slashing your wrists. Overdosing on Advil. Overdosing on Tylenol. They also noted the time you almost jumped out your second-story window. But until I got your chart from the Douglas, I didn't know the exact dates: August sixth to August tenth. In other words, always on or around August eighth, the day Dr. Laura Lee was killed."

Her eyelids clamped down but didn't open.

"Lots of people try to kill themselves, Reena. But I doubt most people have your burden of guilt. It must be terrible, holding that inside for the past eight years."

Were those tears beading the roots of her eyelashes? I was too close to pull back now, but a tiny needle of compassion for Reena pricked me. "Talk to me, Reena. That's what I'm here for."

Her lips cracked open. Her breath puffed out, hot and fetid. I waited for her to speak.

26

H er eyes opened, at long last. She studied me, making no move to clear away the sleep crusted at the corners of her eyes.

Her curly brown hair was matted by the pillow. Her skin was flaking, and she seemed to have lost weight. Her cheeks looked flaccid, making her nose more prominent. Finally, she whispered, her voice rusty with disuse. "I'm scared."

"Of what?"

She turned her head toward the door and fell silent.

I gestured at it and, at her nod, I closed it. The dull thud resonated through the room as I made my way back to her side.

Her eyes filled with tears. "I have to talk to someone. I'm going crazy." The tears began dripping on her pillow in fat white splotches.

I placed the tissue box next to her hand and leaned forward.

She mopped her eyes and rasped, "You look so much like her."

I became very still. I needed her to say it. "Who?"

"You know."

I shook my head.

Finally, she said, "Laura."

"Laura Lee."

She nodded.

I wanted to wait her out. I wanted to be patient. On the other hand, Wendy could still burst in at any moment. I took some deep breaths while Reena sobbed quietly, ripping tissues out of the box. After a minute or two, I asked, "What happened?"

"I was in that borderline group. It was supposed to *help* me." Her mouth jerked once, twice.

"The one with Laura and Dr. Ven."

She nodded and blew her nose, unsurprised that I knew. "All it brought me was—" Her mouth worked again.

My breath was growing short. I tried not to look at my watch.

"I wish I could take it all back. I wish I could take it all *back*!" Her voice broke on the last word.

Should I touch her hand? Would she let me? I pushed the tissue box toward her again and said, "What happened?"

She shook her head and stared up at the ceiling. The plastic-covered pillow crackled with her movement. The tears leaked straight down from the corners of her eyes. "I can't tell you."

"Why not?"

Her lips moved, but the sound was almost inaudible. "...kill me," I thought she said.

"No one's going to kill you."

Her eyes darted to meet mine. "Ha!" she barked. Her expression was bizarre, a mix of scorn and terror and defiance and something else I could not read.

We both heard footsteps then.

Reena's eyes widened before she clamped them shut and lay still. I scooped up her balls of tissues, barely registering how gross that was, before Wendy pushed open the door and called, "Reena? How come this door is—oh." For a second, she looked alarmed to see me before her face smoothed out.

Wendy and I hadn't spoken since our bike rack confrontation. My shoulders tensed. I stood up, the snot rags balled in my fist, acutely conscious of the box still on the bed and the tell-tale dampness of Reena's sheets. "Hi, Wendy. I was just trying to talk to her."

She crossed quickly to my side. I had to fight the urge to step away from her. Instead, I shoved the tissues in my pants pocket.

"Any luck?" she asked.

I shook my head. "I'm concerned about her, though. She seems to have a lot of mucous discharge today." I thought I sounded convincing.

"Is that bad?" Wendy bent over Reena and touched her forehead, smoothing back her locks.

"Well, I might mention it to the internal medicine team."

"She's supposed to go over to psych."

"Yes, I know."

"Maybe she shouldn't. If she's still sick." Wendy's hand shook a little and she shoved it in the pocket of her cut-offs.

"I'll mention it to the team." Part of me wanted to get the hell away from Wendy, even though she was playing nice today, at least in front of Reena. But the other, stronger instinct was to get Reena alone again. I decided to wait Wendy out. "Have you noticed anything that you're concerned about?"

Her lower lip jutted out. "Well, the fact that she's not getting any better."

I nodded as neutrally as possible.

She seemed to inflate with rage. "Are you going to do anything about it? Or are you just going to keep nodding and smiling and switching her to different wards because you have no idea what's going on?"

I clamped down on my tongue and tried to act all psych-y about it. "I know this must be very difficult for you and your mom."

"You don't know jack shit. None of you do!" She snatched the tissue box off the bed, from beside Reena's thigh, and her arm jerked back like she was going to whip it at me.

I automatically threw my arm up to block her.

Her lips drew back in a snarl, but she hesitated.

I watched her while silently calculating how fast I could reach Reena's bedside phone to dial a Code White.

Wendy read the determination in my eyes and brought the tissue box down toward the bed.

I relaxed for a millisecond before she ripped up the cardboard box, tearing it open with her blunt nails.

The last few tissues fell out in a lump beside Reena's thigh. Wendy seized them and shredded them, too. The tissue bits floated down on the bed and on Reena's legs like limp, second-rate confetti.

The entire time, Reena didn't twitch. She was a better actress than I'd given her credit for. Maybe I would be, too, if my foster sister was this cuckoo.

Wendy's chest heaved up and down. Her breathing filled the room. Her hands were still clenched in fists and she glared at me, daring me to take her on.

I eyed her carefully. She did not want to back down. Neither did I, but I wasn't willing to fight about it. Not unless she was about to harm one of us.

Abruptly, the energy seemed to drain out of Wendy's body. She put her hand to her forehead. "Oh, my God. I think I'm going nuts."

Since I was on psych, I felt like I should say something wise. But because I really wanted to agree with her, I was stumped. I nodded and said, "Hmm."

She grabbed my hand, pressing her warm, sweaty palm against mine before I extricated myself. Wendy said, "I didn't used to be like this, I swear. This isn't me."

"Hmm." I had no idea what her baseline was like, but I had to try and help. Not for the first time, I wished I actually got trained in counselling instead of winging it. "Would you like to consult our service today?" She'd probably have to register in emerg or something because she wasn't registered as a patient, even though she was a patient's family member.

"Oh, my God, I'm, like, begging you for help, and you ask me if I want to consult your service? No wonder Reena's still a fuckin' vegetable!"

Wendy looked ready to shred my face. I backed away from her, toward the only door. I'd have to talk to Reena later. Wendy was just too volatile. "What would you like me to do instead?"

"Oh, forget it! Just save my sister, okay? That's what you signed on to do, now do it!"

"You're absolutely right. I'm sorry, I need you to help me with some paperwork. Could you come with me?"

"I said no!"

I stared at her until she blinked. Then I said, as gently as possible, "She needs your help. Come with me to the nursing station. It will only take a minute."

"You guys are so useless," she said, but she let me lead her away while I formulated a plan. Maybe the psychiatrist on call would talk to her. At the very least, Nancy would chat with her in the ER. I didn't trust Wendy alone with Reena.

27

I plastered the last of my notices around St. Joe's and popped into the Renaud Bray bookstore. Most of the books were in French, but I needed to calm down. I tested mechanical pencils with fat orange lead. I picked up notebooks shaped like cats. I found "*le consummateur*," this yellow-covered guide to shopping in Montreal that both Tucker and Tori had recommended, but I put it back down because I didn't want to be reminded of them.

At last, I started walking back to my apartment, ready to think about Reena. What was she really afraid of? Was it really Wendy who was nuts the whole time? Or, like Dr. Gatien had mentioned a week (a lifetime?) ago, was it some weird *folie à deux*?

What had Reena been about to confess?

When I passed *Péloquin*, I heard a woman yelling, "Dr. Zee! I mean, See! I mean, doctor!"

The voice sounded dreadfully familiar. For a second, I sped up.

I heard sandals slapping the sidewalk behind me. "Doctor Sze! Please!"

The "please" stopped me. Reluctantly, I spun on my heel.

Wendy advanced on me with a pleading look.

"Wendy! Aren't you talking to Nancy?" The psychiatrist on call made me bring Wendy to emerg. Nancy promised she'd give her some "crisis counselling."

Wendy shook her head. "Forget that. Did you do this?" She held one of the Michael Martinez posters in her hand.

I was so surprised, it took me a second to recover my voice. My heart banged in my chest "Do you know him?"

"He's my ex."

I gave her a look.

"He was! That was before—" She stopped herself. "Look. I used to go out with guys. It's okay to experiment." She sounded like she was quoting someone. "I mean, who cares. Do you want to know about Mike or not?"

Every time I saw this girl, she changed on me. Right now, she was trying to be helpful, and if she hadn't gone psycho on me twice already, I might have bought the smile. She even had dimples, deep slashes in both cheeks that shouted, trust me! I'm cute!

I was starting to think she was the real borderline, not Reena. I paused to think. Mrs. Lee would want any lead pursued and if Wendy was talking to me, she wouldn't be terrorizing her foster sister. "I do. But, like the ad says, we want the Michael Martinez who was in the borderline group therapy at the Douglas—"

"Yeah, yeah, he was in Reena's group. That's how I met him."

That silenced me. Could it be that easy? Put up a few ads and we'd find the sociopath from eight years ago?

She smoothed the ad over her leg and smiled at me again. "You're helping Reena, I don't mind helping you. How much is the reward, anyway?"

Mrs. Lee hadn't given me the specifics. I didn't really want Wendy bugging her, but I said, "You'll have to call the number and ask. It's like Crimestoppers. We pay for information that leads directly to him."

"I think I have his number. He's on Tumblr." When I looked blank, she said, "It's a social networking thing. Interested?"

She had me. She knew it. Her grin widened to reveal perfectly white, even teeth. She jerked her head at the Nickels diner across the street. "I'll tell you about him over a cup of coffee."

I followed her into the diner, where she ordered black coffee and wanted to pay for my Orangina. "My treat, 'cause I've been such a cunt," she said.

I tried not to flinch as I handed the cashier some money. I wasn't taking anything from Wendy.

She laughed and paid for her own. "You don't like that, eh? You'd probably call me, I don't know, something Latin. Or maybe you'd spell it out. B-i-t-c-h?"

Now I knew she was yanking my chain. I dropped in a chair outside the door, away from most of the crowd, and asked, "Do you really know Michael Martinez?"

She leaned back in her chair, spreading her knees like a guy. She cackled. "You can call him Mike, you know. Everybody does. And he doesn't go by Martinez anymore. It's Martin. It's this acting shit. He figures Martin is easier to remember and it works in English and in French. I told him, it's easier to forget, too. You want to stand out on your audition."

I waved all that away. "How did you get to know him?"

She rolled her eyes. "You want my c.v. or something? Just hanging out, I guess, with Reena and Jodi and, well, the rest of the crew. He was cute, I had this thing for older men, boom, bam, thank you, ma'am. Or I guess it should be thank you, *man. Now* it's ma'am." She laughed again. She reached in the pocket of her short-sleeved blouse and flipped open her cigarette pack. Her lighter was silver, not a disposable Bic. It had an angel molded on the side, which would have been cheesy except the angel's eyes were chips of red glass. She noticed me staring. "Nice, huh? It was a present. A lot nicer than a bra or a bucket of KFC, eh? So anyway, was that all you wanted to know?"

I shook myself. This information was falling into my lap and I should direct it, but I needed to gather my thoughts. "What did you think of him?"

"He had a big dick?" She rounded her lips over her cigarette and managed to make it look phallic. "No, seriously, it was about average. But he was a nice guy."

I rummaged through my brain for the antisocial traits. "He was charming?"

"Yeah, I guess. He knew how to talk his way into your pants, if that's what you mean." She tapped her cigarette into the ashtray. I tried not to inhale, but enough other people were smoking outside that her cancer stick hardly made any difference.

"Did he love you?" That popped out of my mouth.

She paused in mid-tap. Her fingers rested on the ashtray. "Yeah, I think—yeah."

"What made you think he loved you?"

She started smoking again, short, hasty puffs. "What does that have to do with anything?" She was having trouble meeting my eyes, all of a sudden.

"I just want to know."

She rested both elbows on the table. "How much was that reward again?"

"You'll have to call the number."

"You didn't say anything about personal questions." She dug in her back pocket for the flyer. "Says right here, 'for significant information leading to his contact.'"

"That's right." But I didn't retract my question.

She traced the M of Michael with the index finger of her free hand. Then the i. Finally, she said to the paper, "Yeah, he loved me. He told me some shit he probably wouldn't have, otherwise. Happy?"

"Sure. You said he's on Tumblr?"

"Let me make sure I've still got it." She scrolled through her phone.

A woman at the next table giggled and pretended to hit her companion. They both laughed. A girl in tortoiseshell glasses bent over her textbook. A customer dropped some change and other people bent to help him pick it up, except a kid who grabbed a loonie coin and wouldn't give it back.

"Got it," said Wendy.

I reached for the phone, but she held it against her chest. "Why are you looking for him?"

"We think he might know something."

"About Laura Lee?"

The name on everyone's lips today. "Did you know her?"

She stubbed her cigarette out, mashing it in the ashtray with unnecessary force before lighting another one. Instead of smoking, though, she stared at the ugly angel on her lighter. "Not really."

I wasn't sure whether to believe her or not. I decided to go for the bird in hand. "Are you going to give me Mike's coordinates?" That's what the French say, *coordonnées* means contact info, and it seems to have rubbed off on the anglophones, like asking people to "close" the lights.

Wendy said, more to the lighter than me, "I guess so."

"Have you seen him recently? We need current information." No way we'd pay for a decade-old land line.

She shrugged.

Since she was the one who'd come to me and she seemed more than a little nuts, I sucked up the last of my juice and dropped a tip on the table. "Well, you've got the number if you decide to call."

"Wait!"

I was already standing. I looked down at her. Her knuckles blanched as she gripped the table, but as she noticed me watching, she made sure to let go and light a cigarette, nice and easy. "I'll tell you about Mike. What do you want to know?"

I played for time. "Why don't you tell me about him?"

"Well, he was the best-looking guy I'd ever seen." She blew a plume of smoke toward my left shoulder. "I think it was his eyes. The way he'd look at you. He really saw you, you know? Not only thinking about himself and what kind of shit he could pull. When he wanted you, he paid attention. You could've passed a lighter under his hands and he'd bat it away." She smiled to herself. "A lot of other guys who were that hot, they'd think they were the shit. But he never did. There was something, I don't know, kind of unsure about him that made me like him even more, you know what I mean? The way he'd check for me if we were at a party?"

I must have made a face, thinking of all the jealous exes out there. But she shook her head. "Not like that. He'd do his thing and I'd do mine. But once in a while, he'd check the room, looking for me. To make sure I was there. I got a kick out of it. He needed me. Me, piece of shit Wendy Redburn."

I felt my eyebrows press together in sympathy.

She snorted and blew smoke out of both nostrils. "Lose the lost-puppy look, okay? It's not that big a deal."

But it was. I'd been judging her by my standards, but she was a foster kid with a past I couldn't even guess at.

She had to smile. "God, you're more pathetic than me. So what else do you want to know? He was tall. Well, everyone was tall to me back then, but I'm guessing he was at least 5'10". Brown eyes, black hair. Nice hands..." She started smoking again, faster. "Ah, forget it. I'll just give you his number. You can call him yourself."

28

I hurried home and called Mrs. Lee from the hallway, almost before I kicked my sandals off. I figured she deserved it after eight years. She was strangely muted while I rhymed off all the contact info. Then she said, "We'll see if he knows anything, Hope."

"But this is the guy Dr. Ven thought was the one! The sociopath!"

Her sigh gusted through the receiver. "Let's see if the number works. But first, we need a plan."

She was right. We couldn't go blasting in and saying, "Hey, did you kill this woman?" even though it would make for a better movie. I said, "Okay. Do you want to call the police, or should I?"

She snorted. "They won't do anything."

"They might. We could show them Ryan's computer model." I checked my email while I was talking to her. Ryan hadn't messaged me, but I plugged in the link on the guy's Tumblr account. It worked. I got a mug shot of a guy with sharp cheekbones and intense blue eyes, like a Calvin Klein ad, but under the heading Michael Martin. It even had his agent info.

Mrs. Lee clucked her tongue. "You said Ryan would bring his model next weekend."

"Right, but we could tell the police about it today." Even to myself, that sounded weak, but I was still staring at Michael Martin's photo. I shook myself and remembered the tombstone picture and my phone log. "I have to show them something anyway. They can contact Michael and bring him in for questioning."

"They haven't done anything for eight years. I don't trust them," she said.

I didn't like the note in her voice. "Mrs. Lee. You're not going to call him yourself, are you?"

She snorted. "Do you think I'm stupid enough to meet with a killer by myself?"

I hesitated. I would never underestimate this woman.

"I'm an old woman. It's you who has to be careful."

"I am."

She laughed and I joined in. No, I wasn't exactly cautious these days.

"Promise me, Hope. Promise me you won't meet him alone."

"I wasn't planning to. But how are we going to—"

"It's been eight years. You wait. You think about this. We need to make a plan."

It sobered me, the fact that she, of all people, was saying this. "All right. I promise. I'll put it together before we talk to the police."

"Yes, that's good. You go outside and take a walk. You need fresh air."

Sometimes, she was so much like my mother. I knew better than to argue. "Okay, okay."

I didn't go for a walk, but I ventured out on my balcony. It was on the north-east side of the building, behind a giant, leafy tree, so it was in the shade instead of the sun. I took some deep breaths, watching the leaves rustle. The metal rail was cool under my hand. I watched a red Saturn trying to parallel park across the street in a space that was about half a foot too small, while other cars zoomed around it. I drank a tall glass of water.

Then I dialed Tucker's home number. I had a great excuse. He was trying to find Michael Martinez, and I'd already tracked him down. Tucker could help support my case with the police.

While the phone rang, I daydreamed about facing down Michael Martinez while Tucker played back-up. Somehow, I imagined Tucker shirtless and tanned while his muscles glistened with oil.

The phone rang for the forth time while one of my neighbours started playing scales on the trombone.

My mind drifted to Ryan. We made a good team too. I wouldn't mind trying again, but not if he was already playing with Lisa. Yes. I know I'm a hypocrite.

The phone rang through to the answering machine. "Hi, you've reached Tucker. Leave a message."

"Hi. It's Hope. Um, how'd it go last night?" With any luck, I sounded chipper as opposed to insanely jealous of Tori. "I have some contact information for the guy we're looking for. I talked to Mrs. Lee. We need a plan. Call me, or I'll try your cell phone." I paused. "Oh, right, you're drying out the battery. I may try your pager. Okay, 'bye."

I made myself wait twenty minutes before I paged him.

I paced around my apartment. I sat on my balcony, listening to the trombonist tackle music from Star Wars. I even cleaned, for God's sake.

I was trying not to think of Alex, the previous dipwad, who specialized in disappearing acts.

Finally, I left the apartment again to grab some groceries, just for something to do. Tucker knew my number. I had my pager.

At 6 p.m., when I was drifting off to exhausted sleep, the phone rang. Jolted, I grabbed it. "Hello?"

"Hope. Sorry I didn't call you before."

Ryan. My heart sank for a second before his mellow voice worked its magic. "Hey, Ryan."

"Did you have a good weekend?"

"Sort of. Did you?"

He paused. "Yeah, I guess. I'd rather have seen you."

"How's Lisa?" I chirped. That unreasonable jealousy had started gnawing at my colon again.

"I think she's all right. She said she was going to call you."

"Really."

"She said she might ask you to join her church."

Bully for her. I hadn't been crazy about going with Ryan. Why would I cuddle up to his latest ex-girlfriend? Before I could remind him that I was agnostic, he said, "I told her you might want to join another church, since she's downtown and you're in Côte-des-Neiges."

Despite myself, I was touched he was thinking about my travel time.

"She asked where you lived. She might send you some info about churches in your area, if that's okay."

I mumbled unenthusiastically.

"Or she might call you. She asked all sorts of stuff about you, if you like to sing, what sort of hobbies. I think there might be a sort of city choir you could join, even if you're not at the same church. You'd probably have to be at United, though."

Lisa sounded annoying, even if I didn't already hate her. "I probably won't have time."

"Yeah, I know. I told her about this case we were investigating. She was pretty interested."

"What!" I sat bolt upright, shocked out of my stupor.

"Well, she wanted to know why I was hanging out with my computer so much, instead of her. She's kind of jealous that way."

I permitted myself a small smile, but it was fleeting. "Ryan, c'mon. I thought you know we weren't going to talk a whole lot about this to other people."

"Lisa's not just anyone. We're really good friends, still."

Epic fail.

"But you're right. Mrs. Lee might not feel comfortable with this. I should have thought. Sorry."

And the Lord giveth back. My cheeks relaxed. "Okay. I mean, I know we didn't say anything officially, but yeah, I don't feel like it's our story to tell."

"Mea culpa. Anyway, we've got better stuff to talk about, right?"

"I thought so."

"I want to show you my computer model. I think it proves she was run down. I'll come and demo it for you and Mrs. Lee next Friday."

"I can't wait to see it." I paused. "You think it's something we could show the police? Like, is it ready for prime time?"

"I think so. I've been kind of obsessed."

"Awesome."

Ryan explained the specs while I rubbed my eyes and tried to wake up. This was why I could never become an engineer. Eventually, I broke in. "Strong work. So you're coming on Friday night?"

"Definitely."

"Great. I'm on call, but we'll work it out. Now, listen. You know Michael Martinez? I've got his phone number."

"Yeah, did Tucker track him down? I gave him some pointers."

"No, Mrs. Lee and I did." I explained. He made suitably impressed noises. "Now the problem is, what exactly to do with this information? I want to go to the police, but Mrs. Lee doesn't trust them."

"Can you blame her? It's been eight years. But you need to talk to them anyway. I'll bring my laptop and show them the model. Okay. Enough shop talk. Have you been thinking about us?"

That woke me up in a hurry. "Yeah."

"And?"

I parlayed, "You want to go first?"

"Sure. I assume you're too paralyzed by lust to speak."

I burst out laughing.

"I'm crazy about you, Hope. I really want it to work out this time."

I sobered fast. "Ryan..."

"No. Listen to me. I let you get away once. I don't want to make that mistake again. I know you haven't made up your mind yet. I know Tucker is part of it. And I know I hurt you."

I buried my face in my pillow. This was so unlike Ryan. He wasn't big on declaring his emotion even when we were together. He said "I love you" and figured I should know the rest.

He paused. "Look, I know you're not perfect. Neither am I. But I wanted you to know where I stood." He sighed. "I wanted to see you this weekend. I had this thing all planned. But Lisa...well, I kind of felt sorry for her."

My heart gave a double-thump. Pity. He must be well and truly off her then. Right? Right?

But still, the other part of my brain said, if he really liked you better, he would've given her the boot and driven up to see you.

"I wrote a little computer program for you."

I tried to process that. "Yeah, the model for Mrs. Lee."

"No, that was for Mrs. Lee. This is something else. It's nothing, but anyway, I'm e-mailing it to you."

I had to love the way these guys were wooing me. Tucker sketched my portrait and Ryan wrote a computer program. "Well, thanks."

"Tell me what you think. I love you, Hope." And he hung up before I could say anything.

Slowly, I replaced the receiver. I wanted to run to my computer. But I delayed it a little, enjoying the suspense as I lifted the receiver one more time and finally heard the rapid beep that someone had left a message.

Tucker.

I clicked over to Gmail with my right hand, and pressed *98 to play back the voicemail with the left.

Sure enough, Ryan had emailed me a message with an attachment. As it downloaded, I entered my phone password to retrieve my message. C'mon, Tucker.

A man's muffled voice said, "You're going down, bitch."

29

That took the foam off my root beer in a hurry.

My phantom caller was back.

As threats went, the gravestone one scared me more. First, it implied death more explicitly. Second, that person knew where I lived and what my name was. But I was able to laugh at the tombstone pic a little with Ryan literally at my side.

Now that Ryan was in Ottawa, and Tucker was incommunicado, it felt like a colony of mice had decided to bungee jump into my stomach.

I pressed *57 before anyone else could call me, and got the message that Bell Canada had traced the call. Chilly comfort. God knows when I'd get that warrant. Maybe after I was already six feet under.

Still, I followed the police's advice. I listened to the message again, saved it and logged it manually. Five seconds long, left at 6:09 p.m., number unknown.

It definitely sounded like a guy, nothing like Wendy. She could have drafted a friend to harass me. But why would she threaten me, especially if she wanted the reward money?

One man who might be gunning for me was Michael Martinez.

He could have figured out who was looking for him and tracked me down first. But that was nuts. Wasn't it?

My next thought was that it was a random call. Like a telemarketer, only crazy instead of someone enslaved by crap wages. But I couldn't kid myself anymore. It was time to take these threats seriously.

What could I do, though? I had nothing concrete, no ID. Bell Canada sends the info to the police, not to the customer.

I tried Tucker again, both home and pager. I hung up when there was no answer.

I called Tori and did leave a message. "Did you guys have a good night? I got another phone call and I'm a little freaked out. I know this sounds dumb, but could I come over? I don't feel like hanging around here."

Then, like it was fate, I called Ryan. He might be able to track the ID down in some techno-magic way. More importantly, he cared about me and wanted me safe.

That calmed me down even before he picked up the phone.

"This has nothing to do with what you just said, but..." I told him.

He said, "Shit. I'm coming over."

I managed a laugh. "No. What would you do here?"

"Protect you."

"Ryan. It's Sunday. You have to work tomorrow, right? You just took a vacation and had to beat it back to work."

"Yeah, but..." He sighed.

My heart sank. He wasn't coming. It was the right thing to do, the smart thing to do, but still. I was alone.

He rallied. "I could come just for tonight."

"It's a two-hour drive each way. You'd just have to turn right around again."

"Yeah, but you could reward me richly while I was there." His voice dipped seductively.

My body flickered in response, despite my incipient panic. Or maybe because of it. They say the sympathetic nervous system is fight or flight, but maybe it's fight, flight, or fuck. "Ryan—"

"It's no big if I have to drive back at two a.m. I'll see you in a couple hours. I love you, Hope." This time, he paused for my response.

I started to cry and couldn't stifle it. "I'm sorry. I don't even know why I'm crying."

"Because you're alone there, you work around the clock, a maniac almost killed you, and another one's threatening you. Do you think it's the same guy?"

"He's in custody." I yanked a tissue out of the box and tried to blow my nose and sob more quietly. Get a hold of yourself, girl.

"Can he send stuff from jail? Or get someone to do it for him?"

I hadn't even considered that. Boy, did I suck as a detective. "I could find out."

"Do it. I guess, in a way, that would be better than someone on the loose who's out to get you."

"Unless he hired someone to come after me?"

"Or just scare you."

Sometimes, Ryan and I thought in perfect synchronicity, even on the bad stuff. I dabbed my face, and managed to get myself more or less under control, except for the beginning of a headache and a clogged nose. "Yeah. Maybe that would be best case. Only one enemy and he's trying to intimidate me."

"I don't like it. Can you stay with someone else after I leave? Or check in with a neighbour every so often?"

"I'm on it." I thought of my messages to Tucker and Tori. Wouldn't that be screwed up, if Ryan was encouraging me to crash with Tucker. Well, murder and intimidation make strange bedfellows.

"Don't go anywhere, and lock your door."

I glanced outside. The sunlight was mellowing into yellow and gold, bright but gentle, with longer shadows and cooler evening breezes. It was one of my favourite times of a summer day, but I didn't feel safe. I was glad Ryan had barred my windows. "Okay."

"Good thing I tightened up your security. Okay, I'm about packed. See you in two. I love you. Take care of yourself, Hope."

One last, hot tear seeped out of my right eye. "Ryan, I can't thank you enough."

"Don't worry about it. I'll be there soon." His voice softened. "First, last, and always."

After I broke the connection, I pressed the receiver to my forehead, wordless. That was what we used to say to each other. First, last, and always.

He and Tucker were both such good men and I was hurting both of them. In theory, I had always liked the idea of a threesome with me and two other guys, both as a sex fantasy, and as a potential reality, as seen on www.polyamory.com. But in this lifetime, with these players, I knew my two men would not settle for that long-term. I would have to make up my mind. Soon.

And I would have to find out who was targeting me. Sooner.

30

First, to clear my head, I ran Ryan's computer program.

A window popped open. It showed a red velvet curtain with sashes, the heavy ones you see in theatres. Two cartoon men stood on either side. When I clicked on one, they opened the curtain and moved off-stage.

At first, the window was black. Then the black churned around, became turbulent, and a picture of me popped out. Me as a kid in a Brownie uniform, cuter than a ladybug. It bugged me that my orange and white scarf was tied with the right wing bigger than the left, but I could see the determination in my eyes and in the way I lifted my chin. I hadn't bothered to smile.

"Take on Me," by A-Ha, started to play in the background. And at that moment, a cartoon bubble popped above my picture, saying, "I am not beige."

While I was still laughing, the picture was replaced by one of me in a slim-fitting evening gown, black satin, slit up to mid-thigh. I was smokin'. Ryan had escorted me to my faculty's formal ball in second year university and told me he loved me. "If everything goes right for the next two years, Hope, I want to marry you."

I blew a kiss at the screen and straightened my spine. No, I didn't know how to sort out my love life, but somehow I felt calmer.

I was not going to die. I was not going to get hurt. Two good men loved me and I was going to find Laura Lee's killer. The fact that someone was threatening me meant I was getting close.

Or, as Ryan had pointed out, the last murderer was still holding a grudge, but let's not quibble.

So when the phone rang again, I snatched it up, ready to do battle. "Hello?"

"Hope." Mrs. Lee's voice hummed with excitement. "I talked to Michael Martinez. He's willing to meet us."

"Mrs. Lee! You promised—"

She paid no attention. "I've been waiting eight years, Hope. Eight years. When every day, sometimes every hour feels like eternity."

That silenced me.

She sighed. "I know I told you we needed a plan. It's the most logical thing to do. But I am so tired of waiting! The police, the detective, the lawyer, and now you. Everyone pats me on the head and expects me to knit at home. I cannot wait any longer when this man may have information about her death. Can you meet us at eight-thirty?"

Oh, my God. I wasn't planning on leaving the apartment, and now Ryan was on his way. That left me an hour and a half to make it there, which made it about the same time Ryan might buzz my apartment if he really kicked it.

Mrs. Lee was still talking. "I chose the Xpress Café half-way between us, in case you wanted to come. Regardless, I will be there."

"Mrs. Lee. This is crazy. You want to meet with the man who might have killed your daughter?"

"I have to, Hope. Whether you come or not. It's the one on Queen Mary." She hung up.

I clapped my hands to my cheeks. Dear Lord. She was not joking.

I called Tucker. To hell with pride. Someone had to go with Mrs. Lee. I'd prefer a giant ninja versed in hand-to-hand combat and assault weapons, but Tucker would do.

No fucking answer at home. I left my number on his pager again, but I was beginning to suspect his pager batteries had died. It wasn't like him to ignore me.

I called Stan Biedelman. He was a reasonably big guy. He answered his cell. "What's happening?"

"Do you want to play bodyguard for Mrs. Lee?" I filled his dumbfounded silence with the details.

Longer pause. "I don't think that's a good idea. You shouldn't encourage her."

"Did you hear me or not? I'm not encouraging her, she's on her way!"

"First of all, my entire family is here for dinner, including my uncle from Moose Jaw, so I can't go. But even if I could, I wouldn't. I'd call the police."

"And tell them what? We're meeting a guy a psychiatrist fingered eight years ago. We have no proof, but he could be dangerous?"

"Yeah, something like that."

I hung up on him and called Tori again. Maybe together, we'd be adequate muscle. In psych, if a patient is acting up, you do a "show of force." I saw it once as a med student. A woman was in isolation, under camera supervision, when she lost it. She picked up the armchair and started ramming it against the safety glass window in the door.

The nurses and orderlies gathered together and walked up to the door. That was the show of force. It doesn't matter if it's men, women, or both, as long as it's a group. At least it worked with that patient. Between Tori, Mrs. Lee and me, in a public place, we'd probably be okay.

Still no answer.

God damn it.

I could not allow Mrs. Lee to meet this potential murderer alone. I didn't care if it was in a public place. It wasn't safe. And she never would have found this guy if it weren't for me. I could not live with myself if she died because of me.

I called Ryan. He, at least, answered right away again. "You gotta be kidding."

"It shouldn't be long. Here's the address. You can meet us there." I rattled the directions. I could hear traffic in the background, so he was already on the road, without a GPS, but I wasn't worried. Ryan was born with a compass in his head, kind of like a homing pigeon. He'd find us.

"Hope, the whole point is for you to be safe. Jesus! I want you to come home to Ottawa."

"No. I'm off, Ryan. I'll see you there. I've got my cell and pager."

I'M NOT A COMPLETE IDIOT. I drove to the Xpress Café instead of walking. And I left messages with Tucker, Tori, and my parents, plus a note on my dining room table saying where I went. Just in case I got offed.

I wasn't worried about myself so much as Mrs. Lee. Everyone was always criticizing my judgment, but now I thought she was the one in more danger. Not only was she grieving and angry and impatient, she may well not want to live anymore.

The Xpress Café was easy to find. A sign with plain, white lettering on a navy background hung over the glass-fronted building. A single, empty, plastic table sat on the sidewalk. I pushed open the door, rattling a jingle bell, but I hardly noticed it, the faint aroma of coffee, or the look from a white-aproned guy behind the counter. A girl paged through her book—no. A couple ignored each other as they read the newspaper—no.

It was only 8:20. Maybe I'd beat them there?

But at the back, near the washroom, I spotted Mrs. Lee parallel to the wall. She noted me out of the corner of her eye, but she kept talking to a pale man with messy black hair.

Michael Martin. I materialized at their side. They were sitting at a table for two, so I kept standing with a fake smile at my face, waiting for the right moment to interrupt.

"—*fi*-nal offer," Mrs. Lee said, accentuating the long i in the first syllable. She looked remarkably calm. Her purse was still looped around the shoulder closest to the wall and her left hand rested on it, a dead giveaway that was where she was holding her money.

Instead of answering her, he turned to look at me. I caught my breath. His eyes were an eerie, light, milky blue, the kind you might see on a Siberian Husky; not what I expected with dark hair and olive skin. He was good-looking—not as arresting as his head shot on his website—but his eyes were a bit close-set, and his forehead a little prominent. He was the kind of guy you might say to yourself "Hey, not bad," if you lined up behind him at the grocery store. Still, something about him set my senses on alert.

"I'll have a soy latte," he said, pushing an empty coffee mug toward me.

I goggled at him. He thought I was the help? Totally unexpected.

So was his laugh. "Just kidding. Coffee's fine." After a beat, he said, "I assume you're her back-up?" He smiled and gave me a quick, appreciative once-over. To my surprise, I almost smiled back before I caught myself.

Of course, antisocial people can be very charming. "Hi, I'm H—Helen."

"Hi, *H—Helen*," he said, imitating my hesitation. "Nice to meet you. I'm Mike, but you probably already know that."

I glanced at Mrs. Lee. Her face really did look inscrutable, but I could sense her anger. "May I join you?" I was asking both of them. I knew it wasn't a coincidence they'd already started. She'd built in time for herself for a one-on-one. Good thing I'd been early, for once.

Her head jerked down in a yes. I started to drag a chair over. "Oh, allow me," said Mike, picking it up and setting it down for me. "Could I buy you a drink? Since I'm about to become a rich man?"

"Not until you accept my offer," said Mrs. Lee.

"I'm fine," I said. "Could you bring me up to speed?"

Mrs. Lee compressed her lips together. She didn't want me to talk. She wanted to run the show. Fine.

Mike leaned back in his chair with his knees akimbo. "Sure. What part do you want to hear? The dinero or the conditions?"

I checked Mrs. Lee's face. She stayed mute. This was why we should have had a plan. I had very little idea what was going on in her head.

"Your Mrs. Lee is very anxious to know what happened to Laura. I'm happy to tell what I know, but I want to be well-compensated for it. After all, you're not the only ones asking."

I narrowed my eyes at him. Had Tucker gotten a hold of him first? Was that why he hadn't been answering his phone?

Mike shook his head and flicked the spoon in his mug. It clanged lightly. "Uh-uh. I want the cash first."

"How do we know you have anything worth paying for?" I asked, as a waitress moved toward us to clear the table.

"Honey," he said, grinning at the waitress, "I've always got something worth paying for."

The server averted her eyes, but the spoon rattled in the cup again as she swept it on to her tray along with some crumpled napkins. "Would you like a refill?"

"Fill 'er up," he said.

I couldn't help thinking he wasn't very smart, talking about money in front of the waitress. She could come back as a witness later, if needed. Maybe we could use his overconfidence against him. I tried to signal Mrs. Lee with a look, but she was so focused on Mike, I might as well have been a pack of sugar on the table.

"Do you accept my offer, then?" Mrs. Lee said.

"Wait." I still didn't know the terms.

"Sure. I've got to check the money, though. No offense."

"Mrs. Lee, please——" But I felt a hand brush against my right thigh and jumped. Mike winked at me. I scooted my chair back, mouth open in outrage, but the next thing I knew, he was sliding an envelope into his back pocket. "I'll be right back."

31

I grabbed Michael's wrist. "You must be joking."

"Hey, H-H-Helen, I've got to make sure it's not Monopoly money, right? I'll be in the men's room."

"So you can climb out the window with her money?"

"You've been watching too many movies." But he covered my hand with his left. "I'll let you come with me and watch."

Oh, God. This was where I needed the Y chromosome and a lot more muscle. "You're not going anywhere." I knew how ridiculous that sounded. One of my best friends once described my build as twig-like. I hung on, acutely conscious of how thick his wrist was, covered in coarse black hair. He wasn't huge, but he was much bigger than me. And I had no right to touch him. If Mike backhanded me, would he be able to claim self-defense?

Mrs. Lee stood up, but there was no way I'd let an old lady break her hip on this. Show of force. I met Mike's eye and said, with as much authority as I could muster, "Count it here."

He laughed aloud. "Who's going to make me? You?"

A Goth girl shuffled by en route to the bathroom. For a crazy second, I thought I could call on her to back me up as needed. But she dropped her paper coffee cup on the table beside us, pale face averted and shaded by her long, dyed-black hair. No help there.

I yanked his wrist forward. He laughed, breaking my grip easily. But with my left hand, I plucked the envelope from his back pocket.

It was thick, neatly sealed, heavy with money.

"Hey!" Mike snatched my wrist, hard enough to grind my radius and ulna together. Teeth gritted, I snapped at the envelope with my free right hand, but he imprisoned that wrist, too.

Mrs. Lee seized the envelope, startling both of us.

Mike dropped my wrists and turned on her, but hesitated. The whole café was watching. The waitress and another clerk stood behind the counter, undecided, but the couple, the studious girl, and a gaggle of teenagers stared at us.

"Just fooling around, folks," Mike said, with a cheery wave.

Everyone watched Mrs. Lee tuck the envelope back in her purse. She nodded and waved everyone away, then took her seat and primly crossed her legs, as if nothing had happened.

Gradually, conversation resumed with a few glances our way. I refused to rub my wrists, even though the left one hurt especially.

"What's the deal?" Mike said to Mrs. Lee through a smile that almost looked genuine. "You want to know about your daughter? Or you want to play 'pass the envelope'?"

"I'll give you some money now," she said. "You can count it in front of both of us. But if you think you can just take our money and run, you must think me a fool."

"Hey, you're the one who contacted me." He spread his arms out and raised his voice. "I didn't come looking for you. And, like I said, other people are asking. I'm a popular guy."

Mrs. Lee didn't stir from her seat. After a slight pause, she asked, "How much are those people paying you?"

"We haven't set a price yet."

"I'll give you fifty dollars right now, before you tell me anything. For every useful piece of information, I'll give you another twenty."

He blew his breath out between his lips. "No way, Grandma."

"Do you know so little?"

"Wouldn't you like to know?"

They stared at each other. Mike and I were both still standing. Only Mrs. Lee sat, seemingly serene. She sipped her coffee.

Finally, he sank back in his seat. "A hundred up front, fifty per tip. If you're too stingy with the $50's, I'll stop talking."

Mrs. Lee nodded, and pulled the envelope and a silver letter opener out of her purse. With great ceremony, she slit the side of the envelope open.

32

"My name isn't Michael Martin. It's Michael Martinez, or it was back then. I was—what, nineteen? I didn't know anything yet."

Old info. Mrs. Lee made no move toward her purse. We watched him and waited for the story to flow.

He ran his hand through his hair. "Ah, shit. I don't know what you want to know. Yeah, I was part of that group—you know, the one Dr. Lee headed with Dr. Ven. I was the only guy, which had its benefits." He grinned, but it dimmed fast. "Too bad they were all nuts."

Mrs. Lee said, "I would like a list of all the group members. That would be worth my while." She slid a notebook and a pen toward him on the table. I glanced at her purse. It was only moderate-sized, but I expected her to pull a tank out of it next.

"Put it on the table first."

She placed the cash, deftly hiding it under her palm, but the flash of red made the denomination clear.

"No. Not where you can grab it back."

She uncovered it and I dropped the sugar bowl over it, leaving my hand over the bowl.

Satisfied, he laid his right hand on the bill and clicked open the pen to scrawl. He was a lefty. "This is what I remember."

I looked over his shoulder. As a doctor, I'm pretty good at deciphering bad handwriting.

Kate

Tracy

Shelley

Sara

Reena

Jodey

My heart rate kicked up. "Wait a minute. Jodi Green?"

He shrugged. "Yeah, I guess. We didn't do last names."

"She came with Reena to the emergency room."

"I'm not surprised. They were, uh—" He smirked and glanced at Mrs. Lee. "—good friends."

I'd known Reena was a lesbian, so that didn't surprise me too much. But Jodi as a borderline? That was how they met? Strange.

Mrs. Lee said nothing, but turned her gaze back to the list. She was not amused.

Mike kept writing, but slower now.

Ann

Portia

"I think that's it. I remember her because her name's like the car, but she made a big deal about how it's spelled different," he said. "But I'd have to think about the others. We had the regulars and then we had the ones who dropped in sometimes. I don't remember them all. Unless they were hot." He smirked some more before filching the $50 from under the sugar bowl.

Mrs. Lee didn't blink, so I took my cue from her and watched him pocket it.

Two seconds later, the Goth girl passed us on the way back from the bathroom, scooping up her coffee. I was glad she hadn't come out when the money was on the table, but it made me nervous that Mrs. Lee had so much cash, and was doling it out in public. No matter how safe the natives claimed Montreal was, it felt like we were begging for a mugging. Not to mention whoever was already targeting me.

Mrs. Lee said, "Okay" and ripped the list off the top of the notebook, folding it neatly in her purse. She took out another $50 and covered it with the sugar bowl, but held her hand over both of them. "That's a good start. Next. Where were you the night of August eighth, eight years ago?"

I held my breath. My pulse beat in my throat. Oh, God, Mrs. Lee. Around us, dishes clanked and a woman laughed, high and excited, but the moment felt suspended.

Then Mike broke into a smile. "That's worth at least a hundred, don't you think?"

I writhed in my seat. The police could ask him for free. But we still had no evidence, and it was Mrs. Lee's call.

Without breaking eye contact, she reached into her purse and added another $50.

Mike nodded and dropped his hand over the sugar bowl. His fingertips were wide and blunt with old scars over two of his left knuckles. At some point in his life, he'd been a fighter. It would not pay to underestimate him.

Beside me, I sensed Mrs. Lee, too, was holding her breath.

His eerie eyes moved from my face to hers and back again.

Just as the waitress returned with his coffee. "Sorry for the wait," she said.

I avoided her eye, hoping she'd take the hint and leave. But Mike said, "Is it fresh?" He slowly ripped open a creamer, stirred it in, and tapped in a little sugar before tasting it. "Coffee's not bad here. Thanks," he said, letting the waitress go. He was enjoying the suspense. He was an actor, all right. But, right as he sensed he was losing me, he handed over the information. "I was bartending."

"What about after the bar closed?" I snapped. Laura was run down after her five-a.m. blade, and Quebec bars close at three.

"It was an after-hours club. I was there 'til seven. Lots of witnesses. Sorry, babe. Oops. I mean *Helen*." The $100 disappeared with hardly a paper whisper. He did handle cash with a practiced ease. The bartending and acting résumé would explain his plastic charm. We could check up on his story, but I instinctively felt like he was telling the truth. So far.

He scrawled on the notepad, ripped off the page, and handed it to Mrs. Lee with a little flourish. "Here are a few of my buddies who were there."

"Thank you," she said.

I fought not to show my disappointment, mind scrambling for another question. If he was upping the ante so quickly, Mrs. Lee might not be able to afford many more strike-outs.

But Mrs. Lee had her bat at the ready. Her voice was flat, the words evenly spaced and unmistakable. "Who killed my daughter?"

33

M ike hesitated. A flicker crossed his face—shame? Caution?—before he slipped back into his usual mode. "What? And no money on the table?"

"How much do you want?" Mrs. Lee's voice shook on the last syllable.

I reached out toward her, but she swung her shoulder away while still focused on Mike. This was between the two of them. I was there as backup, and as a courtesy, nothing more.

Mike stirred his coffee and sipped it. I got the feeling he was delaying not to be a jerk, but because he was making up his mind.

Mrs. Lee slipped her hand in her purse and grabbed some bills. She slapped them on the table without looking at them. I saw a flash of brown and a man's face: hundreds, then. She was breathing hard, almost panting.

My heart broke. I concentrated on glaring at Mike instead.

Finally, he met her eyes once before turning back to his coffee. "I'll tell you one thing. I don't know for sure." He made no move toward the money.

I opened my mouth, but Mrs. Lee was quicker.

"But you know something?" she demanded.

He shrugged and sank into his seat. "I'm not sure."

"Tell me!"

I winced at the rawness in her voice. She was only two steps away from a howl.

"I told you. I don't know." He stopped. "But I'll tell you, the guy who stole the truck—this chick asked him to. He didn't want to. He was gonna go straight." He spoke to the table.

I held my breath. I knew, and I was pretty sure Mrs. Lee knew, that "the guy" was Mike and we were talking about the car that had killed Laura Lee.

"So, okay, he did it anyway. He left it in a parking lot and went to work. The next day, he found out...it was that truck. The police found the wreck back in the same parking lot."

He threw his napkin on the table and stood up so fast, his chair rocked on its hind legs. He took a deep breath, muttered something, and marched out of the café without a backward look.

I jumped to my feet. I might have been able to catch him. But I happened to glance at Mrs. Lee. She was crying silently, rivulets streaming down her face, eyes hazy with pain. The last batch of money was still sitting on the table.

When I looked up again, Mike had disappeared.

I thought I knew who the murderer was, and it wasn't him.

I folded the money. It was crisp. I tried not to imagine her going to the bank and withdrawing the bills, praying it would buy her justice. "Mrs. Lee. We have to go." I tried to push the money into her palm.

She brushed me away. "He said sorry. That's what he said. *Sorry*."

"Mrs. Lee."

"Laura. Oh, Laura." She folded her arms around herself and bent in half. "Oh, my beautiful girl. Oh, my heart."

I shoved the money in my pocket and rubbed her shoulder, wishing I knew what to say.

She groaned, just a puff of air, but I smelled sour coffee and despair. I folded her in my arms. She stiffened. Then she sobbed so hard, my shoulder grew damp, my arms ached from holding her up, and her agony made my body rock, too. I felt people looking at us, but I studiously ignored them until I saw one in particular, framed in the doorway.

Ryan.

He marched toward us. At the sound of footsteps, Mrs. Lee pulled herself off of me and groped for a napkin to blow her nose.

"Thank God you're here. Can you take her home?" I said to him. It was not a time for hello kisses and profound thank-yous, especially since my pager started to scream.

"Yeah, no problem."

I showed him the lists of buddies. "I can't explain right now, but these people are Mike Martinez's alibi. Do you think you'd be able to start to check them out? Or at least make copies so the police can do it?"

"Hope..."

"I know. I know we have no idea what we're doing. But I've got to try." I checked my pager, expecting the long-lost Tucker. Instead, it was the case room.

34

I tried to block out thoughts of Mike Martinez while I snapped a single sterile glove on my right hand and swished my index finger in clear Muco gel.

Mrs. Valdez clenched her teeth and arched her back while I stood between her legs in stirrups. Her thin blue gown was the only shield between us. I could smell briny amniotic fluid and the sharper, metallic scent of blood.

Her husband murmured in Spanish while the nurse chanted, "One. Two. Three..."

I glanced at the beeping fetal heart monitor, which flashed one-ten, one-twenty. Normal. The heart tracing was reassuring. The single fluorescent light at the head of the bed illuminated Mrs. Valdez's cheek while our blurred shadows danced on the walls.

For once, I was grateful for the switchboard's incompetence. They hadn't tracked me or my pager down until Mrs. Valdez was hooked up to an IV and an epidural and, according to the nurse, she was already seven centimetres dilated. Theoretically, I would verify the dilation after she finished her contraction. But in all honesty, I'd probably poke around and then repeat whatever the nurse had said. I didn't know much 'bout birthin' no babies.

At last, Mrs. Valdez relaxed. The nurse took her hand off the abdomen, where she'd been palpating the uterus, and nodded at me.

I said, "Sorry about this. It will only take a minute."

Mrs. Valdez didn't even open her eyes.

I tried to be gentle as I inserted my finger up the folds of her vagina and probed the softened edges of her cervix.

Mrs. Valdez moaned. Mr. Valdez clutched her hand and glared at me.

I retreated, stripping off the glove into the garbage. "Seven. It won't be too long now." Although, for a primip (first-time mom) and a baby estimated at over eight and a half pounds, that was debatable.

I eased my way out of the room, while the husband gathered a few ice chips and handed them to my patient. She turned her head away from him.

The door swooshed closed behind me. At the nursing station, a few nurses chatted over charts and coffee while the unit clerk avoided my eye. Where did the OB residents and med students hang out? Before I could ask, my pager went off again. This time, it was a non-hospital phone number.

The unit coordinator waved me toward a call room in the back hallway. I peeked in the empty OR suite, a bathroom, and a dirty utility room complete with commodes, before I found the call room.

There were two single beds, one for a med student, one for a resi-dent, one dirty window, and a desk with a lamp and an old copy of William's Obstetrics. The med student bed was rumpled but empty. Presumably its occupant was working or eating dinner. Sometimes, housekeeping didn't bother making the beds for us, which was pretty disturbing. I chose to sit at the desk to punch in the number.

Tucker answered. "I've got to talk to you."

"About what? Why didn't you answer my calls?"

"I found the guy we were looking for."

Tucker didn't want to say Mike's name aloud. I wondered where he was; I hadn't recognized the phone number. "I already found him. Mrs. Lee and I interviewed him."

"What are you talking about?"

"Michael Martinez, a.k.a. Mike Martin. The guy Dr. Ven thought was antisocial. Isn't that who you're talking about?"

"Yes, but how could you have talked to him? I was just with him."

"When?"

"Met up with him half an hour ago."

I checked my watch. It had taken longer than that for me to see my OB patient. "He saw us first, then. Did you pay him?"

A long, telling pause.

"Because we did." Mike Martinez was making a killing off of us, no pun intended.

Tucker cleared his throat. "Anyway. I want to talk to you about it."

"You want to bring it to the case room? My patient's about to deliver."

He burst out laughing. "God, Hope. You never stand still, do you?"

"Try not to. Are you coming?"

"See you in ten or twenty. Unless your patient's delivering then."

"She's a primip at seven centimetres. I'll see you soon." I hung up with a smile. I'd been worried about Tucker, no matter how I played it.

I passed by the case room to make sure Mrs. Valdez wasn't about to push without me. Her face glistened with sweat. The baby moved, making a muffled noise on the monitor. The nurse adjusted the external monitor, which was, as far as I could tell, a loudspeaker strapped to Mrs. Valdez's belly. I backed out again. Not yet, but soon.

I felt twitchy with energy. I walked past the other labour rooms, past the triage room, and past a woman waddling toward the elevator on her husband's arm. I bent my head over the water fountain. Lukewarm, rusty water was better than nothing. When I lifted my head, Tucker was lounging against the wall, staring at me with a McGill clipboard tucked under his arm.

I almost shrieked. My hand did fly to my chest, as if I were a Southern belle. In other words, a humiliatingly girly reaction.

Tucker laughed so hard, he thumped his free hand against the wall and laughed some more.

"Shut up." I strode past him to the call room. He followed, still chuckling. He was looking fine, in a short-sleeved blue denim shirt that showed his distal biceps and well-muscled forearms, but looks weren't everything. Personality and ability to answer phone calls counted for a lot.

He shut the door. The room felt a lot smaller and quieter than it had a few minutes ago, and I caught a whiff of dirty sheets or socks or both. He'd probably think it was me. I stood by the door and crossed my arms. "So what's your big news?"

Tucker dropped his clipboard on the desk and perched beside it, nudging aside the phone with his rear end. I closed my eyes. Now was not the time to notice his ass. "First of all, let me dazzle you with my detective work. You know what I was doing last night?"

Tori, I thought, which was pretty unworthy of me. "Dazzling detection?"

"Basically. Tori and I buttered up Dr. Ven, so he'd let us take a look at Mike's file. He wasn't that keen on it because of patient confidentiality, rah-rah-rah, but Tori convinced him we were doing a case study on borderline personalities and needed access to the records."

"Tori did that?" I'd never seen her out-and-out lie.

"Yeah." Tucker grinned. "I had no idea she was so good at laying it on. She went on about the importance of psychiatry at St. Joe's, and how we needed to improve our program here. I guess now we know how she gets her stellar evaluations. Anyway, she convinced him. He took us over to medical records at the Douglas, and let us take notes, but not photocopy anything. So I got Michael Martinez's past contact info and his next of kin. I managed to get his number through his cousin."

"Not his parents?"

Tucker shook his head, frowning a little. "It's a bad story. Anyway, I tracked Mike down and convinced him to meet me tonight. But he blew me off at the last minute. Later, he called me and said he was at Côte-des-Neiges, if I wanted to come."

"He paged you?" How come Tucker had answered that page and not mine?

He grimaced. "My pager died. I wasn't carrying it because I'm not on call. I bought a temporary cell to use with Mike, and I got so caught up, I didn't check my home messages until I was on my way over here. Sorry."

"It's okay." Not what you'd expect to hear from someone professing true love and undying devotion, but I understood getting caught up in an investigation. "Was Tori with you?"

He grinned, flashing a fine set of incisors. "Jealous?"

I shook my head a little too hard. "Curious. She didn't answer her phone, either."

His smile widened. "Nah, she's on call, and you know Tori. She doesn't answer personal calls on call."

I bypassed his knowing attitude. "Okay. So you met with Michael."

"Yeah. So did you, sounds like. You want to go first?"

I shook my head. "Shoot."

"He's got an alibi for that night. There really was an after-hours club called X-TC, and he worked there. Ryan's tracking down the contacts you gave him, but it looks legit."

I waited a beat before it sank in. "My Ryan? Ryan Wu?"

"Yeah. I called your house first and he answered. Is he a permanent resident?"

It was my turn to grin. "Jealous?"

"Hell, yeah." He smacked his fist into his palm. "After I pummelled him, he agreed to be my data slave and look this stuff up."

I quirked an eyebrow. "Good job."

"Okay, fine, he was already on it. After he took care of Mrs. Lee."

"Great." That was awfully quick care of Mrs. Lee, but maybe she'd insisted on a ride straight home. That sounded like her. I felt a surge of affection for Ryan, king of the computer. I kicked off my sandals and sat on the clean bed, cross-legged. I glanced around the room to make sure no one could overhear, and lowered my voice for good measure. "So have you figured out who killed Laura?" I waited for him to say, No, who, you wise woman?

He nodded. "I think Mike might have hired someone."

Mike? *Qué?* "How'd you figure that?"

Tucker ticked the points off on his finger. "He stole the car.

Sounds like he admitted that to you and Mrs. Lee, from what Ryan understood. But he was smart enough to get himself an alibi while someone else mowed her down."

"Why would he do that?"

"This is the part I didn't tell you: he was sexually harassing Laura, and she was threatening to go to the police."

35

Tucker filled in my stupefied silence. "Mike was obsessed with Laura. He came to the first meeting because his doctor made him, but once Laura started heading it, he never missed a Monday. He started reading up on borderline personality and suggesting group activities. When that didn't work, he moved to asking her out directly. She told him she didn't date patients. He dropped out of the group shortly thereafter. But you know those calls Mrs. Lee said Laura was getting? I bet it was him."

It was certainly new information, but it went against my own hypothesis. So I challenged him. "How'd you get all that? I bet he didn't tell you."

"Dr. Ven. Laura told him someone was harassing her, but refused to give the details. He didn't piece it together until afterward."

I pushed the pillow aside to lean against the wall while I contemplated this. Tucker blew on his knuckles and pretended to polish them on his shirt. I'd forgotten that move from kindergarten. I tossed the pillow at him. "Why would he decide to kill her?"

"Isn't it classic? *'If I can't have you, no one can.'*"

I chewed my lip. "He didn't strike me that way."

"You probably felt sorry for him."

I straightened, stung. But it was true. Part of me had somehow sympathized with him.

Tucker frowned. "Don't get sucked in. That's what happened to Laura."

I didn't like the implication that soft-hearted women like us got run over by men who "loved" them. "I can look after myself."

"I'm sure."

The speaker behind the bed crackled to life, making me jump. "Dr. Zee? Are you there?"

Tucker gestured at me to press a red button below the speaker. I fumbled for it. "Yes."

"Just checking. Dr. Zahrad called again."

It wasn't my fault switchboard hadn't been able to find me, but Dr. Zahrad, the staff on call, obviously wasn't amused. "Okay." I fluttered my eyelids at the ceiling and Tucker grinned.

The speaker blared again, "He said he'll be in when the patient is at nine centimetres and that you should keep him posted."

"Thank you."

A burst of static replied. After it died down, Tucker shook his head. "They keep you on a short leash."

"No kidding. I gotta get back and show my face." I did want to get back to Mrs. Valdez, but I also wanted to figure out all this stuff with Michael Martinez, and I knew that if she got close to delivering, they'd page me stat.

I tried to think. Was Tucker right? Mike had some sort of motive and had at least contributed to the means. But whose blond hair was in the car? Or was that a red herring?

Tucker said, "I'm going to call the police. They can talk to Dr. Ven about it and check Laura's phone records for Michael's old phone number. There's one more thing I got from Dr. Ven that I have to give back to him—well, Tori was the one who sweet-talked it out of him." Tucker reached for his clipboard and slid something out from under his sheaf of notes.

It was a group photo, taken outside on a sunny day much like this one. I sucked in my breath when I saw Laura in a white coat. On her right, at the edge of the group, I noted a balding, South Indian man with glasses, no doubt Dr. Ven. On her left, Mike Martinez flashed his teeth in a practiced smile. He was standing a little close to Laura. She had her arms crossed and her smile looked slightly forced. I felt a pang of sympathy for her. But I felt relieved that it was the same guy I'd met tonight. At least Mrs. Lee hadn't shelled out her money to an imposter.

I scanned the group until I found Reena kneeling in the front row. She smiled with her lips still covering her teeth. Her eyes were uncertain. Her face was younger and rounder and she wore more eye makeup than a K-pop star. More importantly, she'd bleached her hair. Even as my heart seized up, I noticed her spiky blond hair was cut too short for her heavy jaw.

I could hardly speak for a minute. A lot of things were coming together. All I could say was, "She bleached her hair."

"Yeah, I noticed that, too. It's funny. We think of Reena as such a pain in the ass, but Dr. Ven remembered her as more a dependent personality. He laughed when he saw the picture because he called Reena and Jodi 'the twins.' Soon after Jodi joined the group, Reena bleached her hair and imitated her makeup and looked pretty godawful."

Bleach.

I said, "We need a DNA sample from Reena Schuster."

"You don't think—"

"I've got my suspicions." I looked at him. "I mean, we have plenty of samples from her—blood, urine, maybe even sputum. But I doubt it's legal to use them."

He lifted an eyebrow. "Especially on your say-so."

I ignored that. "I remember a forensic pathology case. They gave the suspect a piece of gum and he spit it in the toilet afterward. They collected it and ran it. The judge ruled it was allowed, not entrapment, because he'd thrown it away."

"Uh uh. You can't go through her garbage, Hope. There's the whole chain of evidence thing, remember?"

Damn. I did remember, from rape kit talks, how important it was to get consent, label, and store everything so it would stand up in a court of law. The police would have to do it.

Tucker narrowed his eyes at me. "You're not going to do anything stupid, are you?"

"How could I? I have a baby to deliver."

"Uh huh." I wore my most innocent expression, *à la* Paddington Bear, but I could practically see him swearing to keep a close eye on me.

I could live with that.

I glanced back down at the picture. Jodi stood in the second row directly above Reena. Jodi's head was turned aside as if someone had called her name while the shutter clicked. From what I saw of her face, she looked startlingly young, narrow-faced like a kitten, pretty in a sulky sort of way. She was wearing a beret low on her forehead. Kind of an odd choice on a summer's day.

My eyes moved back to Laura's image. Her posture was impeccable. She looked directly at the camera with no hint of coyness or shyness. Here was a woman with nothing to hide and, I would have guessed, little to fear in her life. Until she got mixed up with this group. And, once again, studying her heart-shaped face and the determined lift of her chin, I saw that she looked uncomfortably like me in that Brownie photo.

I put it down. "I gotta get back to my patient."

Mrs. Valdez's moans shifted to a high-pitched keen.

"Hold your breath," said the nurse. "Use it to push." She hoisted Mrs. Valdez's leg in the air and gestured at the husband to grab the other. "Push! Push! You can do it!"

Mrs. Valdez strained, red-faced, with her eyes screwed shut. The baby's scalp descended toward me, a few centimetres from the perineum, but soon its dark, wet hair retreated.

"Don't stop now! You've still got some left! Come on!"

"You're doing a great job," I chimed in, but Mrs. Valdez shook her head and groaned. Her hair was matted to her temples with sweat.

Her leg flopped. The nurse shoved it back in the stirrup and said, "Okay. We'll try the next time. Don't worry. There's a reason they call it labour."

True dat. I wasn't sure how much Mrs. Valdez could understand, even if we spoke Spanish or Portuguese. From her glazed eyes, she was orbiting Planet Exhaustion right about now. TV tends to focus on the glory of the baby, without all the pain and pushing. Not to mention the poop. Before going into medicine, I hadn't realized that they used to give women enemas so it would be nicer for the staff. Fortunately, I only witnessed a log once. The nurse instantly swept the stool into a towel and from there into a tray so we didn't have to watch it or smell it.

Dr. Zahrad passed by. He was a short, peppy man, with prematurely grey hair. He examined Mrs. Valdez, conferred with me and the nurse, and buggered off to watch TV.

My own montage was running through my head. If only we could get DNA samples, we could implicate Reena in the vehicle. If only she would give them voluntarily. If only we had enough evidence to bring to the police.

If only she confessed.

Beep-beep-beep said the baby's heart on the monitor. The heart rate dipped to ninety. We all eyed the monitor, but the red numbers hesitated before they blinked back up to one-thirty.

The nurse and I sighed with relief and shared a brief smile.

Reena was still at the hospital. What if I were to pass by her room tonight, after delivering this baby?

"Here we go again," said the nurse. "Come on!" She gestured at the husband. Simultaneously, they each lifted Mrs. Valdez's legs. She closed her eyes. The fat on her thighs jiggled.

Mrs. Valdez gritted her teeth. The tendons in her neck and the veins on her forehead bulged. "Uhhhh!" Tears leaked from her eyes.

"Come on, you're great, it's fine, let's go. The baby's almost ready to come out. Come on, baby. Say hello! Say hello to your mommy!"

"Hi, baby!" I chimed in. I really didn't know what to say.

Mr. Valdez spoke in Spanish.

Slowly, excruciatingly, the baby made progress. At some magic moment, the nurse called Dr. Zahrad and unfolded the delivery cart, revealing stainless steel instruments and bowls, blue paper drapes, and cloth gowns.

For a moment, I felt nostalgic for the OR. I have always loved the surgical dance. The sterile gown, where you twirl around and the nurse holds the gown's tie, wrapping it around you. The ritual of saying what size gloves you wear and plunging your hands into each one while the nurse snaps the cuff over your wrists. The metal instruments on the tray. The beam of lights angled just so. Painting the patient's skin with iodine or chlorhexidine and draping the surrounding area. Picking up the scalpel to make the first incision.

In another life, a life where I could always put my career first, where I could press snooze on my biological clock without worrying about the consequences, where my back didn't freak out after standing with a retractor for two hours—in that life, I would be a surgeon.

I snapped back to reality as the baby's head began to bulge the perineum. It wasn't crowning yet, but it was close. Dr. Zahrad pushed open the door. "Massage her!" he snapped to me as the nurse gowned him up.

I fumbled for the packet of Muco gel.

"Not that! You're sterile! Wait, I'll get it for you," said the nurse before I made contact. "Stand there for a minute. Don't push," she said to Mrs. Valdez, and then to Mr. Valdez, "Tell her not to push!" She tore open the packet and squeezed a blob onto my fingers. "Go!"

Gingerly, I daubed it on the vaginal opening.

"Didn't anyone ever teach you?" snapped Dr. Zahrad, reaching around me to pull at the lips of the vagina.

I shook my head.

"Where did you do your medical school?"

"Western."

He rolled his eyes at the nurse. "Western."

Mrs. Valdez groaned and clutched her husband's arm.

"PUSH! PUSH! PUSH!" they chorused. I joined in.

"Come here," Dr. Zahrad said, grabbing my hand. "See how the skin is blanching? There is too much pressure. I don't want to have to do an episiotomy. Massage, massage, massage! You don't want her to have a tear!"

The nurse squeezed two more packets of Muco. Imitating Dr. Zahrad, I hooked two fingers inside her vagina and pulled at the skin closest to her anus, trying to stretch it out.

"The baby's coming!" called the nurse. "Tell her the baby's coming any minute!"

And then, in a gush of blood and more salty-smelling amniotic fluid, the baby's head pushed at the rim of her vagina.

"Stop pushing! Stop pushing!" they chanted.

"Control it," Dr. Zahrad muttered at me. "Push back. No tearing. No tearing."

The baby's head eased out, slippery with white vernix. I spotted little black curls. Its squashed little face pointed toward the floor. Then it rotated slightly and its arms dangled. I grabbed the chest and held the baby's body as its hips and legs came into the world.

I swooped it onto the mother's stomach gently. I heard a roar in my ears.

Mrs. Valdez reached toward her warm, pink-brown-white baby. Its eyes were open. Its mouth smacked once as the nurse swabbed it dry and wrapped it in a warm blanket.

"Just a minute," said Dr. Zahrad, handing me a clamp.

I clamped the umbilical cord where he pointed with his finger. Dr. Zahrad clamped it again, about an inch away, after milking a bit of the blood out in between. Then the father cut the cord and we all stared at the folds between the baby's legs.

"It's a girl," said Dr. Zahrad.

Mrs. Valdez burst into tears and scooped her daughter close, kissing her. Her husband watched both of them, laying his hand tentatively on his new baby's back. The nurse snugged a hat on her.

I blinked back tears.

When all was said and done, this was a miracle. I felt privileged to be in the room. This was life. This was creation. This was love. This was motherhood and fatherhood and daughterhood.

I had to do what I could to honour that sentiment.

Dr. Zahrad nudged me, pointing to a bloody gash in Mrs. Valdez's perineum at six o'clock. "She has a second-degree tear. We will need to repair it after she delivers the placenta."

I nodded and stepped between her legs to apply gentle pressure to the dangling end of the umbilical cord.

Mrs. Lee had lost a daughter. Mrs. Valdez had gained one.

When I was finished here, I would pay Reena a visit.

36

"Ryan," I said, as soon as he picked up. "I'm almost done here. There's one thing I need to do, and I'll be right home—"

"Hope. I'm on my way. I'll see you in five. Where are you?"

It was 10:55. He was right. He had to get back to Ottawa. I glanced down toward triage and saw Tucker's lean figure walking toward me. Man, oh man. Or rather, men oh men.

I made a quick calculation. I wanted to be alone with Ryan, and not in the stinky residents' room or the weight room where someone might burst in on us. "There are usually some empty call rooms on the sixth floor. I'll meet you by the elevators. It's deserted, but page me if you don't see me."

"Done."

I hung up and faced Tucker, who was smiling at me so intimately the unit clerk and two nurses gave us curious looks. I beckoned him down the hall, past triage, toward the elevators. "Tucker—"

He smacked a kiss on my cheek. "Feels good, doesn't it?"

I stopped short, and not only because his lips and the smell of his body made me want to sink my teeth into his bare shoulder.

"Doesn't it feel awesome, delivering a baby? I may do OB for the rush, even though everyone says I'm nuts. Including you."

I shook my head, feeling guilty that my rush had turned back into my primary obsession already.

"Aw, I can see it in your eyes. You look bee-you-ti-ful!" He lifted me up and swung me around in a circle.

I squealed. I could picture him lifting me wrong, throwing his back out, and me having to drag him down to emerg for Toradol. I banged on his shoulder, but he spun me around again, faster. The dingy yellow walls and orange carpet whirled, and suddenly I was afraid I'd be sick.

The elevator dinged. Tucker stopped and set me down. I wobbled, but fortunately the elevator swooshed open to reveal no one. I laid a hand against the control panel. Before I left, I had to explain. "Tucker, Ryan's coming to meet me."

"Great. I'd like to see him too."

I scowled at him as best I could while my head still felt a bit like an egg yolk swirling in a sea of albumin.

"Seriously. He's a good guy. Not as good as me, of course—"

I pressed the button for the sixth floor. "I appreciate all your help. Especially the picture. Now go away."

"Hey, I waited all this time." He lounged against the wall, his hip bone curving dangerously close to my hand. I dropped my arm back to my side before my fingers traced the outline of his hip through his pants.

"Yeah, you did. Thanks."

"I took you out. I wined and dined a psychiatrist. I bribed a psychopath. And you think you're just going to blow me off while you take your ex-boyfriend—illegally, by the way—into a deserted call room?"

"Well, yeah." I had to grin at him, though. "You said you'd wait for me, right?"

"Yeah. And I said, not forever. I should have added, not as a chump."

I raised my eyebrows. He wasn't half as romantic at St. Joe's as outside of it. "I'm just saying goodbye to him before he goes back to Ottawa. You trust me, right?"

He raised his fist to his lips, his pinky extended like Mini Me in Austin Powers. I wasn't sure what that meant, except that he looked ridiculous. The elevator binged open for me.

"Well, like it or not, I'm on my way." I stepped inside and waved at him.

He stepped into the elevator with me.

"Tucker—"

He parroted my tone. "Like it or not, I'm coming with you."

I crossed my arms and faced the stainless steel door of the elevator after I pressed button number six. "This is ridiculous."

"I agree. When are you going to figure out Ryan's a side order and I'm the main event?"

That bought him some eye contact. "Does that mean I get to enjoy you both at the same time?"

"Ouch." He thumped his chest. "Hoisted by my own bad metaphor. Or is it a simile?"

"Metaphor."

"Oh, I love you brainy girls. My point is, I'm coming with you." The elevator stopped at six and he held the door open for me. "After you."

I decided arguing was futile and went for out-walking him. I can speed-walk past guys almost twice my height without breaking a sweat, a useful talent in medicine. I gunned past him, searching for an empty room. The security guards are supposed to lock everything up, but sometimes they slip up.

On the other hand, sometimes they don't have enough rooms for all the students and residents on call and someone ends up sleeping in the residents' room. I couldn't bear to meet Ryan in a room reeking of garbage, while people scarfed down French fries and blasted videos.

On the other hand, he might prefer that to Tucker as our chaperone.

Tucker kept pace with me, not too difficult as I kept trying the handle of each call room door, even if the navy sign was slid to "Occupied." He said, "What, you don't have a room?"

I ignored him.

"I guess you didn't have time, hunting down killers and all."

I rattled a doorknob extra hard, gritting my teeth.

"What would you say if I told you I hadn't turned in a call room key?"

I stopped at stared at him.

"They're supposed to call you if you forget to return it, but..." He shrugged and smiled.

"Are you sh—" I bit off the word. I swore too much. "Are you playing with me?"

In answer, he dug his hand in his left pocket but didn't take anything out to show me.

I narrowed my eyes. Call room keys are fair-sized because they have a hard plastic room number attached to a key ring. I hadn't noticed any bulges in his pockets, and I had checked him out pretty thoroughly earlier. "Why would you help me when all you've been doing is antagonize me about meeting Ryan?"

"Well, you know I like to tease you, Hope."

"Do you have the key or not?" I heard a toilet flush down the hall and realized I was perilously close to bellowing. People were trying to sleep.

He rummaged his left pocket, then his right. I was tempted to search him myself until the curve of his mouth told me that was the whole point. I put my hands on my hips. "Let me guess. You don't have the key."

He shrugged. "It's true, I forgot to turn one in. But I guess I forgot to bring it. I didn't realize you were up for some sixth-floor hanky-panky."

I whirled on my heel and marched across the hall to try the next room.

"Hope!" Ryan called from the end of the hall.

I practically broke into a run. The old carpet muffled my footsteps. "Thank for coming. I totally appreciate it." I expected Tucker to keep pace with me, even beating me to Ryan, but he'd melted away. Maybe he'd discovered his conscience.

Or maybe he was eavesdropping. I tugged Ryan back toward the elevators and pushed the door open into the stairwell.

The plaster was crumbling off the walls, but at least it kept a door between us and Tucker. "How are you?" My voice echoed up and down the flights of stairs.

He frowned at me. "This is kind of weird. Why don't we find a call room, like you said?"

"They're all locked. I might be able to find a teaching room unlocked, if security hasn't gotten to it. They're kind of careless on internal medicine." I pointed down the halls.

He shrugged. "Nah, I don't have time. Okay, first things first. Mrs. Lee is okay. I took her to the police."

"You did!"

He raised his eyebrows at me. "Yeah. I thought someone should involve them and I convinced her to tell them what she knew. They're probably going to reopen the case."

I grabbed his arm. "Really? That's great!"

"It was never officially closed, just archived, and they're interested in interviewing Michael Martinez. The officer, Luc Tremblay, also mentioned the possibility of doing more DNA testing on the blond hair from the vehicle. It's probably not Michael's, with a name like Martinez, but it might be a lead. The technology's a lot better now."

I closed my eyes. "I should have gone to them sooner." I wanted to tell him my suspicions about Reena, but first I was sidetracked by guilt.

He squeezed my hand. His hand was warm and dry and felt exactly right in mine. "You couldn't know."

"Yeah, but it's not my job to anticipate what they might or might not want to do. I should give them the information and let them decide. It's just like I hate when patients come here having diagnosed themselves on the Internet."

He shrugged. "Probably true. But I got the feeling it was a special case with Mrs. Lee. On one hand, they're sick of seeing her. On the other hand, they don't dare miss anything."

"Still. I should have gone to them before. You're the only one who's been smart enough to follow the rules."

He smiled and kissed me, a light peck on the lips. "Thanks. And hello to you too."

I smiled back. I wanted to kiss him more, and harder, but not in the stairwell. "Thanks for driving all the way down to look after me, and then bringing Mrs. Lee to the police."

"Hey. You're worth it."

We kissed some more, longer and lingering. He weaved his hands through my hair. I rubbed my cheek against his, not caring if Tucker or anyone else saw us. Ryan was a hero. A quiet one, one who did the right thing without a big hoopla, but a hero nonetheless.

Ryan was the one who drew away first to rest his chin on top of my head. "There's just one other thing."

I sighed and waited for him to tell me he was turning into a pumpkin.

"You know that picture of the gravestone in your mailbox?"

I nodded. How could I forget? I pulled back to see his face, still holding myself in his arms.

Ryan wore a wrinkle between his eyes. I wanted to smooth it away with my fingertip, but he looked too serious as he spoke. "I thought it looked familiar. I searched for it this week. You wouldn't believe how many cemetery pictures people post, but anyway. I found it in Alexandria. You ever been there? Halfway between Montreal and Ottawa?"

I shook my head. "I don't get off the highway."

"Neither do I, but once Lisa wanted to go to this china clearance place, and we ended up puttering around. Anyway, I'd bet you a silver dollar it's the same tombstone. The quality of your copy isn't great, but it looks like the same angle and everything."

I nestled my head in his shoulder again. "Good work. If I had a silver dollar, I'd give it to you." My paranoia and fear decreased an order of magnitude when I was in his arms. "But what are you saying? Do you think someone in Alexandria is targeting me?"

He shook his head. "No. Since it's online, someone could have downloaded it."

"Where was the original photo from?"

"That's the strange thing. That website had been taken down, so I could only get a crummy copy off someone else's website. But I gave it to the police and I'm going to keep looking."

"Thanks, Ryan. I'll bring them the paper copy ASAP." I thought about asking him for the specs so I could investigate it myself, but he and the police were already on it. I wanted to concentrate on Reena Schuster.

"My pleasure." He bent to kiss me again. Our bodies molded together. He ended up pressing me against the wall. I had both arms wrapped around him before I surfaced for air again.

"Ryan..."

He touched my hair gently. "I wish I could stay."

"Me too."

"Maybe I could stay until four a.m., and then drive back to Ottawa."

I was touched by the yearning in his voice. "You could. I don't know about the traffic, though. I'm on call next weekend, but we'd still see each other." Reena flitted through my mind, but I could be persuaded to spend a few hours with Ryan instead.

My pager went off. I stifled a curse as its beep echoed up and down the stairwell.

Ryan closed his eyes. "I thought your patient already delivered."

"I know, but I guess if something goes wrong, she's still my patient." Part of me wondered when or if the OB consultant would ever take over. Was I going to get called at three a.m. for Tylenol and Gravol, too? I'd have to ask, but in the meantime I unclipped the pager from my waistband and checked the number.

He sighed. "I'd better go."

"I know."

"I love you."

I stayed silent, trying to frame my answer.

"You don't have to say anything. I just wanted you to know."

I looked at him. "I've always loved you, Ryan. You know that."

"But?"

The pager felt warm in my hand. I said, "I don't know. Is it possible to love two people at the same time?"

He shook his head.

"You're old school, though, Ry. I know it's not something the church teaches, but I wonder. I feel like I could love you and medicine and..." I didn't say Tucker's name, but we both knew what I was thinking.

That made him smile a tiny bit. "You were always wondering. Some people are wanderers. You're a wonderer."

I smiled back.

"I think you'll be coming back to me, though."

His confidence turned me on. I kissed him in reply. It was a long and lingering kiss that allowed me to breathe in his breath, taste his tongue, and slide my hands down his back to reach his ass.

I never said I was a saint.

And, after a hesitation, I felt Ryan smile before he cupped my ass back.

When he finally let go, I could hardly walk straight to make it out of the stairwell and answer my page.

"Hello, is this Dr. Sze?" a nasal, francophone, male voice asked. He sounded as if he were holding the receiver away from his mouth.

"Yes?" I half-sat, half-collapsed in a chair under the wall-mounted phone I'd located on the medicine floor opposite the ward.

"Are you looking after bed 1411?"

I sighed. "Is this about Mrs. Valdez?"

"No, no, it's about a Dr. Tucker. That handsome resident? The one for whom you should forsake all others?"

It took me a second to clue in. "Tucker. Is that you?" Of course it was. I clenched the receiver in my hand and thought of Ryan navigating his way back to Ottawa. "John Tucker, I am going to kill you."

"No, no." But he was starting to laugh and lose his accent. "You mean you are going to love him and perform a striptease, very slow and sexy. Don't worry, you can wear your greens and pretend you are a doctor too. Dr. Tucker likes this sort of thing—"

I hung up on him. And then, even though I still wanted to kick him, I had to laugh. He always made me laugh.

My pager went off again, but I ignored it. Ryan was probably already unlocking his car door. For a second, I imagined the moon shining on his upturned face as he glanced back at the hospital, wondering what I was doing. And I imagined Tucker chortling as he paged me again and again.

Sure enough, my pager went off. I stopped it at the first beep.

DUPLICATE, said my pager.

"Screw you," I said back to it. I had a date with Reena.

37

First, I checked Reena's chart. Psych wouldn't accept her until she was completely medically cleared. Normally they take an internist's word for it, but this time, with the patient trapped in a supposed coma, they'd asked for neuro to weigh in. Neuro had deferred it until Monday.

In other words, the different services were playing games (what the book *House of God* might call buff and turf), and Reena was still where I'd left her.

I knocked on the door.

No answer, of course. It was after visiting hours, she was playing possum, and possibly genuinely asleep at eleven thirty-six p.m.

I glanced nervously down the hall, and knocked again. One of the nurses had been doling out medications as I checked the chart, but so far no one had really paid attention to me. I wanted to keep it that way. I pushed my way in, and made sure the door closed behind me.

The bedside light illuminated a spot on the floor. I wondered why they bothered burning electricity for someone who didn't open her eyes, but it made it easier for me to navigate to her side and ease myself onto the chair at the far side of the bed, next to the window. "Reena," I whispered. "It's me. Dr. Hope Sze."

Her breathing stayed slow and even, heaving the blankets up and down. Her arms stuck out over the blankets. I wondered if her arms got cold or cramped, staying like that for hours, until someone moved her. I couldn't imagine a situation that would make me fake a coma for a week unless it was extremis, like a concentration camp. "Reena. I know you're awake."

The cracked lips stirred and her fetid breath wafted out at me.

I sat back.

She gave a ghost of a laugh. "Scared you, huh?" Her eyes opened, wincing at the bedside lamp.

She was only twenty-nine, around my age, but she looked prematurely aged, the way anorexics do. "You got me," I said.

"What do you want this time?"

I licked my own lips. "To talk to you about post-traumatic stress."

She started to scoff, but stopped, and I knew I had her. For a few seconds, anyway. I carried on. "I've got it, too. I jump when someone slams a door. I have nightmares. I replay the scene over and over again, wondering if I could have done something, anything else. Sometimes I think the only thing worse than living through it is reliving it for the rest of my life."

Her forehead wrinkled. "Whad'ja do?"

A good therapist would deflect the question, but I wanted to draw her in. "This guy tried to strangle me, and he almost got away with it." I realized my hand had drifted up to my throat and dropped it back down to my side.

"Oh, yeah, I read about that. The whole 'detective doctor' thing." She rubbed her nose, sniffed, and rubbed it again, clearly not impressed.

I changed tactics. "What about your thing?"

"What about it?"

A tacit admission. She hadn't denied the PTSD. "You might want to talk to someone about it."

She yawned and had enough manners to cover her mouth. "Jodi says I've got plenty of friends. I don't need to talk to you."

"True." Although she wouldn't keep coming to emerg if she

weren't desperate for something her friends weren't giving her. "But I'm here, and I know what you're going through."

"What are you doing here, anyway? It's the middle of the night."

"I was in the neighbourhood, delivering a baby. And we're alone. No nurses, no Jodi, no Wendy. Just us."

She yawned and pointed and flexed her toes. "A nurse might come in."

"Probably not. They're getting ready for sign-out." At her blank look, I explained, "The night nurses come on at midnight, so the evening nurses have to get ready with their notes and explain who each patient is and what's happening to them."

She yawned again and scratched her nose. "So that's what they're doing. I thought they all went on break or something. For, like, hours."

I smothered a smile. Doctors always tease nurses about going on break. But I had to get Reena back on track. "Do you want to talk about yourself? Do you have nightmares or flashbacks?"

She shrugged and ducked her head, but not before I saw anger crease her face. "Well, it's not like I was in Afghanistan, but yeah, been there, done that. Someone slams a car door and I'm whipping around. The phone rings and I wake up screaming. I try to sit with my back to the wall. I try not to go out at night." She twisted her hands in her lap. "My friends are sick of talking to me. But what else is new? My frickin' doctors are sick of talking to me."

"What do you think we could do to help?"

"I don't know."

"I think you do know, but you're scared to say it."

Her dark eyes darted toward me and away again.

"We can talk about the symptoms as much as you want. Or you can finally unload what's behind it all." I paused. She blinked hard, avoiding my eyes. We both heard footsteps patter by in the hallway and the high-pitched, steady beep of another patient's blocked IV. I continued. "Eight years. That's more than a quarter of your life. Aren't you sick of keeping it to yourself?"

She glared at me. "Are you accusing me of something?"

"No." Not yet, anyway. "Just offering to listen. That's why you kept coming to emerg, right?"

She rolled over and yanked the sheet on her bed until it loosened from under the mattress. For someone who'd been lying in bed for a week, she seemed pretty strong, pushing herself to half-sit up on the pillows. "I wanted good drugs."

I waited.

She glared at me. "No one would give me any."

I waited.

"You think you can trick me, but I don't think you know shit."

"Maybe. I know a little bit, though. I know you've been scared of me ever since you saw me, and that I look a lot like Dr. Laura Lee."

With a small gasp, she wound the end of the sheet around her wrist.

"I know that you got even more upset when I dropped an envelope with Mrs. Lee's name on it."

She tightened the sheet hard enough to indent the muscles of her forearm.

"And, after it became clear Mrs. Lee was my patient, you refused to see me at all. I thought you were being difficult. I didn't realize you were scared."

She unwound the sheet a little. The skin had blanched, surrounded by red inflammation. Old scars criss-crossed her wrist. "You just want me to confess," she mumbled.

Now I remembered her saying that to me when we first met. I'd thought she was being a typical psych patient, over-dramatic and annoying. But now I understood something quite different. I saw the new weariness in her voice, as well as the slope of her shoulders and the re-ratcheting of the sheet around her wrist.

"No, Reena," I said, as gently as possible. *"You* want to confess."

Her eyes met mine suddenly. "You think you can get me off? I've got a huge psych history."

I tried not to recoil. She wanted to plead "not criminally responsible," what used to be called criminally insane. Somehow, I hadn't expected that.

But I didn't have to like Reena. And my testimony would be irrelevant. Any lawyer would get a hot-shot psychiatrist to assess her, not a resident doing a six-week psych rotation. I still had to coax a confession out of her, or at least lead her to give one to the police. So I tried to look agreeable. "They'd definitely have to consider your psych history."

She dropped the sheet for a second. It flapped against the side of the bed. "Yeah. Not just the borderline and dependent personality bullshit. I've got depression. That one doctor thought I might be schizophrenic, and another one said maybe schizoaffective. And I was on a lot of drugs, you know?"

It took me a minute to realize she meant medications, but maybe she was thinking street drugs, too. "Sure."

She grabbed the dangling sheet and stretched it between her fists, ripping it out further from under the mattress. "You don't care."

I did care, but I was starting to think I'd made a mistake. I'd thought I could usher her toward the police, or at least agree to talk to them if I sent them to her room. But maybe I was muddying the confessional waters and angering her. I'd better bail. "Reena, look. If I didn't care, I wouldn't be here."

She narrowed her eyes. "I know what you care about. Murder, right?"

I jumped a little. She smiled. I raised my chin and said, "Do you know anything about it?"

"Hell, yeah. Arrest my foster sister's ass. She's the one who gave me the drugs! The Haldol that almost killed me," she added impatiently, at my blank look.

"Okay." That time she ran out of the emerg, she was demanding drugs. Today, she thought she could get off because she was taking drugs, plus now she was accusing Wendy of giving her drugs. Again, I wondered if I were getting anywhere.

"That's attempted murder, right? Isn't that what you were asking about? Because you *care* about me so much?" Her lips twisted. She waved me away when I tried to speak. "She knew I was allergic. I almost died when I was fifteen because this crazy psychiatrist thought I was psycho and gave me Haldol. I wear a Medic Alert bracelet and everything, see?" She shoved back the striped sleeve of her shirt to show me the heavy links. "It's all over my chart, too. So when Wendy gave me those little white pills, you bet your ass she did it on purpose."

Mrs. Schuster and Wendy had both danced around how Wendy had found Reena and brought her to the hospital. They'd never specified how Reena had gotten the drugs in the first place. It was plausible. There was only one problem. "Let's say that she did. Why did you take them?"

"'Cause I hate that little bitch and I wanted her to freak out!" She laughed, low and ugly. "Yeah, I know what you're thinking. Why do I hurt myself and think it'll hurt other people? That's what all the head-shrinks say. Well, I don't give a flying fuck about myself. If she ends up burning in hell because she killed me, it'll be worth it."

I tried to piece it together. Say it was true. Wendy offered her Haldol, and Reena was nuts enough to take it, to punish her. How did that tie in to Laura?

Reena sure didn't help. "She was shitting herself when I was in ICU. Sometimes she held my hand and cried. It was great."

"And now that you're on the ward?"

"Ah, she thinks I'm getting better, especially because they're booting me back to psych. I'll show her ass. That fucking bitch, that little squaw whore, that filthy cunt, I could rip off her tits and choke her with them!"

Suddenly, I couldn't breathe. They say depression is anger turned inward. I'd never understood it before, but now I saw rage that scared me. I stood up and backed toward the door.

"She stole everything! My parents, my name, my girl—everything! And what is she? A foster kid! You take them in for the money and give them the boot when they're eighteen. But my parents actually fell in love with her and tried to adopt her!" She swiped her tearless eyes with the back of her hand. "God damn them. God damn them all."

I hovered above the chair, torn between leaving and listening.

"Ah, you don't believe me. No one does. No one except—" She bit her lower lip hard enough to draw blood. A ruby drop gathered on her lip as she paused. "No one. That's right. No fucking one."

If she hated Laura Lee like this, I had no doubt she would run her down. With pleasure. Now I was worried about Wendy. I rubbed my temples where my head was starting to pound. I'd heard of opening a can of worms. This was more like a nest of vipers.

She rubbed her nose. Blood smeared up her arm.

"I have to go," I said.

"Sure you do. Everyone has to go. Everyone has something to do. Even me!" she screamed so loud I bet they could hear her at the nursing station as I rushed for the door.

38

I still felt smothered when I sat in my car, keys dangling in the ignition, and tried to make sense of things.

One thing was clear. Reena was furious. At Wendy, at her mother, at me, at herself. That rage could not be self-contained. It had to go somewhere.

Was that what happened eight years ago? She exploded and ran Laura Lee down? Was she the woman who maneuvered Mike Martinez to steal a car for her?

I wouldn't have banked on her doing that kind of advanced planning, but I wouldn't have bet she'd be able to fake a coma for a week, either. She had a lot more willpower than I'd have credited her.

It was after midnight now. Too late to call Mrs. Schuster. It was possible to call Wendy, but Reena was not about to break out of St. Joe's and murder her tonight.

I brushed my hair back from my temples and laid my forehead on the steering wheel. I would call the police first thing in the morning.

There was only one thing nagging at me. I couldn't quite formulate it, but uneasiness sat in the pit of my stomach.

I turned on the ignition. The Ford Focus's engine turned over. I began to nudge my way out of my space, checking the rear view mirror as I reversed. Péloquin Street was otherwise deserted. Reena's voice beat in my ears.

She hadn't seemed depressed to me. If I'd met her on the street, I would have said "pissed off" or "crazy." But maybe there was some black hole at the centre of it. I didn't understand. I never would.

I shifted back to drive and signalled my way out of the space, shoulder-checking, even though no one was there.

Reena's frantic, furious voice raged on.

I'll show her ass.

I swerved into Péloquin and stopped at the light. My pager went off, so I clicked on it to see a different extension, not OB and not psych. I rolled my eyes. Who was Tucker play-acting now? I'd call him when I got home. After I took a shower and washed all the Reena off.

Reena. Off.

Reena. Offed.

The light turned green. A truck rumbled up behind me, but I stayed still.

I don't give a flying fuck about myself.

The truck honked.

Everyone has to go. Everyone has something to do. Even me!

Oh, shit. I screeched a right turn on to Côte-Ste-Catherine.

I had to get back to the hospital right now.

I pulled into the same parking spot, dashed into the hospital, and sprinted up the five flights like it was a code.

A tiny Asian nurse wheeling a BP machine spotted me at the end of the hallway. I ignored her and ducked into Reena's room, banging it open with the flat of my hand.

The nurse called, "Wait. What about—"

I screamed.

Reena was hanging from the curtain rod.

39

She swayed slightly and gagged.

Her eyes bulged in her reddened face. She was already turning blue around the mouth.

The curtain rod creaked and bent, but still held her a good three feet off the floor. She clawed at the white sheet noosed around her neck.

I ran at her. Four minutes. Four minutes until her brain cells died from asphyxiation.

The chair was overturned next to the radiator. I didn't take the time to set the chair on its feet. I scaled the radiator, my sandals nearly slipping off the narrow, painted metal bars, but I managed to stay upright and hoist her weight against gravity, relieving the pressure.

We swayed. Her gown was wet with what smelled like urine and I didn't want to think what else. Pain shot down the right side of my back, but I clung to her.

I was screaming the entire time.

The nurse burst into the room and stopped dead at the door, her mouth open.

"HELP ME!" I yelled, my throat already raw. Reena began jerking in my arms. I couldn't tell if she was seizing or trying to get away, but I bit my tongue as I clung to her. My ankle twisted. My knees buckled.

But I managed to hang on. Just.

The nurse glanced back at the door. "I—have to—"

"Do you have SCISSORS?" I screamed. "Cut her DOWN!"

She dug into her uniform pocket, excruciatingly slow. I imagined Reena's brain cells saying *sayonara*, popping off one by one, while the nurse righted the chair and stood on it, her legs trembling so hard, the chair rocked. Even with the chair, there was no way she could reach.

She bit her lip and jumped off the chair.

"No!" I yelled, but she was already punching the call bell next to the bed, while I tried to hold Reena's weight up off her neck.

"GIVE ME THE SCISSORS!"

She dashed back, scissors aloft. I did my best to hack through the sheet, one-handed, but all I was getting was cramps in both arms while some of Reena's weight rested on my legs.

The call system squawked. "Code Blue, code blue!" yelled the nurse. Too late, I remembered we could have dialed 55555 to trigger a code right away. I kept sawing away with the scissors, but I couldn't hold Reena much longer. Even my neck was cramping up. Tears dripped down my face and the side of my neck. "Get—up—here."

"I can't reach!"

I pulled Reena over to make room on the radiator. Reena wasn't moving or groaning anymore. Good sign? Bad sign? I had no idea anymore. Hesitantly, the nurse levered herself up.

"PULL DOWN the CURTAIN ROD."

She stretched her hand up. "I can't!" She was even shorter than me.

"She's DYING! JUMP!"

She leaped up and grabbed the curtain rod. It sagged and finally broke under her and Reena's weight. I couldn't hold her anymore.

Reena tumbled to the floor and I fell on top of her, catching myself on my hands and knees. My neck and back seized up. I gritted my teeth against the pain and raised my head to look into Reena's dilated pupils as the emerg team burst through the door with the crash cart.

40

I never thought I'd get caught. Especially by something as stupid as a broken arm.

   I dropped into a little ER that Reena knows because she used to come here for psych. Her parents live around here, and the waiting time's short because no one else wants to go to this little shithole. Okay, fine. All they have to do is put a cast on my arm and give me some good drugs. Anyone can do that. We go in and the nurse sighs when she sees us, but Reena points at my arm. "It's not me this time."

   The nurse looks at Reena like she's shit and me like I'm vomit. "Do you have a hospital card?"

   The one hospital card I already have in this name has the St. Joseph's logo. Neat-o. I dig it out. It's so old it's cracked in half. The nurse makes a face and says the clerk should have given me a new one. Whatever.

   The nurse takes one look at my arm, checks my pulse, and gets the doctor to sign an X-ray requisition. That way, while I'm waiting to see the doc, I can have my X-ray too. Good thinking.

   I have to wait in the hall a long time to get the films, and they do my arm and wrist because my wrist hurts, too, and Reena and I laugh and look at my skeleton pics until we get bored and keep taking smoke breaks, *waiting for my turn for the doc. Short wait, my ass. It's, like, four hours until I finally get in a cubicle.*

"Hey, it's Laura," says Reena, pointing out the open door. Sure enough, it's the Dr. Laura who runs the borderline clinic with Dr. Ven. She's wearing a white coat and has her hair up in a ponytail, but it's the same girl. Reena and I trade looks. For some reason, I'm bothered she's working here, but I shrug it off.

Then I hear her talking to the nurse in the hallway. "Oh. I know this patient. At least, I think I do. Do we have the old films?"

You can practically hear the nurse rolling her eyes. "Do you need one? Her arm's broken."

"I always like to compare."

Reena and I look at each other. Same old slowpoke. Wouldn't know how to take a dump if she hadn't read a study about it first. We're going to be here another hour, easy.

Reena touches my good arm. She's feeling sorry for me. I could get an easy fuck out of this, except I wouldn't enjoy it. "Can I adjust your sling or something?" she asks.

"Nah. But my ice is melted again. Can you get that?"

While Reena's out doing that, I try to read a five month-old Maclean's magazine. Reena gives me the ice and pats my good hand. She's all shy when we're in public. It's cute. I whisper in her ear what I'm going to do to her when we get home. She cracks up. There's no way with a broken arm. Feels good to joke around anyway. But my arm hurts more and more. Seems like forever I've been sitting on this green vinyl examining table.

I stand up and pace, even though my arm is killing me. The nurse frowns and closes the door on me, like I'm disturbing the peace.

"You could ask them for a Tylenol," Reena says.

I shrug.

She stands up. "I'm gonna ask them."

Sometimes I actually like her. She's such a pain in the ass, but when she does it to other people, it's great.

She opens the door. I hear Laura's voice. "...seen this before? Today's film clearly shows growth plates, but on the X-ray from two years ago, they're already closed. I've never heard of ossification like this."

My scalp prickles. They're talking about me.

"And the seaside bone in the index finger..."

She's found me out. Holy shit, she figured it out somehow from the X-rays that I stole the ID. I leap to my feet. Awkward, with only one arm, and it jars the fracture, but I clench my teeth and jerk my head at the other door. The door to the hallway.

Reena turns. "Wait, they're coming over—"

I'm already running. I have to make a plan. I don't know what it's gonna be, but for now, I'm running. Running, running, running. As fast as I can. Can't catch me, I'm the gingerbread man.

∾

"So you're a hero," said Tucker, much later, after I'd showered, changed into fresh greens, and collapsed on the emerg resident's bed. The bed sagged under his weight as he sat within arm's length. "Heroine. Whatever."

I shook my head, too weary to speak.

"You figured out Reena did it and still saved her life."

I shrugged.

"I know she might not make it. But now at least she has a chance."

Yeah. A chance at a real coma. Mrs. Schuster would no doubt bake a cheesecake to thank me for interviewing her daughter and triggering her last, most dangerous suicide attempt.

He pressed a cool washcloth on my brow. It was the cheap white terrycloth from the emerg, but it felt so good. More tears leaked from my eyes again. I didn't bother to wipe them away.

"You're a good woman. I love you."

I shook my head. Right now, I didn't feel good, loveable, or loving. If anything, I felt like I was still missing a piece of the puzzle.

"Do you want to stay here, or I'll take you home?"

I didn't even glance at the four white walls or the bedside tray that served as a table. "Home."

∾

I FUMBLED with the keys to my apartment and stared at them, trying to figure out which one unlocked the door. It was one of two brass ones. Choosing the right one, at this moment, seemed at least as hard as the Medical College Admission Test question about a waterwheel.

Tucker swiped the keys from me and unlocked the door on the first try. "I'll see you in. You've been through enough."

I nodded and toddled through the open door.

Tucker shoved his hands in his pockets and hovered in the entry. I realized he wasn't going to come in. Part of me was relieved. The rest of me was disappointed. His mouth was moving. I tuned into his words. "Well, you delivered a baby and saved a life. Not bad for a day's work."

I nodded, eyelids sandy with fatigue. "You too." It might not have made sense, but I'd been impressed he'd run to the code right on the heels of the emerg team. He even put in a femoral line. A triple lumen. He had good hands.

I didn't check my watch to see how late it was. I was so wiped, I could hardly remember how to breathe.

He kissed my forehead. "Go to sleep. I'll cover for you tomorrow. You're on emerg, right?"

I stirred. He couldn't cover. He had his own clinic to do. "But—"

He pressed his index finger to my lips. Despite everything, his skin felt good against mine. I had the sudden urge to lick his finger. His nostrils flared. We stared at each other in the dim light of the hallway.

Finally, I nodded and he dropped his hand back down to his side.

"Lock the door," he said.

I did. I threw the main bolt and the tiny one in the floor. I listened to his footsteps echo down the stairs. The apartment door squeaked open and closed again. Tucker was gone. The night was over. I could finally sleep.

My stomach growled.

Oh, no. I really needed to crash. I was beyond exhaustion. But sometimes I had to eat first, or I'd wake up feeling sick from the void in my stomach. A piece of cheese or bowl of cereal would do.

I kicked off my sandals and walked to the kitchen. I didn't bother to turn on the light as I stepped through the kitchen doorway. I could make out the bulk of the fridge from the street light spilling in from the window above the sink on my left. I swivelled to face the fridge and yanked open the door, letting the cool, humid air bathe my face. Hmm, I'd forgotten about that jar of pickles. I reached for it, and a foreign sound caught my ear.

Someone's intake of breath.

But I'd already locked the door behind Tucker.

My skin prickled.

I slammed the fridge door.

A woman stepped out of the wedge of space behind the open kitchen door, where she'd been hiding. Almost casually, she knocked the kitchen door shut, trapping us together.

I screamed.

Her wig was so dark, it nearly matched her black T-shirt and chiffon skirt. It was the Goth girl I'd vaguely noticed at the cafe earlier tonight, but she threw her shoulders back and I recognized her face and her movement.

It was Jodi Green.

"Nice place you got here," she said in a high, child-like voice, as if she wasn't breaking and entering. As if she hadn't worn black leather gloves on a summer night.

Her smile scared me the most. Her perfectly even white teeth looked so sincere, so unconcerned.

I lunged for the only door.

Her right hand shifted. She showed me an open switchblade. The blade was at least six inches long.

I caught myself and hung back, my breath rasping in my throat. I had no doubt she would kill me, given a sixteenth of a chance. The trick was not to give her the chance.

I screamed again.

She tsked and advanced on me. "Is this how you usually treat your guests? I don't think so. Anyway, your neighbour's out, and I don't think anyone else gives a shit. Do you?"

Instead of answering, I gauged my chances of getting to a phone. My cell was in my backpack by the front door, but for my landline, I kept a cradle hung on the wall behind her right shoulder, on the other side of the door.

She laughed. "Just try it."

There was only one way out from the kitchen: the door she was blocking. No, wait. She'd moved my table away from its usual place beside the wall.

The fire escape!

I remembered the cyclist I'd seen with Ryan. In my mind's eye, I saw Jodi coast into the garage, and then casually climb the indoor fire escape stairs straight into the kitchen of my otherwise-fortified apartment.

She followed my gaze. "Yeah, that's how I got in. I like the bars on the windows, though. When I see Ryan, I'll tell him, nice try. Good for keeping you in instead of me out."

I tried not to react to the fact that she knew his name. Oh, Ryan. So smart, so thorough, so careful—but neither of us suburban creatures were accustomed to apartment buildings equipped with fire escapes.

"And I'll thank Tucker, too, for dropping you off at the door." She shook her head. "You're a real ho, you know that?"

I started. I've never been called a ho in my life. But I knew she was trying to provoke me. I said nothing.

"Good silent treatment, though. Aren't you going to ask me how I did it?"

Great. Now that I'd wasted my time on Reena, Jodi wanted to confess. I nodded. At least it would distract her while I calculated how to escape a galley kitchen with her two feet away from me, blocking the main exit.

She'd shifted the table to the far wall. I could try and knock the table at her while I went for the fire escape stairs, buying enough time to run to the basement.

"You could try it," she said, reading my mind again. "But I barricaded the door on the other side. I do love girls backed into corners."

I tried not to think about how it would feel to be trapped in the kitchen corner between the wall, the table, the flimsy metal shelving unit, and Jodi with a knife.

She grinned at me, running the blade along her finger. "I'm good with this. Borderlines are famous for slashing themselves, right? I think it's more efficient to practice on someone else, though."

My heart thumped twice in my chest. I'd better distract her. "Is that how Reena got those cuts on her arms?"

She made a face. "No, she did that herself. That girl was born to get stomped on."

"And you had the right size combat boots to do the stomping?"

She grinned. "Pretty much. So did you figure it out, finally?"

"I figured out you got Mike to steal the car for you. Though why you didn't get him to do the hitting and running, too, I wasn't sure."

"'Cause there was only so far I could push that pussy on the stat-rape charge. Car theft was as far as he'd go, no matter how much I tried to convince him." She tested the blade along her thumb. It was eerie, talking to her in the shadows of my kitchen. I listened for foot-steps overhead, toilets being flushed, or other signs of life in the building.

Nothing.

Either no one was home, no one was awake, or they were all minding their own business.

I took psych in undergrad. I'd heard about Kitty Genovese, murdered in a New York City apartment courtyard while a hundred neighbours watched. They never even called the police afterward.

I could not rely on the kindness of strangers. I had to get myself out. Now.

"So you leaned on your girlfriend instead," I said.

She rolled her eyes. "Yeah, Reena practically wears a dog collar anyway. But she's so unpredictable, you know? I had to go along to make sure she'd get the job done." She grinned and stabbed the knife in the air toward me.

So Reena did the running over and Jodi played the passenger. I leaned back and pretended to be casual while I added, "And because you wanted to watch."

She smiled. "You're smarter than you look."

"Thanks," I said, even though it was hardly a compliment.

What if I headed away from the doors, into the heart of the galley kitchen?

There was only one reason I'd do that. I tried not to look, since I seemed to be telegraphing my every thought, but I kept a knife block beside my sink, behind the appliances, where the kitchen counters ended. Jodi needn't be the only one with a knife.

The problem was, despite my dissection experience, I hardly ever deboned a chicken, let alone used a knife as a weapon. And I did not particularly want to hoist myself on to the counter, scramble into the sink and try and smash my way through a second-story window.

But I would if I had to. It was very clear to me, as my blood hummed through my veins, that I wanted to live.

The kitchen wasn't big enough for the two of us. It was so narrow that I could touch the fridge and the gas stove at the same time. I could hear her breathing.

"I'm sure you're sick of hearing this, but you do look like her. At least, like her when she was alive. Not so much when she was a broken piece of meat, but we'll see about that, right?"

Bile rose in my throat. I swallowed it back down. Her. She wouldn't even call Laura by name. "What are you doing here, anyway? You're always getting people to do your dirty work. Make Mike steal the car. Make Reena run her down. Make Wendy give Reena the pills."

She beamed under her white Goth makeup. "Oh, you noticed that too? I see why you're a doctor. Yeah, I'm a bit of a control freak that way. But it's so hard to get good help these days."

It was eerie. The jokes, the digs. It was all a game to her. In her eyes, I didn't matter. I wasn't a person, just an obstacle. For the first time, I truly understood the lack of empathy at the heart of a psychopath. "They took care of Laura, didn't they?"

"Yes, but so much drama, I decided it was easier to do it myself."
She smiled. "And, as you say, I like to watch."

I could not suppress a shudder.

"I think there's this saying in medical school, see one, do one, teach one?"

We do say that. It bothered me that she knew it. She knew a little too much about everything. "Why did you kill Laura Lee?"

"Oh, so you're still behind the times on that one?"

"I just want to know."

She shrugged. "I thought you already did. It was silly. I went to St. Joseph's with a broken arm, and somehow, after the X-ray, she figured out I wasn't Jodi Green."

The ortho paper on growth plates. That's why Laura had filed it under psych. I almost wanted to laugh. "Jodi" was smart, but even she couldn't figure out how to make her growth plates look like the woman's who rightfully owned that ID.

"She started asking a lot of questions. I mean, crazy bullshit stuff, like where I was born and if I'd had my tonsils out. She asked for a blood test, supposedly in case I needed a transfusion after the fracture, but c'mon, I broke my arm, not my brain, okay? She was onto me."

True enough. Laura must have pulled the real Jodi Green's chart and tried to cross-reference all the details. I bet that the real Jodi was a few years older and her growth plates had closed already on previous X-ray. Since your growth plates don't open up again, she figured out that "Jodi" was an imposter.

Laura's straight-A attention to detail had gotten her into med school and into the morgue.

"So I killed her," said Jodi, "just like I'm going to kill you."

Before the last words were out of her mouth, she leapt at me with the switchblade.

I screamed one more time and flung the fridge door open like a shield. I braced it with my hands and planted my legs to shove it forward and knock her off-balance.

She spun to take the brunt on her shoulder, but I used the momentum to push her back toward the door.

She recovered fast, pushing the door back against me.

I grunted. She was stronger than I was.

I released it abruptly. She stumbled toward my feet as the fridge door fell closed.

I dove next to the sink, grabbed a pan from the drying rack and smashed it on her head, hard enough to ring like a gong. The force of impact zinged up my forearm to my elbow.

She howled and stabbed at me with her knife.

I managed to deflect part of it with my left arm, but the tip slashed across my thigh. Everyone says adrenaline blocks out pain, but it burned me like an SOB, drawing a mangled shriek from my lips.

I smashed her head again, this time so hard that the pot turned sideways on its handle, and my arm ached only second to my thigh. A slow but steady stream of blood soaked my pants and pooled under my foot, but I ignored it as I transferred the pot to my left hand and grabbed another, more solid pot from the rack.

Jodi grunted, holding her head for a second. Then she said, in a tone more frightening in its quietness, "That's it. I'm going to kill you, bitch."

Like you weren't already, I thought, but saved my breath.

She followed. She was cornering me into the sink and the window above it. I was either going to have to fight my way past her or smash my way through the second storey glass. Neither was particularly appealing, especially since, as a good Chinese girl, I'd slipped off my sandals at the front door while Jodi was still in combat boots.

So I charged her. She screeched and slashed at my eye. I jerked my head back, but she managed to catch my ear.

"My ear!" I screamed, and slammed the pot against her right arm. I clipped the counter on the way, so it wasn't as hard as I would have liked. She grunted and held on to the knife.

I smashed the other pot into her nose.

She choked on the blood fountaining out of her nostrils, and in that split-second of her blind pain, I shoved her aside.

She tripped me.

Not too difficult, as I slipped in my own blood, and maybe hers— no universal precautions here. I tried not to imagine what kind of infectious diseases a murderer might carry. I dropped my pots to catch myself before my face slammed into the floor.

I heard Jodi hiss with delight a second before her knees hit the ground behind me. Instinctively, I rolled on my back, but she was on top of me with the knife, her mouth stretched in a bloody rictus of victory.

I only had one chance.

I yelled, "FIRE!" I grabbed the edge of the oven door and swung it down on her. I managed to bash it against her left shoulder—not hard, and not hitting her knife hand, but enough to make her duck.

Then I bucked my hips upward. She clamped on to me with her knees and slashed the knife.

I whipped my head to the side, screaming incoherently now.

While she raised her arm for a death blow, I bucked again. She fell toward the fridge, and I managed to kick her off me.

I threw myself on my stomach and scrambled to my feet, toward the door. She launched herself at my bad leg.

I howled and grabbed the phone off the wall. I slammed it into her head as she reached for her knife. The cheap plastic split, so I dug my hands into her hair and slammed her head into the linoleum as hard as I could. Once. Twice.

Finally, her hands loosened, and I scrambled to freedom.

EPILOGUE

I ached all over. I couldn't even go to the bathroom without help. Twisting to grab the toilet paper was like an Olympic event.

But I was alive.

Alive, while Reena slumbered on in a genuine coma and Jodi Green, or whatever her real name was, smoldered in jail.

My parents had taken me home to Ottawa. My mother was in heaven, bringing me bone soup and gruel in thirty-degree weather, while my father showed me *Just for Laughs* gags. Kevin tried to trick me into doing his summer school homework.

Ryan brought me movies and more sunflowers. It hurt too much to hug, so he kissed my hand, my eyelids, my intact ear, and the other few body parts that didn't throb. "I'm sorry I didn't block your fire escape."

"How were you supposed to know? My parents are ready to put the landlord through the meat grinder."

He made a face. "I was the one on the ground. Anyway. I'm still not a hundred percent sure why Reena and Jodi ran Laura down."

"Laura figured out that 'Jodi' was an imposter who stole someone else's ID. I think Laura was already suspicious, but then she saw that

'Jodi's' X-rays didn't match the real Jodi Green's, who was a few years older, so her growth plates had already closed. Since you don't suddenly start growing again, Laura knew 'Jodi' had committed identity theft, but she wanted to prove that the X-rays weren't mislabeled before she brought them to the police. And that's when 'Jodi' got Reena to run her down." I sighed. "I wish I'd figured it out sooner myself."

"You did awesome." Ryan licked his lips. "At least you won't have to worry about the phone calls and graveyard pics anymore."

I'd almost forgotten about them. "Yeah, Jodi's in jail and Wendy's not her bitch anymore."

"No." He examined his feet. "It was Lisa."

I goggled at him. Little Lisa?

"I knew she'd taken a picture in the graveyard in Alexandria, so I went through her iPhoto library and found the picture. It was the same one. I confronted her." He scratched a mosquito bite on his arm. "Anyway. She won't be doing it anymore." He raised his eyes to me. "That's past, right? We can do better."

I knew he was right. We could do better.

The question was, would we?

Tucker came to visit next with books, chips, and chocolate. He wiggled my left big toe. "You still got sensation?"

I nodded.

His face sobered. "You were lucky."

I nodded again.

"And brave. And beautiful. And totally kick-ass."

I smiled.

"You're the one," he said, more softly.

I shook my head, but before I could speak, he said, "Don't talk. I'll read to you. I know smart girls like you have good taste. How about CJEM?"

He actually pulled the familiar green-blue Canadian Journal of Emergency Medicine cover out from under his arm.

"You are kidding me."

"Garbo speaks. Well, if that's not your cuppa, your parents told me you like Little House on the Prairie."

"Bring on *Farmer Boy*." I settled back into my pillows and fell asleep before he read about Alonzo's teacher defeating the bullies.

So both men were willing to kiss me all better, but both were also willing to wait. Near-death has its privileges.

Tucker came whenever he could get away from the hospital long enough to make the drive. Ryan stopped by most evenings. We watched *Despicable Me*, Wallace and Grommett, chick flicks— anything but murder and mayhem.

Mrs. Lee brought me a kiss, homemade dumplings, and a card. Inside, she'd tried to imitate a patient history.

Pt. ID: Hope Sze

CC: wounded in the line of duty

Diagnosis: courage, fortitude, and speedy healing

She signed it *"With love and profound thanks, Regina and Laura Lee."*

I smiled.

She held my hand, trying not to squeeze too hard. "Now I can let her go."

We both cried, smiled, and cried again. For some reason, I thought of Mrs. Valdez's baby girl and wished her luck. Then we ate dumplings with chili garlic sauce.

We were alive.

We could rebuild.

It was enough.

∿

WELL, it totally sucks to be in jail. I can't believe I left a hair in that car. I was so careful with my wig.

Even my lawyer says the DNA evidence is going to put me away. But anyway. Onward.

I don't want to be like ninety-nine percent of the girls here. It's a loser-pa-looza. Waa waa waa, my boyfriend got me to smuggle drugs, and I'm the one who got caught. Woo woo woo, he beat me up so bad, I had to shoot him. They can't see beyond their acne scars and instant mashed potatoes.

But there are one or two other girls like me. Smart girls who knew exactly what they were doing. Now they're doing their time, but it means they have a lot of free hours to think. A lot of hours to plan. A lot of hours to make sure they get it right the next time.

One of them is hot, too. We could do a lot of damage together.

READER QUESTION

Why is this book called Notorious D.O.C.?

AUTHOR REPLY

Because Notorious B.I.G., considered one of the most influential rappers of all time, inspired comedian Margaret Cho to name her tour Notorious C.H.O. I saw that tour movie, loved it, and called this book Notorious D.O.C.

It's a meta joke, but doesn't make sense if you don't know rap. The title also references Hope's notoriety. She can't escape her reputation as the medical doctor who tosses criminals behind bars after smashing them in the head with a frying pan.

AUTHOR'S NOTE

Massive thanks to Bruce Kahn, the police officer who reviewed the details; Dayle Dermatis, who read an earlier version and introduced me to the acronym TSTL; and Camden Park Press, Dr. Greg Smith, Céline, and RN Margaret MacDonald for proofreading. As usual, this is a work of fiction. All errors are my own.

If you liked this book,
1. Please sign up for my mailing list at www.melissayuaninnes.com for a
free gift.

2. Leaving a positive review makes spring flowers (and authors) grow.
Thanks! You rock.

www.melissayuaninnes.com

ABOUT THE AUTHOR

Melissa Yi is an emergency doctor with an award-winning writing career.

She was shortlisted for the Arthur Ellis Award for the best crime story in Canada and the Derringer Award for the best mystery story in the English language.

www.melissayuaninnes.com

ALSO BY MELISSA YI

Code Blues (Hope Sze 1)

Notorious D.O.C. (Hope Sze 2)

Family Medicine (essay & Hope Sze novella combining the short stories *Cain and Abel, Trouble and Strife,* and *Butcher's Hook*, which are also available separately)

Terminally Ill (Hope Sze 3)

Student Body (Hope Sze novella post-Terminally Ill; includes radio drama *No Air*)

Blood Diamonds (Hope Sze short story)

Stockholm Syndrome (Hope Sze 4)

Human Remains (Hope Sze 5)

Death Flight (Hope Sze 6)

Graveyard Shift (Hope Sze 7: release date November 1, 2019)

More mystery & romance novels by Melissa Yi

The Italian School for Assassins *(Octavia & Dario Killer School Mystery 1)*

The Goa Yoga School of Slayers *(Octavia & Dario Killer School Mystery 2)*

Wolf Ice

High School Hit List

The List

Dancing Through the Chaos

Unfeeling Doctor Series (Melissa Yuan-Innes)

The Most Unfeeling Doctor in the World and Other True Tales From the Emergency Room (Unfeeling Doctor #1)

The Emergency Doctor's Guide Series (Melissa Yuan-Innes)

www.ingramcontent.com/pod-product-compliance
Lightning Source LLC
Chambersburg PA
CBHW071425260626
47170CB00008B/2591